NOW YOU SEE

Max Manning worked as a crime reporter for several years, before moving on to Fleet Street, where he worked on several international newspapers – including the *Daily Telegraph*, where he was a news sub-editor for sixteen years.

Max is now a full-time writer living in Essex. He is married and has three grown-up children.

NOW YOU SEE

MAX MANNING

WILDFIRE

First published in 2017 by WILDFIRE
An imprint of HEADLINE PUBLISHING GROUP

1

Cataloguing in Publication Data is available from the British Library

Paperback ISBN 978 1 4722 5155 8

Typeset in Dante MT by Palimpsest Book Production Ltd, Falkirk, Stirlingshire

Printed and bound in Great Britain by
CPI Group (UK) Ltd, Croydon CR0 4YY

Headline's policy is to use papers that are natural, renewable
and recyclable products and made from wood grown in well-managed
forests and other controlled sources. The logging and manufacturing
processes are expected to conform to the environmental
regulations of the country of origin.

HEADLINE PUBLISHING GROUP
An Hachette UK Company
Carmelite House
50 Victoria Embankment
London EC4Y 0DZ

www.headline.co.uk
www.hachette.co.uk

For Valerie, Becky, John and Sarah

Prologue

*S*he hears herself breathing, quick and shallow. She knows what's coming and there's nothing she can do.

Tears sting and she blinks hard. Dusk is falling like a grey shroud and the undergrowth is thick with gloom. It's an unseasonably warm September evening, but still she shivers.

He smiles and holds his phone up in his right hand. She can't tell whether he's taking a photograph of her, or a selfie. All her attention is focused on his other hand.

He steps round and behind her, moving so swiftly it makes her head spin. The heat of his body burns through the thin fabric of her dress. He positions the phone in front of her face so she can get a good look at the screen.

It takes her a second to recognise the woman in the photograph. Her skin is paler than usual against her short, dark hair, the blue eyes startlingly wide.

'You're very photogenic, but you should have smiled,' he says. 'You've got a beautiful smile.'

Her heart races and rivulets of sweat run down her spine. Maybe, she thinks, maybe there is still a way out of this.

'Why me?' she says, her voice part whisper, part sob.

He laughs softly and she feels his breath hot on the back of her neck. 'This is so much bigger than you.'

She wants to run, but her legs are shaking so badly she can barely stand. She opens her mouth wide. The scream doesn't come. Her breath has been sucked from her lungs. She tries to step away, but he grabs her right forearm, his fingers digging into the flesh.

He releases his grip and stands so still, so silently, she lets herself believe, for a fraction of a second, that he has gone. But all hope dies in a moment. He's there, and the stillness and the silence mean he's ready.

Hot tears spill down her cheeks. Her vision blurs, but she sees. She sees a dark-haired child learning to ride her first bicycle, her father cheering her on as he runs, arms outstretched, ready to catch her should she fall.

She recalls the excitement of her first kiss, the tenderness of her last kiss. She regrets the precious days she's wasted, never saying the things she wanted to say. She feels the warmth of her mother's hand.

1

Detective Chief Inspector Dan Fenton thought he'd seen it all. He stared at the images on the computer screen and shook his head in despair. It was the first time he'd looked into the eyes of someone who knew they were about to be murdered.

A second picture, taken later at a side angle and low to the ground, showed the same woman on her back, her arms splayed, her torso slick with blood and her legs crossed neatly at her ankles. In the background, the faint silhouette of a line of trees snaked into the distance.

A message typed next to the photographs read:

The world certainly looks different through the eyes of a killer. #IKiller

Fenton lifted a hand and massaged the back of his neck. They had a murder, showcased online. A 'before' picture and an 'after' picture of the victim. An email sent by the killer generously providing a link to his handiwork. What they didn't have was a body. Yet.

His thoughts were interrupted when the office door swung open. Detective Sergeant Marie Daly paused to tug at her ponytail before stepping in.

'The online team are trying to trace the source of the email,' she said. Daly never used more words than necessary. Fenton valued that. He also trusted her to make good decisions under pressure.

'How long is it going to take to get this stuff taken down?' he said.

Daly shrugged. 'It's a fake Instagram account, boss. Created in the UK with the username @IKiller. We've put in a request, but it could take twenty-four hours. It's already been viewed by several hundred people.'

Fenton glanced at his watch and swore under his breath. Another long night at the office. Another broken promise. He slid his chair back and stood, resting his hands on the desk.

'Whoever did this couldn't wait to flaunt it.' He jabbed a finger at the computer. 'We need teams searching every park in the city, every open space large enough for that many trees. Cancel all leave and get every available officer out there looking. I want that body found.'

Daly nodded and left the room. Fenton sat down, lifted his hands to his face and rubbed his eyes gently with the tips of his fingers. What kind of mind could do that to another human being? God help us all, he thought.

2

The key to everything was finding her. I'd been searching for a long time without knowing exactly who I was looking for.

That was a great moment for me. Strike that. The word great is far too weak. It was a prodigious, life-changing moment.

I'm still feeling the joy. Yes, that's the word. The public love my work. I knew they would. It's hard to resist a glimpse into the darkness.

I can't blame myself for what I've done, for what I have yet to do. Guilt is a concept I've never understood. It gets in the way of true creativity, stops you doing things you want to do. Imagine not having a conscience. Think about it. Wouldn't life be so much easier? Admit it.

A veil has been lifted. Life promises so much more for me now. I'm free to follow my path.

3

Fenton pushed through the journalists, ignoring their shouted questions and turning his face from the flashing cameras.

Two police constables guarded the Gore Road entrance into Victoria Park. As Fenton approached the iron gates, a photographer wearing a beanie hat and leather jacket stepped in front of him and raised his camera.

Fenton swerved slightly and turned his left shoulder, knocking the press man off balance, forcing him to step aside. The discovery of the body hadn't been made public, yet the media had arrived mob-handed. Fenton would make it his business to find out how the news had been leaked.

Passing through the gate, he stressed to the uniforms that on no account should any reporters be allowed in. To the left, about fifty yards away, a constable stood by a line of white tape sealing off a triangular area of undergrowth that filled the gap between two towering plane trees.

As Fenton approached he was struck by how fresh-faced she looked. Probably a new recruit, he thought. He flashed his warrant card and a smile. 'You're the one who found the body?' he asked.

The constable's face reddened. 'That's right, sir.'

Fenton nodded, ducked under the tape and edged through a narrow gap in the shrubbery. The woman lay on her back in a small clearing. He moved close to her feet, putting himself where the killer must have stood to take the photograph. The copper-coin smell of blood turned his stomach as he moved beside the body and squatted to take a closer look. The victim appeared to be in her late twenties. Her eyes stared at the sky, lifeless and shiny. Like a doll. Fenton resisted a sudden urge to walk away. He needed to do his job properly.

This was somebody's child. Somebody's baby. When he'd first joined the force, arresting the bad guys, doing his bit for society, felt good. It was all about winning and proving yourself. After the birth of his daughter that changed. One day she'd be out there on her own. Taking bad guys off the streets had become even more important. It felt personal.

Dragging his eyes away from her face, he checked her hands. They were small and clean. No obvious defence wounds. No attempt to fend off the blade. Her dark blue skirt was hitched up around her thighs. He could see no sign of sexual assault, but the pathologist's report would provide the details.

He stood up and slipped through the undergrowth back on to the path. The police constable stood to attention. Fenton lifted a hand to acknowledge her and started walking back to the gate. After a dozen or so strides he paused, took a few deep breaths to clear the smell of death from his airways and gazed across the park.

The morning sun hovered low over east London's tower blocks, its rays glinting off the surface of the boating lake. A thin line of mature oaks curved north to south across the green space, their leaves already changing colour. At that time of day, the park would normally be bustling with people.

A white van approached through the trees. It turned on to the grass and pulled up beside Fenton. Ronnie Oliver, New Scotland Yard's most experienced crime scene manager, and a younger, taller woman climbed out, both already wearing white forensic overalls.

Built like a pitbull, Oliver squared up to Fenton, his jutting jaw level with the detective's chest. 'Don't tell me you've contaminated my crime scene,' he said.

Fenton shrugged. 'Okay, I won't. I had a quick look that's all.'

Oliver curled his upper lip and glanced at his colleague. She turned away and stared at the scenery. Fenton guessed she'd seen her boss lose it before. He admired Oliver's passion for his job and his obsession with protocol, and most of the time was prepared to indulge his tantrums. 'I had a look, but I didn't touch anything. I'm in charge of this investigation remember.'

Oliver scowled. 'You could be the Prime Minister for all I care. Don't come near my crime scene again unless you're wearing a fucking forensic suit.' With that he strode off, his colleague scurrying after him.

It was going to be another long day and, unless they struck lucky, an even longer night. Fenton pulled his mobile phone out of his jacket pocket. The call was answered after the sixth ring. His neighbour sounded flustered. 'Bad timing,' she said. 'We're late for school.'

'Tina, I need a favour.' Fenton paused, hoping for a positive response. He didn't get one. 'Something's come up and I'm going to be late. Very late. Can she sleep over?' The silence on the other end stretched. When his neighbour finally spoke, her words sounded clipped.

'It's early. How do you know you're going to be so late?'

'You'll see it on the news. It can't be helped. I'm sorry.'

'You know this can't go on, don't you? It's not fair.'

'I'll sort it. I'll call the agency.'

Fenton waited for at least thirty seconds before he realised the call had been terminated. He took that as a yes.

He was staring at his mobile's blank screen, momentarily paralysed by guilt, when he heard footsteps. He turned to a frowning pale face, topped with cropped reddish hair. 'Everything all right, sir?'

Detective Constable Ince had been on the team for less than six months. In that time Fenton had come to appreciate his youthful enthusiasm. 'You were the first detective on the scene?' Fenton said. It came out more of a statement than a question.

Ince nodded. 'Ten minutes after the uniforms found her.

Made sure the area was sealed off straightaway.' He paused for a few seconds, running the fingers of his left hand across his forehead as he tried to come up with something to impress his boss. 'I think she's probably been there all night because the park closes at dusk and the gates are locked. I remember thinking there was a lot of blood.'

Fenton kept the disappointment off his face. He was good at that. He'd had a lot of practice. Sometimes first sight of the body can provide a gem, a little nugget of information that can help break a case. Not this time.

Ince rubbed his forehead harder and pressed on. 'She wouldn't have been visible from Gore Road, or from inside the park, because of the undergrowth, but she would probably have been found by a dog walker if we hadn't got there first.'

'We need the victim's ID confirmed,' Fenton said. 'I know I can trust you to get it done quickly.' He watched as Ince walked away, a spring in his step, his head held a little higher.

4

It's amazing how a simple act can have such complex consequences. Predictably my Instagram post was wiped, but not before plenty of admirers shared it around. The ripple effect is a wonderful thing.

The one negative is I'm the only one who knows it was me. I'm not good at pretending to be humble.

The police are running around trying to look like they know what they're doing, but they've nothing to go on. Find the motive and you'll find the killer? No one finds me unless I want to be found.

The thing is, I have more than a motive. She was the first step on my journey. That's the beauty of the relationship between predator and prey. It's not personal. What does that say about me? It says I'm a cold-hearted son of a bitch. Did I plan it? Her death yes, but not what it unleashed.

People like me. They always have. The deluded souls think they know me. If I put my mind to it I can charm the pants off most people. Pay them lots of attention, show genuine interest in their pathetic little lives. Keeping up the pretence is hard, but I'm good at it. It's my camouflage, my weapon of mass deception.

I know that if I want maximum impact I've got to be inventive. When you're in the entertainment business, you've got to up the ante. Your audience always wants more.

5

All of the belongings she'd left behind went into three cardboard boxes. Blake lined them up in the hall near the front door. She wouldn't have to venture far into the flat when she came to pick them up. It'd be better for them both.

He walked down the narrow hall into the living room. At least he didn't have to buy new furniture now. She'd hated his old two-seater sofa and the tiny television set he rarely switched on. Most of all she'd hated the running machine positioned in the centre of the room.

Blake sighed and shook his head. He missed her. He missed the warmth of her smile, her touch, her kindness. If he begged her to come back she probably would, but he'd ruled that out as an option. The best thing he could do for her was let her go. He stepped on to the treadmill, pressed the start button and began jogging. After a couple of minutes, he upped the pace and settled into a steady run. As always, he found comfort in the whirring of the electric motor and the rhythmic pounding of his feet.

By the time the tenant living in the flat below started jabbing a broom handle against his ceiling, Blake was dripping with sweat, his vest and shorts sticking to his skin. He checked his watch. Ten more minutes and he'd reach the four-mile mark.

When the knock on the door came, Blake was warming down with a brisk walk. He stepped off the treadmill, wiped his face with a hand towel and answered the door. His neighbour, a portly, middle-aged man with thinning grey hair, stood on the threshold. Arms held rigid by his side, he took in Blake's sweat-stained shorts and vest and snorted. 'Every day. Day after fucking day.'

'I've finished,' Blake said. 'It's done.'

'It's got to stop.'

'It's stopped. You won't hear a thing for the rest of the evening.'

'You're setting off the wife's migraine.'

'How many times do I have to say it? I've finished.'

'We can't hear the bloody telly.'

'Funny you should say that, because I can hear your television all the time.'

The neighbour unclenched his fists, wriggled his fingers and clenched them again. 'We're not putting up with this you know. Why don't you run in the park or something, like a normal person?'

Blake shrugged and started to close the door. His neighbour edged forward a couple of inches, a defiant look on his face despite the fact that at six foot two, Blake was taller, fitter and twenty years younger.

'I'm warning you for the last time, mate. This has got to stop.'

'Or what? What are you going to do?'

'I'll tell you what I'm going do,' his neighbour said, puffing up his chest like a strutting cockerel. 'I'll take it up with the fucking landlord. That's what. We pay rent, you know. We got rights.'

Blake shivered, his skin clammy with cold sweat. 'The landlord's a prick and you can tell him that from me,' he said, slamming the door in his neighbour's face.

He spent longer than was necessary in the shower, but running hot water was one of the little luxuries Blake appreciated since his return to civilisation. After dressing, he sat at the kitchen table with a glass of beer and powered up his laptop. Before he could check his emails, there was another double knock at his door.

The first thing Blake had done after moving into the flat was to disconnect the doorbell. You can tell a lot about an unexpected visitor from the way they knock. He stayed seated, waiting to see if the caller gave up or tried again. The second knock was a triple rap, loud and impatient. Blake walked slowly to the door, pulled it open a couple of inches and peered through the gap. A young man with reddish hair cropped close to his skull, wearing a brown suit that hung loose on his wiry frame, stood next to an older, stern-looking brunette in a police uniform.

The man flashed a Metropolitan Police warrant card.

'Detective Constable Ince and this is PC Price,' he said. 'We're looking for Adam Blake.'

'You've found him. Well done. Good detective work.'

Ince hesitated and glanced at his colleague for support. She kept her eyes on Blake.

'May we come in, sir?' she said. 'We need to speak and we don't want to do it out here on the doorstep. I'm sure you can appreciate that.'

Blake got the impression that she had done this sort of thing hundreds of times before. 'If this is about the noise then it's a bit over the top.'

The detective lifted a hand and rubbed his chin. 'It's got nothing to do with noise.'

Blake let go of the door, gestured with a nod for the police officers to follow, and led them down the hall. The police-woman and Blake sat on the sofa. Ince stood facing them, next to the treadmill. 'You run a lot then?' he said, nodding towards the machine. Blake responded with a shrug.

'I understand you recently had a relationship with a woman named Lauren Bishop?'

Blake couldn't keep the surprise off his face. 'What's this about?'

'A few questions first, Mr Blake. How long were you and Lauren in a relationship?'

Blake twisted in his seat to face the policewoman, in the hope of getting some sense out of her. 'I don't understand,' he said. 'We were together for almost a year. She moved out six weeks ago.'

'When was the last time you saw her?'

'We haven't spoken since she left. She's supposed to pick up a few bits and pieces. They're in those boxes in the hall.'

The police officers exchanged a look that made Blake feel uncomfortable. 'What's going on?'

'Lauren Bishop is dead,' Ince said. 'Murdered. Her body was found early yesterday morning in Victoria Park.'

Blake shook his head slowly. An image of Lauren splayed, bloodied and lifeless, flashed through his mind. He opened his mouth to protest that they must be mistaken, but instead he sucked in a mouthful of air and swallowed it along with his words. He looked at the police-woman. She studied him, trying to assess his reaction. He gave her nothing except for another shake of his head. 'It's probably best that you to come with us to the station to answer a few more questions.'

'It can't be her,' he insisted. 'Not Lauren.'

'I'm afraid it is,' Ince said. 'Her sister has identified the body.'

Blake shot to his feet, swayed like a drunk and toppled back on to the sofa. He wanted to shout that they'd got it wrong, to accuse them of lying, but deep down he knew they were telling the truth. When he did speak, his voice wavered. 'I begged her to stay,' he said. 'She should have stayed.'

Ince nodded to his colleague and she stood up. 'We'd like you to come down to the station to finish our interview,' he said.

Blake followed the officers to the door. Lauren was dead. Never coming back. He'd loved her, but it hadn't been enough. He had nothing to fill the emptiness inside. If only they knew, he told himself, they'd understand.

6

Fenton rested his elbows on his desk and opened the pathologist's report. The autopsy hadn't turned up anything unusual. Cause of death was there for everyone to see. Lauren Bishop's throat had been cut, her right external jugular vein and left carotid artery slashed, her windpipe severed. Death would have been rapid, a combination of massive blood loss and suffocation.

He flicked through the pages, skimming the text. He'd already read the report twice, but he wanted to make sure he hadn't missed anything. The arterial spray blood pattern on the soil made it likely that the woman had been murdered where she was found. Apart from bruising on her right forearm, there were no other wounds.

Fenton balled his right hand into a fist and twisted the knuckles against his left palm. The victim either walked willingly across Victoria Park with her killer, in which case she might have known him, or he'd lain in wait and pounced when she passed by.

There had been no reports of screams and the lack of

defence wounds showed Lauren Bishop didn't try to fight for her life. Fenton wasn't surprised. In recent years, many stress experts had renamed the fight or flight response fight, flight or freeze. Fenton knew, all too well, that many victims of violent crime, male or female, found themselves paralysed by fear. Like a deer in the headlights. He tried to visualise the killer brandishing the knife and forcing Lauren into the cover of the undergrowth. Time of death had been narrowed down to between 7 p.m. and 10 p.m. The twenty-seven-year-old was a nurse at the Homerton University Hospital, a twenty-five-minute walk from Victoria Park. She'd been due to work a night shift on the day she was killed. Her stomach contained the remains of a light meal and blood tests showed she hadn't been drinking.

Fenton closed the report and thumped the desk hard. New Scotland Yard's cyber team had failed to trace the source of the email, and the photographs of Lauren Bishop and the I, Killer message were still being viewed and shared online. He had officers watching hours of footage from CCTV cameras around the park but, so far, they'd had no luck.

He leant back in his chair and surveyed his office, one of the benefits of his rank. You wouldn't get a double bed in it, but he had everything he needed: desk, telephone, computer and a run of filing cabinets. The pale blue walls were bare and a glass partition gave him a view of the squad room. Fenton was pleased to see only three of his team hunched over their computers. In his experience, cases were rarely solved by desk jockeys.

Detective Constable Ince sauntered into view, crossed the room and walked straight into Fenton's office. 'Evening, boss,' he said, perching himself on the edge of the chair on the other side of the desk. 'We've traced the ex-boyfriend. He's in the interview room.'

Fenton fixed Ince with a hard stare, speaking only when he noticed the detective's face colour. 'Has anyone ever told you that it's normal to knock before entering an office, especially your boss's office? And for the record, you should wait to be invited to take a seat.'

Ince jumped to his feet and stepped round behind the chair. 'Sorry. Wasn't thinking. Mind on the job and all that.'

Fenton flapped a hand dismissively. 'Just remember next time. Now tell me about this ex-boyfriend.'

'His name is Adam Blake. He says he used to be a journalist. I've got someone checking that out. He claims he last saw Lauren six weeks ago when she walked out of his East End flat. He says he spent the night of the murder, all night, in the South Pole.'

He paused and grinned at his boss's raised eyebrows. 'The South Pole pub, on the Mile End Road, a few hundred yards from his flat. We're also—' Fenton held up a hand, stopping Ince in mid-sentence, turned to his computer and tapped away at the keyboard.

'You mean this Adam Blake?' he asked, jabbing a finger at the computer screen. Ince walked round the desk and squinted at a photograph of a tall man being escorted off a military aircraft by two soldiers carrying automatic rifles.

'That's definitely him,' he said, a puzzled look crossing his face. 'He's down the corridor.'

'Blake is a suspect?'

'Well, we're checking his alibi. But he is an ex-boyfriend of the victim. She dumped him a few weeks ago. That's a motive right there.'

Fenton's eyes were still on the screen, scanning the news story that accompanied the photograph. Ince leant closer and read the first few paragraphs. 'I didn't know any of that, boss. I usually only read the sports pages. Does this make him less or more likely to have murdered his ex-girlfriend?'

Fenton groaned. 'Don't assume it's got any bearing on the case at all. Follow the evidence. Look for a motive. If his alibi is confirmed then he's in the clear. But I want his involvement cleared up before the press get a sniff. They'll have a field day.'

Ince stood and started backing towards the door. 'I'm on it, boss.' Fenton clicked his fingers. It had the desired effect, stopping Ince in his tracks.

'Has he seen the post, the photographs? Does he know about them?'

Ince shrugged. 'I doubt it. Unless he was the one who took them.'

'Change of plan,' Fenton said. 'I'll do the interview. You can watch and learn. Give me ten minutes to make a telephone call.' Ince nodded and left the room without another word. Fenton reached for his telephone and dialled his home number. The new nanny needed to stay late on her first day.

22

7

Sitting and waiting to be questioned brought back a lot of bad memories for Blake. The walls of the New Scotland Yard interview room were painted a sterile white. The single light bulb hanging from the ceiling lacked a shade. He shifted uncomfortably in the chair, his knees higher than his hips. Blake reached for the plastic cup on the table, blew hard on the brown liquid and took a sip.

An image of Lauren's mutilated body surfaced again. He pushed it away, back to where it couldn't hurt him. The door opened and the red-haired detective constable entered followed by a taller man with flecks of grey in his dark hair. The older detective sat on the chair opposite Blake and introduced himself. 'Detective Chief Inspector Dan Fenton. I'm leading the investigation into the murder of Lauren Bishop. You'll understand that as her ex-boyfriend we have to talk to you.'

Blake studied Fenton's face. He was clean-shaven, but thick bristles were starting to break through the skin. His eyes were sharp, despite the shadows under them.

'I understand,' Blake said. 'I want to help.'

'You last saw Lauren about six weeks ago?'

Blake nodded and looked across at Ince. 'That's right. I haven't seen or heard from her since.'

'Why did you break up?'

'I guess she couldn't put up with me any longer. I don't think I'm an easy person to be with. I'd warned her, but she didn't listen.'

Fenton paused to consider the best way to frame his next question. 'Your relationship was troubled?'

Blake slumped in his seat. 'It was good. You know, strong. Most of the time. She was sure we could sort out any problems, but in the end, she found it too hard to handle.'

'What couldn't she handle?'

'Me. I suppose.'

Fenton stood up and slowly walked round behind his chair. 'Were you ever violent towards her?'

Blake understood the detective's point, but that didn't make it easier to hear. 'I can lose it sometimes, like anyone can,' he said. 'But I never laid a finger on Lauren. Never.'

Fenton took a long look at the man sitting in front of him. He'd seen that empty stare many times before.

'I gather you're not working as a journalist now,' Fenton said.

Blake shook his head.

'I can understand that.'

'You're obviously a very understanding man.'

'What do you do for money if you're not working?'

Blake wondered why his personal finances were relevant, and for a moment thought about refusing to answer. Instead he decided the quickest way to get out of the room was to cooperate.

'I had a bit of money put away and I was paid well for my story. Enough to buy a house. Converted it into two flats. I live in the top and rent out the one below.'

Fenton nodded. 'Do you own a laptop, computer, smart-phone?'

'Laptop and phone.' Fenton caught Ince's eye. 'We've got both, boss. The techies are looking at them as we speak.'

Fenton's instinct told him that Blake wasn't the killer. At the same time, he knew better than to rule anyone out on gut feeling alone. He made a mental note to get Daly to apply for a warrant and search Blake's home for hidden devices.

'I'll leave Detective Constable Ince to finish the interview,' he said. 'We've got a few more inquiries to make, then once we've confirmed what you've told us about where you were at the time of the murder you'll be allowed to go.'

Fenton walked to the door, hesitated and turned back to face Blake. 'One last thing,' he said. 'The killer photographed Lauren before the murder, and took another after. He posted both online. We've had the account shut down, but you know the internet. Once it's out there, it's out there. Take my advice. Don't look.'

Blake dropped his head and stared at the dregs of his coffee. 'Lauren,' he whispered.

8

Fenton pulled up outside the school gates, regretting his decision to use the five-minute drive from home to break the news to his daughter that the new nanny would be moving in.

He switched off the engine and turned to the passenger seat. Tess looked up at him, her lips stubbornly clamped together, her eyes watery and red-rimmed. He reached across, took her hand and squeezed gently. 'I know this is difficult, I understand, but I need someone to help look after you. I wish I didn't.'

Tess dipped her head, stared at her shiny black shoes and sniffed loudly. 'Why can't you pick me up from school every day?'

Fenton sighed and rubbed his eyes. He hadn't had more than a couple of hours' sleep. 'I wish I could, Tess, but you know that's not possible. Why not give Marta a chance? She's nice, isn't she?'

Tess chose not to answer. 'Why does she have to live with us?'

'It makes things easier, that's all. Easier for her and us.' Fenton didn't want to explain that giving the nanny a rent-free room meant he had to pay her less. When he and Josie bought their first home in the north London borough of Islington they'd had two salaries coming in. Life together had been good. Tess came along six months later and life got even better. But cancer doesn't give a shit.

Tess pulled her hand away, keeping her eyes fixed on her feet. 'Where is she going to sleep?'

Fenton frowned. 'She'll have the spare room. It's plenty big enough.' Tess sniffed again, wiped her nose on the sleeve of her blazer, and released her seatbelt.

Fenton kissed his daughter's damp cheek, reached across and opened the passenger door. He watched her join the stream of children walking through the gates. Before disappearing from sight, she stopped and looked back. He waved and she rewarded him with half a smile.

His day went downhill from there. A steady drizzle slowed the traffic to a crawl. He arrived at the station thirty minutes later than he'd intended and his mood worsened with the news that he had a meeting with a press officer.

It was important to manage media coverage in murder cases, but he resented spending time on it. Fenton found the press officer waiting for him in his office. Ray Partington had joined the Yard's media team four months ago and Fenton had heard good things about him from people whose judgement he trusted.

Slipping into his chair, Fenton noticed the other man

looking pointedly at his watch. He decided not to apologise for arriving late. 'I've got a lot to do so let's make this quick and painless,' he said. 'It's the usual story. We need to keep the coverage going in the hope that a witness will come forward. That shouldn't be a problem, should it?'

Partington slapped a hand on the pile of national newspapers he'd placed on the desk. 'There won't be a problem keeping the press interested. The killer's Instagram post has gone viral. The papers are all over it, but I guarantee they'll soon be desperate for a new angle.'

Fenton sat back, crossed his arms and gazed across at the press officer. Partington wore a dark suit that matched his hair and a blue tie several shades paler than his eyes.

'There's nothing new I want to give out yet,' Fenton said. 'Keep doing what you're doing and make sure that the press keep putting out appeals for anybody who might have seen something.'

Partington tilted his head to one side. 'I understand, but if we don't come up with something new soon they'll assume the investigation is floundering.'

'They can assume whatever the hell they want. I don't give a damn.'

'Look, all I'm saying is that if the papers decide you're not doing your job properly things will turn nasty very quickly.'

Fenton tried to smile, but failed. 'You know your job,' he said. 'Keep the press happy while getting the coverage we need to help the investigation.'

Partington had the sense to realise that the meeting was over and headed for the door. Fenton watched him shake his head as he strode down the corridor, then pulled the pile of newspapers across the desk.

Most of the tabloids had put the murder story on the front page, using the headline *I, Killer* above the 'before' picture. The quality of the image was poor because it had been grabbed off the internet, but the terror on Lauren's face made Fenton's chest ache.

He picked up the *Express* and turned to page two, where an article invited readers to go to the paper's website and take part in a vote on whether they would view similar posts if the killer struck again. Fenton screwed the paper up and dropped it into the waste paper bin by his desk.

He pulled one of the so-called 'quality' papers over and found the story on page three. He was relieved to see that the only picture was a press office handout of a younger, smiling Lauren. The story too, had been angled away from the gory details of the murder. Under the headline *Killer Exploits Social Media Link To Moral Decay*, the article condemned the rush to view the I, Killer post, and the speed with which it was shared by hundreds of Instagram users and spread to Twitter and Facebook. Fenton read the first few paragraphs, nodded in agreement and pushed the paper aside. 'More like anti-social media,' he muttered.

He turned to his computer, grabbed the keyboard and googled I, Killer. 353,437 results in 0.76 seconds. How fucking depressing. He deleted I, Killer and searched for the *Express* website. The result of the poll flashed at him in a green box at the bottom of the home page. Seventy-eight per cent of readers would view pictures of I, Killer's next victim. Fifteen per cent voted no. Seven per cent undecided.

Fenton clenched his fists, stifling an urge to punch the screen. Instead, he stood and scooped up the newspapers, hurled them into the bin and kicked it so hard it bounced off the wall, spilling its contents across the floor.

9

Marta Blagar stared at her reflection in a shop window. Her green eyes were small and watchful. Youth kept her complexion fresh, but if you looked closely you could see signs of stress. She touched the dry patches of skin on her cheeks and traced the tiny lines radiating from the corners of her mouth. Lying went against her nature and the thought of being exposed kept her awake most nights.

The prospect of her family losing the roof over their heads scared her more than anything. The money she sent home every month paid the rent. Marta checked her watch. She had ten minutes to get to the school to pick up Tess.

She turned into Upper Street and, as always, couldn't help but marvel at its opulence. There were stores full of designer clothes, supermarkets crammed with food products from all over the world, and trendy coffee shops buzzing with gossip as customers sipped their skinny lattes while nibbling carrot and courgette cake. Compared to the Bucharest suburb where she'd been brought up, Islington was paradise.

Marta walked with her head held high. She had landed a

job and had made such a good impression she'd been asked to live in after only a couple of days. Her room was small but comfortable and, best of all, rent-free. Her employer was an important police officer and always respectful towards her. She hated lying to him.

The agency had checked her passport, and European Union freedom of movement rules meant she didn't need a work visa. The lying began when she filled in the application form. She claimed to have been registered as a nanny back in Romania. Whether they believed her or not, they didn't ask any difficult questions. They were happy to add her to their list, find her a position and take their fee. At the start of the interview with Tess's father, she had been so scared of rejection she blurted out that she was from Latvia. Her outburst made Mr Fenton smile, but he didn't question her assertion.

During her first few months in London, Marta discovered that opportunities for an unqualified Romanian woman were limited. Romanians had a bad reputation. She'd been advised, by a Polish barman, eager to get her into his bed, that her best chance of earning good money was to make the most of her physical attributes in the city's strip clubs. The club owners, he explained with a smirk, preferred hiring foreign women because they were usually desperate and easy to control. She said no to taking her clothes off for a living, and no to taking her clothes off for the barman. Instead, she became a Latvian.

Marta turned left and increased her pace. She couldn't

afford to be late. By the time she reached the school gates, the pupils were already flooding out. She searched their eager faces, but there was no sign of Tess.

From the first day, the girl had been hostile. No one could replace her mother. Marta understood that. She also understood that Mr Fenton struggled to handle his daughter's grief because he was still busy coping with his own. Pushing through a tide of chattering schoolchildren, she crossed the gates, scanning the road. Cars parked bumper to bumper lined the kerb. Elegant Georgian terraces crowded in on both sides of the street, which rose sharply for four hundred yards.

On the brow of the hill, contrasting figures caught Marta's eye. A man wearing black jeans and a dark hooded top stood in front of a young girl in school uniform. Beneath the hood, the peak of a baseball cap was pulled down over the man's face. He towered above the girl, his upper body bending forward as they spoke. The girl was facing away, her blazer and matching skirt swamping her slender frame. Breaking into a run, Marta called Tess's name and waved her right hand above her head. They must have heard her, but neither the man nor the girl turned. Marta could hear herself breathing noisily through her mouth, more from panic than exertion. She called out again, and this time the girl looked back down the hill. The man stooped lower and whispered into the girl's ear before turning and striding confidently away.

Marta slowed to a walk, forced herself to smile and stretched out her right arm, inviting Tess to take her hand.

The girl kept her hands clasped behind her back, a triumphant look on her angelic face.

Marta took a deep breath, but her heart still raced. 'Your father will not be happy that you wandered off on your own. You must not leave the school grounds without me.'

Tess's mouth twitched with the beginnings of a smile. 'You were late. Dad won't like it,' she said. Turning with a skip, she walked back down the hill. Marta followed a pace behind, panic rising in her chest. If she could sort this out between them, maybe Mr Fenton wouldn't need to be told anything.

'You must wait for me at the gate, if I am delayed. Always, you must wait.'

Tess didn't bother turning around to answer. 'Dad says your job is to look after me, but you weren't there. Why weren't you there? He told me he hired you from a top agency because he wanted the best care for me, a professional. Being late isn't being very professional. Is it?'

Marta edged alongside the girl, and dropped a hand to touch her shoulder. 'A few minutes late. I could not avoid it. Still, you must not wander off on your own. You especially must not go off and speak to strangers. Your father will be cross with you, I think. Perhaps, if you promise not to do such a thing again, it will be better if we don't tell him this time.'

Tess stopped walking and looked up, wrinkling her freckled nose. 'Maybe it would be best, but it's wrong to tell a lie, isn't it?' Marta didn't answer. Tess took the awkward silence as proof she had scored a point.

'Anyway, the man wasn't a stranger. He was nice to me. He knows Dad.' Tess wrinkled her nose and thought hard. 'He said I should tell Dad to take care of the little things. What does that mean?'

Marta gave Tess another reassuring pat on the shoulder. Mr Fenton was a reasonable man, but very protective of his daughter. How would he react to the news she'd been accosted on the street by a creep?

She tried to keep calm, but her bottom lip quivered. 'I don't think it's worth worrying him, do you? You know how much he worries about you. There's no need for me to tell him this time. I know you will not do this thing again. What do you say?'

Tess paused for a moment as she considered the pros and cons of getting her nanny, herself, or both of them into trouble. 'Let's make a deal,' she said. 'You don't tell that I left the school gates on my own, and I won't tell that you were late.'

Marta didn't hesitate. 'It's a deal.'

10

Blake pressed the doorbell and waited nervously, one arm wrapped around a large cardboard box, the other holding a battered suitcase. The flat was on the second floor of a low-rise complex overlooking the Poplar Dock marina. Across the water, the towers of Canary Wharf shimmered in the sunshine.

A Docklands property with a water view was way out of Blake's pay league. The door opened and for a split-second he thought Lauren had come back from the dead. Leah Bishop waved him in. The flat was spacious, open plan and sparsely furnished. 'Put the stuff down and I'll sort it out later,' she said. Blake did as he was told and took a hesitant step back.

Leah let him suffer a long, uncomfortable silence before she spoke. 'Is that it then? You're going to do a runner?'

Blake looked down at the watch on his wrist and fidgeted with the strap. 'Truth is, I don't know what to say.'

'I thought you might want to talk about Lauren. Thought it might help both of us.'

Blake closed his eyes and took a deep breath. 'I'm so sorry,' he said.

'Sorry for what?'

'Sorry she's dead.'

'It's not your fault, is it?'

Blake shrugged. Leah's resemblance to her sister had thrown him off balance. He struggled not to stare. The same short black hair, blue eyes and open face.

She sensed his confusion. 'I'm nearly two years older, but we were always being asked if we were twins. It annoyed the hell out of both of us.'

Blake nodded. He wanted to go, but at the same time he needed to stay. 'Lauren was a beautiful, kind person. It was my fault,' he said. 'All my fault.'

'I know.'

'I'm sorry.'

Leah shook her head. 'Sorry doesn't fix anything.'

Blake took a tentative step towards the door. 'I'd better be getting back.'

'Back to the running machine? Can you believe Lauren told me she was jealous of your running machine?'

Blake raised his hands. 'I didn't come here for this.'

'Why did you come?'

'Because you called. Asked me to bring her stuff. Remember?'

'Don't mind me,' she said. 'This is hard.'

Blake nodded. 'We both cared for Lauren.'

Leah tilted her head, gave him a curious look and allowed

herself a wistful smile. 'I'm coping. I think. I don't suppose it'll sink in completely until the funeral.' She paused to blink back tears. 'I heard you were questioned by the police.'

'You heard right.'

'I suppose the police had to check you out, being the former boyfriend.'

Blake was uncertain where the conversation was going, but he was sure he didn't want to go there. 'I had to answer a few questions. Then they let me go. Like you said, it had to be done. Routine.'

Leah tried to smile again. Instead, her bottom lip quivered and tears pooled in her eyes. 'I keep asking myself, why Lauren? She was a good, caring person. She didn't deserve it. And all those people desperately searching out those terrible pictures. I don't understand it.'

Blake took a couple of deep breaths. He remembered the hurt in Lauren's eyes the day that she left and his throat tightened. He could have talked her round. Leah sniffed loudly and he realised she expected him to answer her question.

'It's down to human nature, I suppose,' he said. 'We've all got darkness somewhere inside.'

'You really believe that?'

'Why do you think drivers slow down to rubberneck at car crashes? Why are we fascinated by horror movies, TV coverage of disasters? Don't ask me to explain it because I can't. The ghouls following the killer disgust me as much as they do you. It just doesn't shock me as much.'

Leah frowned and gave him a drawn-out look that was

impossible to read. He guessed it meant she thought his answer profound, or incredibly stupid. He'd put money on stupid. He moved to the door and reached for the handle. He was wondering how to say goodbye, when she called out, her voice strangely upbeat.

'I'll let you know when then? Give you a call?'

'Let me know when what?'

'Time and date of the funeral, of course.'

Blake found himself nodding and stopped. 'There's no need. I'll leave that stuff to friends and family.' Leah's back stiffened and she lifted her chin, something Blake had seen her sister do many times.

'She loved you,' she said, her voice cracking. 'You lived together. Don't you feel anything for her? She might have made excuses for you but, believe me, I won't.'

Blake dropped his gaze to the floor. 'I haven't got any excuses. Lauren was special to me. She always will be. I never wanted her to leave. She chose to go and I don't blame her. But I'll grieve in my own way. I'll leave the funeral to family.'

'I'm the only family she has.'

Blake didn't intend to be cruel, but he didn't want to leave any room for negotiation. 'Like I said, I'll leave the funeral to the family.'

Leah bit down hard on her bottom lip. The distress on her face almost persuaded Blake to change his mind. Almost. She approached him in silence, prised his fingers off the handle, opened the door and waited for him to leave.

11

Big Ted they called him. They thought it was hilarious, especially after a couple of cans of extra-strong lager. He'd always been small for his age and through school had to put up with all the usual, unoriginal insults: short-arse, midget, shrimpy.

One benefit of his size had been he'd always been able to pass as younger than his real age. Not any more. Eleven months sleeping rough had taken its toll. His boyish face had developed more wrinkles than an elephant's scrotum and his greying hair resembled a badger's arse. That was what his mates said anyway. The crowd he usually dossed down with would snigger when he tried to insist he was only twenty-eight.

He needed to teach them a lesson. They'd notice his absence when they gathered around the soup vans at Lincoln's Inn Fields tonight. Later, they'd start to wonder where he'd got to, feel guilty, maybe even worry about him. It'd teach them not to take him for granted.

Sleep rough on the streets for a decent length of time

and you soon become skilled at predicting what the weather's going to do. Big Ted knew the banks of cloud settling over the city would stick around and prevent the temperature from falling more than a few degrees. He placed a couple of flattened cardboard boxes on the concrete, snuggled up between two wheelie bins and covered up with another two bits of cardboard. The spot he'd picked was perfect. Tucked away in a brick archway under Blackfriars Bridge on the north bank of the Thames, he'd be sheltered from the wind and rain if the weather took a turn for the worse.

Without the warmth of the bodies of his mates, Big Ted expected to feel the cold a bit more than usual, but he'd come prepared. He reached into the pocket of his ragged duffel coat and pulled out a large bottle of cider. A third of it had already found its way down his neck, but there was more than enough left to anaesthetise his brain, numbing his body against the chill and discomfort.

He unscrewed the top, took a long swig and tried to remember if he was sleeping on the streets because he drank too much, or whether he drank too much because he was homeless. The truth was, he didn't give a shit anyway. All he cared about was getting his so-called mates to start showing him the respect he deserved.

Placing the bottle carefully on the concrete beside his makeshift bed, he rolled on to his side and curled up in a ball. The bottle top slipped from his fingers and rolled slowly out of the archway. He swore under his breath, but decided it could stay where it was. The cider was going to be finished off soon. There was no danger of it going flat.

Closing his eyes, he took a deep breath and listened to the soundtrack of the city at night. The constant drone of traffic over the bridge was underlined by the hum of the structure vibrating. Car horns sounded intermittently and, somewhere in the distance, a police siren wailed. There was always a siren wailing somewhere.

12

*T*he sound of footsteps surprises him because there is no reason for anyone to visit his rat hole. Lying still, he holds his breath and listens. His heart flutters like a trapped bird. He feels a sudden urge to piss and squeezes his thighs together. Maybe, he thinks, it's Bonehead or Jezzer, looking for him after his no-show at the soup vans.

The bottle of cider flies over his head and smashes against the back wall. The liquid runs down the brickwork and pools under one of the bins. He twists up on to his knees. 'What the fuck are you doing?' he yells. 'That stuff costs money.' A face peers down at him. Big Ted looks into the eyes and shudders. 'I asked you a question, mate,' he babbles. He raises his voice, hoping to attract someone's attention. 'That's my last bottle. I need it to sleep. Bet you've got a bed to go back to.'

He breathes a sigh of relief when the man dips his hand into the pocket of his coat. The fool accidentally kicked over his cider and is ready to hand out some cash. When the man lifts his hand, a warm trickle runs down Big Ted's right leg and drips on to his trainer.

The knife flashes like molten silver. Big Ted tries to shout, but the only sound that comes out of his mouth is a wet gurgle. He crumples to the floor, gasping for breath. Strong hands roll him on to his back. Fingers grasp a handful of hair, yanking his head back. A thick wetness spurts on to his shoulders and chest.

The pain kicks in, blurring his vision, but he sees the man pull something else from his pocket and hold it in front of his face. 'Let them see,' the man says.

13

Blake rarely watched television. He preferred to switch on the treadmill and run. He particularly avoided news programmes. They reminded him of too many things he was trying to blank out.

After falling out with Leah over the funeral, he'd been surprised when she had phoned to let him know she'd been asked by the police to make an appeal for information about Lauren's murder at a live press conference. She sounded nervous and Blake suspected she'd been hoping he would offer to attend the event with her. He didn't. Over the years he'd taken part in hundreds of press conferences. He didn't want anything to do with that world any more.

Wearing baggy shorts and a running vest, Blake perched on the sofa and fiddled with the remote control. It took him a few seconds to find the right channel. Leah Bishop sat in the centre at a long table, her shoulders hunched, her face pale. The sight of her, so vulnerable but at the same time resolute, twisted his insides.

Sitting on Leah's left an overweight, grey-haired detective

pulled a tissue from his pocket and wiped beads of sweat from his brow.

Journalists who arrived too late to get a seat pressed against the side and back walls. To the far right of the table, a dark-haired man in a suit whispered into the ear of a woman in police uniform.

A barrage of camera flashes signalled the start of the conference. In unison, Leah Bishop and the detective raised a hand to shield their eyes. Clearing his throat, the detective lowered his head to his microphone. 'Good evening ladies and gentlemen,' he said. 'My name is Detective Super-intendent Bob Bell. This press conference has been arranged to assist the investigation into the murder of Lauren Bishop, who was stabbed to death in Victoria Park, Hackney. We will start with the victim's sister. She will be making a simple appeal for witnesses, not answering questions. Any questions you have should be directed at me. Of course, there will be some operational details that I cannot disclose.'

He waved towards the younger man in the suit. 'When we have finished, additional material and assistance will be provided by our press officer, Ray Partington.'

Clearing his throat again, Bell wiped his top lip with his sleeve and turned with a nod to Leah. Blake knew well the pressure of being in the spotlight and couldn't help but admire her courage.

She glanced down at her script. 'My sister Lauren was murdered as she walked in Victoria Park on the evening of September twenty-eighth. She was a kind and gentle person who didn't have a bad bone in her body. The police are working hard to find her killer and I am making this appeal today in the hope that someone out there can help.'

She paused for a moment and, her eyes brimming with tears, raised her head to look, as instructed, straight down the lens of the television camera. 'If you saw anyone or anything strange in the park that evening, or if you know anything or have suspicions about who might have killed Lauren, please, please, please, contact the police. We need to catch the person who killed my sister. My innocent sister. Even the smallest, seemingly insignificant piece of information could prove crucial, so please, please, don't be afraid about coming forward if you think you can help.'

The end of her statement brought another barrage of camera flashes, followed by a flurry of questions. Flustered, she turned to the detective for help. He raised a hand to try to bring order to the room, but ended up having to shout over the clamour.

'As I said earlier, all questions must be directed at me. I'll answer them if I can. As usual, please give your name and the media organisation you are working for. Who wants to go first?'

Every journalist in the room stuck up a hand. Bell pointed at a woman in the third row.

'Yvonne Dixon, BBC London. How exactly was Lauren Bishop killed?'

'She was killed with a knife. I can't give you more detail than that.'

'It's true that the killer slashed her throat, isn't it? Everybody has seen the pictures on the internet.'

Bell blanked her and jabbed a finger at a reporter in the front row.

'David Jackman, *Evening Standard*. The killer must be lapping up all the attention and laughing at the police investigation. He's committed murder and put it on the internet for everyone to see.'

Bell shook his head. 'We're on top of this case. Let's get back to the appeal for information.'

Without waiting to be invited, a female reporter in the front row jumped in. 'Jo Forlong, *Daily Express*. Instagram say the pictures of Lauren Bishop were viewed by more than eight thousand people and given close to twelve hundred "likes" before the account was shut down. This killer is making the police look incompetent, and at the same time seems to be building a fan base.'

Bell wiped his brow again. 'We're working to try to solve the murder of Lauren Bishop and that's why we called this conference today. The gentleman in the red tie.'

The *Daily Express* reporter ignored the brush-off. 'What about urging the public to boycott these pictures and any new ones the killer might post?'

The detective chief superintendent squirmed in his seat and pointed again at the journalist wearing a red tie.

'Nick Gordon, Press Association. Any fool can see that . . .' He stopped in mid-sentence to pull his phone from his pocket. At the same time, a chorus of email alerts pinged, dinged and chimed around the room. Every journalist reached for their mobiles. The Press Association reporter had to shout to make himself heard over the growing babble of excitement. 'My news editor says I, Killer is trending on Twitter. Pictures of a new victim posted.'

Bell threw his hands up. 'That's it. We're done, conference over,' he said.

The camera zoomed out, but Blake kept his eyes on Leah. She bowed her head to hide her face, but he could see her body trembling. The camera immediately zoomed back in for a close-up of her grief.

At that moment, the press officer walked over to Leah and knelt beside her. Blake leant closer to the screen as Partington offered her a tissue. She took it and dabbed at her eyes. Partington gently touched her elbow, helped her to her feet and led her away.

Blake snatched up the TV remote and pressed the off button. He felt a strange mixture of relief and stabbing envy that someone had realised how distressing the event had been for Leah. He stepped on the treadmill, started to run hard and think even harder. What kind of person kills for pleasure? Would you have to be insane or simply evil?

Evil existed. He knew that for a fact. He'd sensed it, stared it in the eye. He pressed the stop button and went in search of his laptop. He found it on the kitchen table and turned it on. Fenton's words, 'Don't look', rang in his ears, but he blocked them out. He found Google and typed in 'Lauren Bishop I, Killer'.

The first half-dozen results were news reports on the police investigation, but the seventh was what he'd been looking for. Someone had shared the original Instagram post with a Reditt forum discussion on 'Why People Kill.'

Blake's forefinger hovered over the mouse, his heart racing. Why did he want to see Lauren's final moments? He had no answer to that question. The sensible thing would be not to look, but he needed to. He took a long, deep breath and clicked.

14

Fenton let Ince drive so he could check out the I, Killer tweet. Reading on the screen of his mobile while in a car always made him nauseous and the photographs only made matters worse.

The account had been set up with the handle @ErikLil and a single tweet posted. *Look into these eyes and know what it's like to play God #IKiller.*

In the photograph, Edward Deere's mouth was twisted into a grotesque smile, the tip of his tongue resting on his lower lip. His eyes were open, the pupils dilated. Fenton had seen enough dead bodies to know that Deere had still been alive when the picture had been taken. Just.

The scent of the tree-shaped air freshener dangling from the rear-view mirror reminded Fenton of the smell of a hospital ward, the smell of grief. No agony can match the final agony of death, he told himself.

Deere's body had turned up within an hour of the tweet, found behind a pair of wheelie bins by a hungover Canadian tourist looking for a hidden corner to throw up in.

Fenton read the tweet again. This time out loud. Ince glanced his way and smiled. 'Sounds pretty crazy to me boss. Why Erik Lil?' Fenton responded with a non-committal grunt. Daly had seen it straightaway, but he was going to have to give Ince a helping hand. 'It's an anagram.'

Ince kept his eyes on the road, his knuckles turning white as he gripped the steering wheel. 'Right, got it,' he said. 'Makes sense. I, Killer has probably been put on Twitter's list of banned usernames.' The same thought had occurred to Fenton. The killer couldn't resist playing to his growing army of admirers.

One thing Fenton felt sure about was that his team would find no connection between the homeless Edward Deere and Lauren Bishop. He'd been selected to die for no other reason than to excite morbid curiosity. Fenton still had his eyes on the screen of his mobile when the car pulled up sharply, jolting him forward in his seat. 'This is it,' Ince announced, his tone overly cheerful for a man about to attend a post-mortem examination.

Fenton looked down at Edward Deere's feeble body, stretched out naked on a steel table, a wasted life cut short. The torso had been sliced down the middle, from sternum to belly, the flesh clamped back exposing the organs.

He regularly attended post mortems and the smell always got to him – a stomach-churning mixture of decaying flesh and antiseptic fluid. The whitewashed walls, harsh lighting and air conditioning made the City of London mortuary feel like the inside of a giant fridge. In the centre of the room stood an examination table and beside it a steel desk on which sat two computer screens.

Instinctively, Fenton raised a hand to cover his nose and mouth, but dropped it to his side when Ince caught his eye and grinned. He looked down at the body again and wondered why the killer had singled out Deere. The homeless man's friends had admitted constantly teasing him about his lack of height. On the day of his murder he'd stormed off in a sulk threatening to never come back, a threat he'd made many times before.

They said Deere had claimed that he'd come down to London from the north-west, but so far his family, if he had any, hadn't been traced. Fenton wondered if there was any point trying to find them. Would they give a damn? Probably not. All the checks had been done and nobody had been worried enough to report him missing.

Deere's limbs and torso were thin and lacking muscle tissue. Fenton studied his face, the light-brown eyes fixed open, the nose small and slightly curved. Cleaned up and in his prime, Deere would have been good-looking in a boyish way. A strip of crisp white linen spanned the width of his shoulders, crossing under his chin, covering his neck. Both detectives turned towards the door as the pathologist, wearing white disposable overalls, entered the room, walked quickly to the desk and switched on one of the computers. 'Sorry to keep you waiting. I know you probably want to get out of here as quickly as possible.'

Alice Drury, in her mid-thirties, was one of the city's top forensic pathologists, with a tongue as sharp as her scalpel. She slipped on a pair of white latex gloves and positioned herself close to the cadaver, facing both Fenton and Ince.

'As you might expect, this is not very complicated,' she said, lifting the linen cloth covering the neck. Fenton turned away for a second, but forced himself to look back. Ince stepped closer to get a better view of the wound.

The pathologist gave Fenton a sympathetic look before turning her attention back to the body. 'I know that, unlike your young colleague here, you're a bit squeamish, so I'll be gentle with you. Cause of death, of course, is this traumatic wound to the neck. Both carotid arteries were severed. The trachea was sliced. It's a toss-up whether he bled to death or suffocated. Likely a combination of the two.'

Fenton suppressed a shudder. 'How does the wound compare to Lauren Bishop's?'

'I'd say the initial cut, the killing cut, is more or less identical. The blade was dragged from right to left both times, suggesting the killer is left-handed. The big difference is that this time the killer sawed at the neck after the initial cut, right through to the cervical vertebrae. The muscle tissue and ligaments in the neck are pretty tough. Sawing through them takes a lot of force and effort.'

Fenton paused a moment to think. 'Does this suggest anger?'

'I'm not suggesting anything. Just giving you the facts.

The murder of Lauren Bishop seemed more clinical. One clean cut.'

'How long would he have taken to die?'

'I'd estimate thirty seconds to a minute, no longer.

Long enough to take a photograph, to capture the last agonies of a dying man, Fenton thought. He lifted his gaze from the body and stared out of the room's single window. The day had turned grey and fat drops of rain ran down the glass like tears.

'Anything else?' he asked. 'Any other wounds, or traces of the killer's DNA? You said the head must have been held to allow the killer to saw through the neck tissue.'

The pathologist moved closer to the computer to scroll through her report. 'It's the same as the Lauren Bishop murder. The killer left no DNA behind. Probably wearing gloves. There were no defensive wounds on the victim's hands or arms. Nothing under his fingernails except dirt.'

Fenton noticed his colleague trying to catch his eye. He nodded and Ince stepped closer to the body and peered at the mutilation. 'Are you able to say anything about the knife that was used?' Ince asked.

'Good question,' the pathologist said, raising her eyebrows at Fenton. 'I was waiting for your boss to ask that one.' Ince looked up and smiled. Fenton didn't smile back.

'We can tell from the span of the initial cut, before any sawing action, that it was a long blade, at least nine inches. A close examination of the skin and muscle tissue that was sawn through shows the blade was definitely serrated. That would have made the sawing action easier. I'd say the length of the blade and the cutting edge used in both killings would have been close to identical.'

Ince nodded and moved back. He glanced at his boss as if expecting a follow-up question. Fenton said nothing and the pathologist took the chance to press on. 'As far as the victim's general health goes, he was surprisingly well considering he was living on the streets. A little undernourished, yes, but all his organs were in good working order, even his liver, and his arteries are pretty clear of plaque.'

She paused for a moment and gave Fenton an appraising look. 'You know, a couple of months living rough on a frugal diet would probably do your cardiovascular system the world of good.'

Fenton had known Drury for almost ten years. They were not quite old friends, but he was fond of her. He put on his best hurt face. He'd always kept himself in good shape.

'One last thing,' he said. 'If you had to put your house on it, would you say Lauren Bishop and Edward Deere were killed by the same person?'

The pathologist stretched out a hand and tapped the computer's keyboard, closing the report file and shutting down the computer. She pulled the thin latex gloves off her hands, dropped them into a surgical waste bin under the desk, and crossed her arms.

'That call's not my job, it's yours,' she said. 'I'm here to give you the scientific facts only, but you've known me a long time and you know I'm not shy about voicing my opinion. In the absence of any forensic evidence left on the victim's bodies it's hard to say, scientifically, that they were definitely killed by the same person.'

She paused for a moment and gently placed the strip of linen back over the corpse's neck. Fenton was unsure whether she had finished or not, but kept quiet to give her the opportunity to say more. She gave him a sideways look and took his silence as an invitation to carry on.

'Having said all that, the method of killing was the same, the knives used must have been almost identical, and the sheer randomness of the murders tells you even more. If you want my honest opinion, and don't tell me you're surprised by this, both murders are the work of the same person.'

Fenton took a long, deep breath, compressed his lips and let the air out slowly through his nose. 'You're right,' he said. 'I'm not surprised.'

15

The drive back to New Scotland Yard was less than three miles, but the heavy rain slowed the mid-morning traffic on Victoria Embankment to a slow crawl. They had been travelling for twenty minutes and still hadn't reached Parliament Square.

Whistling under his breath, Ince drummed the steering wheel with his fingers in time to the squeak of the windscreen wipers as he edged the car forward a few feet before applying the brakes. Fenton glanced across at the detective constable. 'Do you have to do that?' he said. 'I can't hear myself think.'

Ince raised his eyebrows and wrapped his fingers around the steering wheel to keep them still. 'Sorry, boss.'

'What are you so cheerful about anyway? You've just seen your second dead body, it's pissing down with rain and we're stuck in a traffic jam.'

The car ahead moved off slowly and Ince concentrated on following it until the traffic rolled to a halt again. 'I enjoyed it, to be honest. Educational. You've probably been to dozens, hundreds maybe. Surely you're used to them by now?'

Fenton raised a hand to his face and rubbed his eyes, pinching the bridge of his nose with his thumb and forefinger. 'I don't like them. I'll never get used to them. They're people. I mean they were people. Sons and daughters, someone's mother or father, brother or sister, wife or husband. I can't see them any other way.'

Ince took his eyes off the traffic for a moment and looked across at his passenger, a half-smile on his pale face. 'I get that, sir,' he said. 'But the wounds, the way the victims were killed, where they were killed, must tell us something.'

Fenton sighed. He found Ince's lack of empathy depressing. 'So, tell me, hot-shot,' he said. 'Sum up for me what the bodies of the victims say about the killer, or killers.'

Ince's smile widened and his fingers resumed their drumming. 'Well, from the line of the initial neck wounds we can say both were killed by a left-hander. From the speed and strength needed to inflict the fatal wounds cleanly, without a struggle, I think we can assume the killer is a man. A tall, athletic man.'

He shot a glance at his boss in search of reassurance. Fenton gave nothing away. Ince focused on the chrome bumper of the car ahead and carried on. 'The two victims are almost certainly unconnected, so we can say they were selected randomly. The killer targets the arteries in the neck. Maybe he has a blood fetish. He likes killing, enjoys it. It probably turns him on even.'

The rain stopped and Ince flicked the windscreen wipers off. 'How am I doing?' The traffic was moving faster now. By the time Fenton spoke, they had reached Westminster Bridge.

'I think you've been watching too many TV police dramas, that's what I think. You're making too many assumptions. Never assume anything. It's a sure-fire way to screw up.'

Ince swung the car right towards Parliament Square. 'I don't know. You tell me,' he said. 'Teach me the error of my ways. I'm always keen to learn from people who've done it all before.'

It sounded like a compliment, but Fenton suspected otherwise. 'Well, after what we've seen and heard today, there is one thing I can tell you. Something I'd stake my reputation on.'

Ince kept his eyes on the road as a set of traffic lights ahead turned red. 'Go on,' he said.

'There's going to be a third murder and there's nothing we can do to stop it.'

Ten minutes later they pulled up outside New Scotland Yard and Fenton's heart sank. Close to twenty photographers and reporters milled around the entrance. Behind them two television news vans topped with satellite dishes were parked bonnet to bonnet at the kerb. Standing in front of the reporters, Partington appeared to be doing his best to field their questions.

Fenton gestured at Ince to drive on to the car park barrier. He had no intention of running the gauntlet of a ravenous press pack. He found Daly in the incident room, busy issuing instructions to half a dozen detective constables. She spotted Fenton standing in the doorway, broke off and followed him into his office. He perched on the edge of his desk and crossed his arms. 'Any progress?'

Daly shook her head and lifted a hand to straighten her ponytail. 'The Twitter account has been taken down, but there's nothing to stop the killer setting up another one.'

'We need to check all the CCTV footage from cameras in the area around Blackfriars Bridge.'

Daly nodded: 'It's being done.'

Fenton walked around behind his desk, gesturing for Daly to take a seat. 'I saw Partington fending off a bunch of reporters out front,' he said. 'What's going on?'

Daly pulled a strand of hair from over her left eye. 'Apparently some of the papers are planning to use tomorrow's editions to call for the officers leading the investigation to be replaced.'

Fenton sat down and swivelled his chair, swinging his knees from side to side. After a few seconds, he stopped. 'Tell me truthfully,' he said. 'Just between you and me. If you weren't a police officer, say you were employed in a bank, or an estate agency, when you got home from work would you go online to search out the terrified face of a woman who knows she's about to die?'

Daly glanced briefly over her shoulder at her colleagues in the squad room. 'I hope not,' she said.

16

I couldn't help myself. I should have taken more care selecting the victim, but he served a purpose. I have to keep the momentum going. My followers need to be entertained.

The human psyche has a dark, primitive side. Most people cower in the comfort of the light. I am not most people. Don't think that those who fear their darkness are superior human beings to those who embrace it. They are not better. They are weaker.

But they can't stop themselves taking a sneaky peek into the shadows. I invite them into my world and they follow. From a safe distance, of course. At least that's what they think.

From here on my prey must be worthy. Planning and selection are the key to satisfaction. This one pleased my public, but didn't satisfy my hunger. Not like the first time.

Should I worry about the police? Not too much. The press conference was a farce, though the sister was interesting.

The police are still appealing for witnesses. What does

that tell me? It tells me that they haven't got a clue what to do next. They will, of course, already have their computer experts trying to track me down. Yeah, good luck with that. No doubt they'll also be consulting criminal psychologists. All psychologists are criminal in my mind. Let me guess what they'll come up with.

This guy has killed at least two people, so he must be a raving psychopath. His internet activity shows he's obsessed with fame. He's a narcissistic manipulator, charming and intelligent, can't empathise with other human beings, and is a sexual pervert who gets his thrills by spilling blood.

Predictably predictable. They're not equipped to out think someone like me. I'm capable of things they wouldn't under-stand. Each of my kills is a step along a path I have plotted for a while now, but killing has always been part of my nature. The strongest, deepest, purest part.

Knowing is everything. I know my prey. I know myself. Self-knowledge is the only true freedom. If you know what you're doing is insane, you must be sane, right?

17

Blake sat in the consulting room, his arms folded across his chest. The woman on the other side of the desk pursed her lips. They stared at each other in silence for what seemed like an age, but was probably no more than a minute. The woman cracked first.

'We're not going to get anywhere if you don't speak.'

'What do you want me to say?'

'What do you want to say?'

Blake tilted his head back and examined an ornate floral moulding in the centre of the ceiling. Two large cracks criss-crossed the decaying Victorian plasterwork. He took a deep breath. 'I'm not sure what I want to say, but when I do know I'm going to need help to say it.'

To Blake's surprise, the woman smiled, displaying a set of white, perfectly straight teeth. 'Well that's as good a place to start as any.'

Looking at Belinda Vale, Blake felt decidedly underdressed. Maybe, he thought, she had a date at an expensive restaurant after work.

NOW YOU SEE

The psychologist tilted her head to one side, making her brown fringe slant across her forehead. 'Shall we move on, Mr Blake? Is Mr Blake okay, or would you prefer Adam?'

Blake shrugged. 'Whatever you want. Most people call me Blake.'

'Good. I'll go with Blake then.' Twisting in her chair, she reached into the top desk drawer and pulled out a blue folder. She dropped it in front of her, flipped it open and scanned the first page. Her slender fingers were bare, except for a single gold band on the third finger of her right hand.

She looked up from the file, nodding as if what she had read confirmed something she suspected. 'Why now?' she said.

'What do you mean?'

'Why have you decided to come for therapy now? After all this time. You were referred to me almost a year ago. You never showed up.'

Blake frowned. 'Are you saying there's a time limit or something?'

'Of course not. I'm simply pointing out that something must have changed. I assume you're here because you want help. You didn't want it eleven months ago. So, tell me what's different.'

Blake wondered if she was genuinely interested, or simply saying what she thought she needed to say to get him to talk. He gave her the benefit of the doubt. 'I think maybe it's time. Maybe I should have done this before, but I didn't.'

Vale nodded encouragement, but Blake fell silent and took another long look at the ceiling.

'We don't have to talk about what happened in Iraq,' she said. 'Not this time. But if we can talk more about why you think you're ready for this, I think that would be useful.'

Blake's jaw muscles flexed. 'Useful to who? I'm regretting coming here already.'

A flicker of irritation crossed Vale's face. 'We're not going to get anywhere if you keep this up,' she said. 'If you're here because you want things to change you need to ditch the attitude.'

Part of Blake wanted to spill his guts, vomit out the poison. A bigger part wanted to keep it hidden. 'I don't know how to do this,' he said.

Vale looked down at the file and turned over a page. 'I tell you what. Let's try simple questions and answers. I'll ask and you respond. How about that?' Blake nodded his assent.

'Right then, where shall we begin? Are you in a relationship at the moment?'

'Is that relevant?'

'It gives me an idea where you are emotionally. Helps build up a picture.'

'No, there's no one.'

'Have you been on your own since coming back?'

'There was somebody. We broke up. It didn't work out.'

Vale glanced down at the file again. 'Post-traumatic stress disorder can be a difficult burden for a partner to cope with.'

'She tried her best.'

Vale picked up a pen and scribbled in the file. Blake strained his eyes to try to read the note.

'How serious was this relationship?'

'We lived together for a while. She moved into my flat. Then moved out.'

'How did you feel about that?'

Blake shook his head. 'That's a dumb question.' The psychologist made another note. 'How the hell did you think I felt? I didn't want her to leave, but I understood.'

Vale shifted in her seat and crossed her legs. 'Would you consider resuming this relationship if the opportunity presented itself?'

'It won't.'

'It may not be out of the question.'

'It is.'

'PTSD can be treated successfully. You've taken the first step by coming here. If we sort out your issues she might be willing to give you another chance.'

'She won't.'

'I understand it's difficult not to be negative in your situation, but why are you so adamant this relationship can't be mended?'

'Because she's dead.' Vale's eyes widened, but she kept the rest of her face neutral. She picked up her pen, rolled it between her thumb and forefinger and put it down again. Blake admired her self-control, but wasn't going to make it easy for her. If she wanted to know she'd have to ask.

'I'm so sorry. Is this why you're here?'

'What do you mean?'

'Is this why you changed your mind about getting help?'

Blake shook his head. 'I don't think so. I hadn't thought about it like that.'

'Do you want to talk about her death?'

Blake linked his fingers and stared at his hands. Vale gave him a moment to think. 'Emotional avoidance is a common symptom of PTSD. Unfortunately, burying your feelings is unhealthy.'

Blake snapped his head up. 'I can do without the jargon. I feel like I'm being lectured.'

'I'm sorry you feel that way, but I meant what I said. It would be a good idea to explore your grief.'

'Not this time.'

'There's going to be a next time then?'

Blake thought for a few seconds. 'Maybe.'

18

After leaving Vale's clinic, Blake headed east along High Holborn, a bustling thoroughfare linking the West End with London's financial district. The late-afternoon sun slanted its rays under a blanket of cloud, gilding the skyline.

The session hadn't been as bad as he had feared. Vale's professionalism impressed him. It was a start and that was all he'd been hoping for. What did he ultimately want to achieve? He wasn't sure.

He'd been walking for about thirty minutes when his mobile phone rang. He dug it out of his jacket pocket and checked the caller ID. An unknown number.

He answered the call with a cursory 'Yes.'

'Hello, Blake, can you hear me?'

He recognised the voice straightaway. He covered his free ear with the palm of his hand. 'The traffic's noisy, but I can hear.'

'It's Leah Bishop. Are you free to meet? I need to talk to you.'

Blake hesitated. 'How did you get my number?' he said.

'How do you think? I'm Lauren's sister. You know, Lauren, your former girlfriend?'

Blake considered pretending that he was losing signal and cutting her off. 'What's this about? I told you I'm not coming to the funeral and given you my reasons. I'm sorry, but that's the way it is.'

'I'm not calling about that. Can you make Spitalfields Market in an hour? Please. It's important.'

Blake cursed himself for answering the call. 'Where do you want to meet?'

Leah sighed. 'Thank you,' she said. 'There are lots of pubs and bars around there. I'll choose one and send you a text.' She ended the call before he had time to say anything else.

It took him forty-five minutes to get to the Red Lion. The exterior promised a traditional East End pub, but inside the owners had gone for the shabby chic look. He spotted Leah in the main bar, a cavernous room with a high ceiling and a dark, pitted wooden floor.

Blake weaved his way through the standing drinkers to where Leah sat on a Chesterfield-style sofa, a glass of white wine in her hand. She looked smaller somehow, crushed by the weight of grief. He sat beside her without waiting for an invitation. She nodded at a pint of beer on the table in front of them. 'That's yours.'

Blake picked up the beer and took a sip. 'Good choice.' The two of them locked gazes. Blake was the first to look away, unwilling to acknowledge the hope that flared in her eyes – the hope that he might be able to help her.

She placed her glass on the table. Blake noticed her hand trembling. 'I suppose you're wondering why I asked you to meet me?' she said. Blake stayed silent. It wasn't a real question.

Leah dipped her head. 'I've been thinking a lot about Lauren.'

Blake took another small sip of beer. 'I think about her too.'

'We have to do something,' Leah said. Her eyes were dry, but her voice shook. 'The man who killed Lauren is walking the streets, bragging about what he's done on the internet. We can't sit around doing nothing.'

Blake raised a hand to his face and pinched the bridge of his nose. Had he heard right? Did she say we? He wasn't sure. 'What else can you do?'

Leah coughed, wrapped her fingers around the stem of her wine glass, slid it a couple of inches to the right and pulled it back again. 'I want to hire you to help me catch her killer.'

Blake's mouth opened, then closed. He tried again. 'Do you know how crazy that sounds?'

'What's so crazy about it? You've got the skills. We need to at least try to do something. Lauren would want us to try. I know she would.'

'We can't.'

'Is that it?'

'That's it.'

Leah's cheeks reddened. She took a minute to compose herself. 'Are you unable to articulate your reasons?'

'I can give you reasons. The thing is, I don't want to. I'm not going to.'

Blake stood. Leah reached out and tugged gently at his wrist. 'Please sit down,' she said. He did as she asked. She kept her fingers resting on the back of his hand and took a deep breath. 'A few weeks before she died Lauren told me she believed you could straighten yourself out if only you'd do something positive with your life. Set yourself a challenge.'

'You mean run a marathon, or climb a mountain?' Blake asked, shaking his head.

'You were a serious investigative journalist, weren't you?'

Blake answered with silence.

'Make finding Lauren's killer your challenge. That's the least she deserves. Did you love her?'

'I really cared about her.'

'Then why not?'

Blake shook his head. 'Leave it to the police. That's what they're for.'

'They're not getting very far. If you find out anything important you can share it with them.'

'Have you seriously thought it through?'

'I really have. Please think about it.'

Blake thought about it. Maybe it was the only way to put things right. He'd failed Lauren in so many ways. She'd given him everything and all he'd offered her was disappointment. He couldn't bring her back. Maybe this could be the next best thing.

He looked at Leah, his lips twisting into a tight smile. 'I need some time,' he said. 'I'm not sure if it's a good or bad idea, but at least it's an idea and I haven't had many of those recently.'

I, KILLER

He thought . . .

19

Fenton stifled a yawn and listened to the press officer. He certainly had a talent for talking.

'The newspapers and TV are going for broke on this story,' Partington said. 'They keep using the I, Killer hashtag. We've lost our ability to control the press coverage of the case – the killer's using social media to set the agenda.'

Detective Chief Superintendent Bell scowled behind his polished oak desk. 'You're admitting you can't do your job, that the force's press office is an expensive waste of taxpayers' money?'

Partington looked across at Fenton, as if hoping for some sign of support. The detective raised his eyebrows, but said nothing. He wanted the meeting over with as quickly as possible. He had better things to do.

Partington wasn't ready to throw in the towel. He pulled his mobile from his jacket pocket and tapped deftly on the screen. 'The second murder sent Twitter crazy. It got several hundred more likes than the Instagram message and was retweeted 20,282 times.'

His patience worn thin, Fenton snapped. 'I don't give a damn about what's happening online. The most important thing is that we catch this killer and I can't do that sitting here talking.'

Bell's scowl deepened. 'We're already being crucified by the media and this case needs to be sorted. The whole thing is making me look like a complete idiot.'

Fenton glanced across at the press officer, who raised his eyebrows. 'I know it's not my job, but I can't help thinking that the killer's social media posts are the key to this case,' Partington said.

Fenton shrugged: 'The cyber team's doing everything they can, but they keep hitting dead ends.'

'That's because it's so easy to cover your tracks. If you keep creating a different generic email address and use the wi-fi at some random coffee shop, or internet café, you're going to be almost impossible to trace.'

Bell lifted his chin and puffed out his not inconsiderable chest. 'The word impossible is banned in my office.'

Fenton slapped a hand on the desk and rose to his feet sharply. 'I've got a murder investigation to run. We're going around in circles here.' He half expected Bell to order him to stay where he was, but Partington intervened.

'Wait a minute, please,' he said. 'There's one more thing I wanted to mention.'

After a moment's hesitation, Fenton sat down. It was the 'please' that clinched it. Partington nodded his thanks. 'I was wondering whether you've got someone monitoring the online comments about I, Killer?' Bell threw Fenton a questioning look.

'Of course,' Fenton said. 'We have a civilian support worker on it full-time.'

Partington winced. 'I thought you might say that. The thing is, this is not a criticism, I'm trying to help, but I don't think you understand the scale of the task.'

Fenton clenched his jaw. He wasn't used to being told how to do his job, but was too professional to put personal pride before the investigation.

'Apart from the I, Killer messages and photographs going viral across social media, people are discussing the murders on message boards and commenting on newspaper websites. We're probably talking tens of thousands of posts, and more every day. The killer could even be joining in the discussions, making comments of his own.'

Fenton took a moment to let Partington's words sink in. If he was right about the size of the monitoring task then they were going to need more manpower. 'I'll check it out right away,' he said. 'Thanks for bringing it up.'

Partington seemed genuinely pleased to have made a positive contribution to the investigation, but Bell took the opportunity to twist the knife.

'Sort it out, DCI Fenton,' he said. 'I need everyone on the top of their game right now.'

20

Back in his own office, Fenton grabbed his computer's keyboard and tapped #IKiller into the search engine. The results filled the screen. He clicked on the top one, #IKiller on Twitter. He had an idea what was coming but the sheer volume shocked him.

Hundreds of the tweets condemned the murders as evil, hundreds accused the police of incompetence, and hundreds more expressed a fascination with the killer and the photographs of his victims. Fenton's heart sank as he skimmed the messages. *Never seen a dead person before #coolcorpses #IKiller; Thanks for sharing. Made my day. Can't wait for the next one #dyingformore #IKiller; Dead good photos. This is so evil . . .but I love it.HaHa #adyingart #IKiller.*

Fenton closed the file and thought about repeating the exercise on Instagram, but couldn't face it. Partington had been right. He needed to assign at least two more bodies to monitor the messages and comments.

He reached into his in-tray and started leafing through a hard copy of the Edward Deere forensic report. There were no spots of blood that didn't belong to the victims, no clothing fibres, no stray hairs, no flakes of skin, no footprints or fingerprints.

Either the killer was extremely lucky, or he'd put a lot of effort into leaving the crime scene clean. Both murders were carried out in locations not covered by CCTV cameras. Fenton suspected there was nothing lucky about that. His line of thought was broken by the sharp rap of knuckle on door. He didn't invite the visitor in, but the door opened anyway and the head of a uniformed constable appeared. 'Excuse me sir, but . . .'

Fenton cut the young officer off mercilessly. 'No, I won't excuse you.'

'Right, sir, sorry, sir.'

'What's your name officer?'

'Mackie, sir. Police Constable Mackie.'

'Well, Police Constable Mackie, can't you see I'm busy?'

Mackie's cheeks burned. 'I didn't realise, sir.'

Fenton prided himself on not being an arsehole boss, but the constable had caught him at a bad moment. 'This is what's called thinking, Mackie. You probably don't do a lot of it at the moment, but if you get out of that uniform and become a detective one day, it's going to be an important skill. When I'm thinking, I don't like to be interrupted. Is that clear?'

Mackie nodded, pulled his head out of sight, poked it back into view, mumbled something unintelligible and ducked out again, closing the door behind him. Fenton checked his watch. He'd been at work for twelve hours. He hoped Tess wasn't giving Marta too much trouble.

He stretched his legs, leant back in the leather chair and closed his eyes. He knew that sometimes killers prey on a certain physical type. People who remind them of the real target of their murderous urges. A mother, father, wife or ex-girlfriend. Each time they kill, they get the satisfaction of revenge. Lauren Bishop and Edward Deere couldn't have been more different. Neither of them was sexually assaulted, before or after their death.

Fenton opened his eyes, sat up straight and took a notebook and pen out of the desk drawer. He flipped the notebook open and wrote, in capital letters, the words FASCINATED BY DEATH.

He wasn't a psychologist, but he'd been around long enough to know that most serial killers are psychopaths, but not all psychopaths are serial killers. Some of the world's most successful men and women, business tycoons and political leaders, have achieved what they achieved because they are charismatic, ruthless, lacking in empathy and manipulative. All classic psychopathic traits.

Fenton tried to imagine the killer's day-to-day life. He probably holds down a job. Maybe even has a wife or family. Nobody suspects what he really is. During the killer's childhood there would be unprovoked outbursts of violence, incidences of high-risk behaviour. By now he'd probably mastered the art of appearing normal. He'd be skilled at aping the emotions of non-psychopaths. Fenton put the pen to paper again and printed the words FAKING NORMALITY.

He reached for his white plastic in-tray, grabbed the autopsy reports and flicked through the pathologist's conclusions. Inevitably, when someone's throat is slit there is an awful lot of blood. Did the killer choose this method because he liked to, needed to, see the blood pumping from the carotid arteries, watch life seeping from the bodies of his victims? Fenton added the phrase A LUST FOR BLOOD to his list.

Did the killer saw at the homeless man's neck in rage, frustration, or out of sheer curiosity? In both cases, the initial cut to the throat had been clean, lightning quick and fatal. The knife wielded from a freestanding position. The victims weren't bound or held in position to ensure accuracy. That would require excellent coordination, strength and speed, and a lot of confidence in your ability to strike a fatal blow. Fenton closed the reports and dropped them back in the tray. He picked up the pen and grabbed the notebook. He paused for a moment before writing the words A TALENT FOR KILLING.

Fenton used the pen to drum a simple rhythm on the table. The internet photographs, the messages, the IKiller hashtags: the killer had an ego the size of a small planet and it was going to need stroking regularly. He stopped drumming and made a final note. OBSESSED WITH FAME.

Fenton slipped the notebook and pen back in the drawer. He fished his mobile out of his pocket and checked for a text message from the nanny about Tess playing up. Nothing.

He headed for the door. Before his fingers touched the handle, it opened slightly and Constable Mackie's head appeared in the gap.

'What now?' Fenton asked. 'I'm off home to read my daughter a bedtime story.'

Mackie edged nervously into the room. 'I tried to tell you before, sir, but you were busy thinking. There's been another woman attacked in Victoria Park. Stabbed in the neck.'

The constable's words took a second to sink in. 'Another body?'

Mackie shook his head. 'She's on her way to hospital. The attack was interrupted by a couple of joggers. They chased the man and held him down until a patrol car arrived. Detective Constable Ince is at the scene, sir.'

Fenton pushed Mackie aside and sprinted down the narrow corridor.

Half a dozen spotlights lit the crime scene. Inside the lights, police tape sealed off a rectangular area of grass. Inside the tape, four scenes-of-crime officers wearing plastic overalls, hoods and face masks crawled in formation. Fenton spotted Detective Constable Ince talking to two female uniformed officers outside the tape on the edge of a children's play area. Both of the women were laughing loudly at something the detective had said. Ince noticed his boss approaching and ushered the uniforms away.

'What have we got?' Fenton asked.

'Attempted murder of a woman in her thirties, sir. It looks

like the suspect tried to slit her throat, she twisted away but wasn't able to avoid being stabbed in the side of the neck.'

'She's alive?'

'The paramedics reckon she'll survive. The blade just missed her left carotid artery. She's in a medically induced coma for now. She was lucky.'

Fenton thought Ince looked as if he was enjoying the gory part of the job a little too much. 'You call being stabbed in the neck and being put in a coma lucky?'

Ince had the good sense not to respond.

'And what about the suspect?'

'The park was pretty deserted, it closes at dusk, but a couple of students out for a run were heading for the eastern gate when they witnessed the attack. They dialled 999, disarmed the suspect and sat on him until the uniforms arrived. I think they were rugby players, sir, you know, big buggers.'

'Where's the suspect now?'

'He's cuffed, in the back of a patrol car and on his way to the station.'

Fenton buttoned up his jacket and shivered. 'What about the weapon?'

Ince grinned. 'We've got it. It's sorted. Once we match the cutting edge to the other wounds, it's done. Case closed.'

Fenton blew on his hands and shivered again. A dangerous man was off the streets. There was no doubt about that, but Ince's smugness made him uneasy.

21

Interrogation could be the hardest and, at the same time, the most satisfying part of a detective's job. There were rules to be followed, techniques to draw on and plenty of psychological plays to snare a criminal in his own web of lies.

Fenton sat in the corner of the interview suite, observing the suspect as Daly, his team's most experienced interrogator, fired off the questions. For thirty minutes they went unanswered. The suspect, tall, muscular and in his mid-twenties, sat upright, his white-knuckled hands gripping the edge of the table, his eyes flickering constantly around the room.

When asked repeatedly to give his name he gave no sign that he'd even heard the question. He said nothing when told he was being questioned in connection with two murders and one attempted murder.

The breakthrough came after a police constable entered the room and handed Daly a piece of paper. She scanned it and passed it to Fenton. Daly stopped pacing and sat opposite the suspect. She tried to look him directly in the eyes, but he shifted his head, just a fraction.

'We know your name is Ellis Taylor. We know you are twenty-six and live at 22a Butterfield Road, Bow.'

The suspect turned slowly to face the two-way viewing mirror spanning most of the wall to his left and stared at his reflection.

'That's not me,' he said. 'I don't know no Ellis Taylor.'

'That's weird, because according to our database, you've got his fingerprints.'

Taylor kept his eyes on the mirror, behind which Bell and Ince were watching in the dark. Daly waited patiently until Taylor turned back to face her. This time he let their eyes lock.

'We've got officers on their way to your flat, others digging deep into your records. Within the hour we'll know everything about you. There's no point playing this game any more.'

'I'm not playing. She deserved to die. She was an evil bitch.'

Daly glanced at Fenton. 'You knew her then?'

Taylor nodded. Strands of dark hair fell from behind his ears, framing his narrow face. 'I knew all about her. She deserved to be punished.'

'Punished for what?'

Taylor twisted his lip. 'The soul who sins deserves to die.'

'What was your relationship with her?'

'I don't have relationships with sinners.'

Daly took a moment to consider her next question. She looked at Fenton again. He gave nothing away.

She turned to address Taylor, only to find him staring at the mirror again.

'If you want we can postpone this interview until we get you a lawyer. You're entitled to legal aid.'

Taylor kept his head still. 'I don't need no lawyer. I've done nothing. Only good things.'

'Stabbing Tanya Reid in the neck is good? Killing Lauren Bishop and Edward Deere is good? We have witnesses. The men who apprehended you saw you stab Miss Reid. We have the knife, we'll be able to match the blade to the murder wounds. You cocked up this time.'

Taylor looked straight ahead and released his grip on the table. 'I must be careful. They're watching me. Watching and listening. Happy is he who does not condemn himself.'

For a moment, Fenton thought he had worked out that the mirror was two-way, but as he watched the corners of Taylor's mouth twitch, fall still, and twitch again, he realised the real reason for his outburst. Paranoia, plain and simple.

Fenton caught Daly's eye and raised a hand. 'The interview is suspended,' she said. 'I think we all need a few minutes.'

Daly led the way into the observation room. Bell didn't wait for them to take a seat. He pointed a stubby finger at the detective sergeant.

'What are you doing taking a break? He's ready to confess to the lot. He can't help himself. Get it out of him before a brief turns up and complicates things.'

Fenton took a half-step, putting himself between Daly and Bell. 'It was my call,' he said. 'I think we should take this slowly. The suspect clearly has psychological problems.'

Bell rolled his eyes and shifted his position. The chair

groaned. 'Obviously, he's as mad as a box of frogs. He was caught in the act. He's not even trying to deny it. I want his confession quick smart so we can get put out a statement confirming we've got our man.'

Fenton knew Bell well enough to know that arguing would be a waste of time. He tried anyway. 'We've got him for the stabbing. No doubt. But as yet we've no evidence linking him to the two murders. Nothing linking him to the killer's online campaign.'

Bell levered himself to his feet with a loud grunt. 'We'll get all the evidence we need, believe me. I want this wrapped up as soon as possible. The guy's been rambling on like a religious nutter, talking about sinners, evil, and quoting the Bible. As young Ince here pointed out earlier, this fits in with the two murder victims being laid out in a crucifix position.'

Fenton looked at Ince and shook his head. 'So now you're taking advice from a detective constable not long out of short trousers? You're promoting him to senior investigating officer?'

'You're in charge of the investigation, but never forget there is one person you answer to. Me.'

Fenton took a couple of deep, slow breaths. 'I'm not saying he's not the killer, but maybe it'd be sensible to wait for the knife test result and the background checks before we push Taylor to confess to anything. He's paranoid, delusional and rambling.'

Bell rubbed his hands together. 'Just because he's crazy

doesn't mean he's not our killer. Surely, it makes it more likely? He said it himself. He's on some mad crusade to rid the world of sinners.'

Fenton turned to the viewing mirror. Taylor, his arms folded across his chest, hands gripping his ribcage, appeared to be hugging himself. During the break he'd been joined by a legal-services lawyer. The pinched-faced woman sat beside her client looking unhappy at being called out.

'I don't think Taylor's attack comes close to matching the two murders. Sure, there are similarities, but that's all they are. The throat wounds to Lauren Bishop and Edward Deere were clean, clinical and fatal. One slash, one dead person. Taylor doesn't seem to have been carrying a mobile phone or a camera. I, Killer was super-efficient, calculating and organised.' Fenton nodded towards Taylor. 'Look at him. That man isn't remotely capable of any of that.'

Bell shrugged. 'I don't want to hear it. He fucked up. I want you asking the questions this time. If he wants to confess to the killings, let him spill.'

Fenton returned to the interview room with Daly in tow. This time the detective sergeant took the seat in the corner. Fenton nodded a greeting at the greying lawyer. She responded with a pout.

He switched his attention to the suspect, treating him to a smile. 'Do you own a mobile phone, laptop, or computer?' he asked.

Taylor laughed: 'They are Satan's tools, holding the masses in their thrall.'

That's probably the sanest thing he's said since his arrest, Fenton thought. 'When did you last eat?'

'I haven't eaten for two days.'

'I can get someone to bring you a sandwich.'

Taylor looked at his lawyer as if he was expecting legal advice on whether he would incriminate himself by accepting the offer of a snack. He didn't get any. 'Not hungry,' he said. 'My flesh is food. My blood is drink.'

Fenton pulled a chair up and sat down resting his elbows on the table and his chin on his hands. 'I take it you're not denying that you tried to kill Tanya Reid?'

'I don't know no one called Tanya Reid.'

'She's the woman you stabbed in the neck.'

Taylor grinned. 'She's marked. I saw the mark.'

'What mark?'

'Marked for cleansing.'

'Cleansing by you?'

Taylor sat up straight, looking from one wall to the next, before settling his gaze on his and Fenton's reflections in the one-way mirror. 'They're always watching.'

'Who's watching, Ellis?'

The smile disappeared and Taylor's face twisted into a mask of terror. 'They're waiting for me to fail. The sins of the world spring from failure. If I fail I'll be marked. If I have the mark, I'll be cleansed.'

Fenton sighed. Taylor's biblical ramblings annoyed the shit out of him. 'Are you telling me you killed Lauren Bishop and Edward Deere because they were sinners?'

Taylor's eyes shifted to Fenton, back to the mirror, then to Fenton again. 'They were sinners marked for death. We're all sinners, but not all of us have been marked.'

Fenton let the statement, a virtual admission, hang in the air. He glanced at the lawyer, half expecting her to earn her money and intervene. She dropped her eyes to study the face of a gold watch on her left wrist and said nothing.

'You murdered Leah Bishop and Edward Deere, slit their throats in cold blood because you thought they were marked for death?'

Taylor sniggered. The snigger evolved into a cackle, bubbles of saliva oozing from the corners of his mouth.

'You don't get it do you?' he said. 'I decide nothing. I don't choose who lives or dies. It's them. I'm their instrument. Their hand of wrath.'

Fenton caught the duty lawyer's eye again. She shrugged and raised her eyebrows. He knew what she was thinking. Her client was crazy. What could she do? You could start earning your legal-aid fee and advise him to shut the fuck up. Taylor needed to be locked up, he needed psychiatric treatment and he'd probably admit to assassinating John F. Kennedy if you asked him nicely.

Fenton was considering his next question when the door flew open. Chief Superintendent Bell straddled the threshold. 'This interview is over,' he said. 'Read him his rights and charge him. Two murders, one attempted murder.'

Fenton jumped to his feet 'I haven't finished the interview. I need another half an hour at least.'

Bell waved a hand as if he was swatting away a fly. 'If I say the interview's over then it's over. This is a waste of time. The man's as good as confessed.'

'As good as isn't good enough.'

Bell glared at Fenton, his cheeks wobbling. After a few seconds, he turned to Daly. 'Get the suspect out of here now,' he barked. 'Get him charged. Lock him up and notify the duty press officer. I want a press release issued within the hour.'

Daly nodded at a police constable standing in the corridor. The officer approached Taylor, placed one hand on his wrist, another under his arm and yanked him to his feet. Taylor's eyes swivelled to Fenton, to Bell, the door and back to Fenton. He whimpered like a lost puppy as the constable marched him into the corridor.

22

Fenton tuned his car radio to a heavy-metal station and turned the volume up as loud as he could bear. It was late, or early, depending on how you looked at it, and the traffic was light. He'd driven north across the city so many times his brain often switched to automatic pilot, leaving him with little memory of the journey. He wasn't a big fan of heavy-metal music, but he hoped the distorted guitar riffs and relentlessly dense bass would drown out the memory of Ellis Taylor's whining.

Marta had left the hall light on and Fenton stifled a yawn as he climbed the stairs. He tiptoed into the kitchen and wondered if he could make himself a sandwich and open a beer without waking Tess. Instead, he crept into his bedroom clutching a glass of water.

He set the alarm on his mobile for 7 a.m. Five hours' rest would be more than enough, but he knew the likelihood of him sleeping for that long was slim. About the same odds as winning the lottery.

Fenton switched off the bedside lamp and slipped under

the duvet. He rolled towards the centre of the double bed, arched his back, stretched his legs and produced a loud yawn. He closed his eyes and tried to clear his head, but he couldn't stop thinking about Ellis Taylor.

Eventually he drifted into a twilight sleep, his thoughts transformed into a series of images of Taylor hunched over the mutilated body of a woman. The sleep was shallow enough for him to be aware he was dreaming, but too deep for him to wake up. Bent over the body, Taylor whimpered. Slowly, he straightened up and turned, revealing teeth and lips stained with blood. Fenton sat up with a start, reached out and switched on the bedside lamp.

He waited until his breathing slowed before settling back on the pillow, stretched out an arm to turn the lamp off, but decided to leave it on. Outside the city was stirring into life and he could already hear the steady hum of traffic.

Shifting over to the bedside table, he checked the time on his mobile. It was 6 a.m. He had to be up in an hour. He closed his eyes and instantly fell asleep. Twenty minutes later his mobile rang. Swearing loudly he grabbed it, checked the ID and accepted the call. 'This better be good, Daly,' he said.

'We need you in, boss. We've got a bit of a crisis and Chief Superintendent Bell wants you to sort it.'

'He can sort it himself. I'm dropping my daughter off at school this morning. It's probably the only time I'll get to see her today. I'll be in after that.'

Daly didn't reply, but Fenton could hear her breathing. 'Did you get that?' he prompted.

'I heard, sir, but I think you'd better arrange for someone else to do the school run.'

'What's happening?'

'It's Ellis Taylor, sir. We finally got access to his health records and he was diagnosed as a paranoid schizophrenic five years ago. He's been in and out of various psychiatric clinics ever since.'

Fenton swivelled until he was sitting on the edge of the bed and yawned down the phone. 'Tell me something that surprises me.'

'The thing is, sir, his last spell inside was two months in the Whitehall clinic, a secure psychiatric unit in east London. He was released because the clinic was under pressure to free up beds. Apparently, his new medications were working well.'

'He didn't seem stable to me.'

'That's just it. When we searched his flat we found boxes of his medications unopened. It seems he stopped taking the tablets four days ago. As soon as he walked out the door of the clinic.'

Fenton thought for a moment. His brain may have been thick with sleep, but Daly's last sentence made no sense. 'Taylor was released into the community four days ago?'

'You've got it.'

'Prior to that he'd been in the clinic for two months?'

'They confirmed the dates.'

'You're telling me he was definitely locked up when Bishop and Deere were murdered?'

'Locked up and dosed up. The shit has well and truly hit the fan here.'

Fenton gripped his phone so tightly the blood drained from his fingers. 'Let me guess,' he said. 'Bell is keeping his fat head well and truly down. It's up to me to face the press and explain why we fucked up.'

Daly didn't respond. She didn't need to.

'I'm on my way,' Fenton said.

23

The sound of the mourners singing 'The Lord Is My Shepherd' carried across the graveyard to where Blake stood behind an iron gate. If asked, he'd find it difficult to explain what he was doing there. Funerals had always disturbed him. Graveside sobbing, awkward small talk and sad silences made him feel uncomfortable.

The City of London Cemetery and Crematorium in Manor Park, east London, has five chapels, three for cremations and two for burials. Lauren Bishop's funeral was being held in the larger of the burial chapels, which was located on the east side of the complex.

Blake's resolve had weakened the previous night. He'd lain sleepless for a long time. He'd initially put his restlessness down to the fact that he had made a second appointment with the psychologist. In the end, he'd had to admit the truth.

The singing stopped and the chapel fell silent. Blake glanced at his watch. He had an hour and a half to get across the city to his appointment. The gothic-style wooden doors of the chapel opened and the coffin containing Lauren's body emerged on the shoulders of six pallbearers. Dressed identically in black suits and black ties, Blake guessed they were employees of the funeral directors. A group of mourners, about fifty-strong, followed the coffin. They were led by Leah Bishop. Head bowed, she walked slowly, a black handbag clutched to her stomach. Blake felt a twinge of regret that he lacked the courage to stand beside her.

He side-stepped to his right to take cover behind a grey stone wall, his head far enough around the gatepost to see the funeral party arrive at the edge of a grassy area dotted with tombstones. Blake noticed that most of the grave markers were shiny and new. Death is relentless, he thought.

The mourners gathered in a circle and Blake watched the dark oak coffin descend into the ground. Two men in grey suits, and a woman in a dark coat with a pony tail, stood several yards back from the grave. The police always turned up at the funeral of a murder victim. Maybe they were hoping the killer would arrive clutching a wreath and weeping tears of remorse. Blake thought that an unlikely scenario.

The day had started out hazy. By midday the cloud layer had burned away, leaving the sky a washed out blue, the autumn sun the colour of old gold. Despite the warmth in the air, Blake shivered. He immediately recalled a saying from his childhood: 'Someone's just walked over my grave.'

As a boy, he'd puzzled over its meaning. The thought that

somewhere in the world his grave waited for him had been scary. And who was this person daring to desecrate his future resting place? Recent events had changed his attitude to mortality. There are worse things in life than death, he told himself, and a grave is nothing more than a hole in the ground.

Leah stood beside the grave, her eyes closed, next to an elderly chaplain. His head bobbed as he read from a prayer book. Blake couldn't hear what he was saying, but guessed it was the usual stuff. Religious platitudes, mumbo jumbo.

He stepped away from the gatepost to give himself a better view of the coffin being lowered into the ground. The ritual left him cold, but an unexpected memory bubbled to the surface. The day they first met, Lauren had laughed at almost everything he'd said. Even when, no, especially when, he'd been trying to make a serious point. That was one of the first things that had attracted him to her. Her laughter. Her laughter, and the way she moved. Blake shook his head and allowed himself a wry smile. Lauren would definitely be laughing if she could see him now.

The chaplain made the sign of the cross, closed the prayer book and slipped it into his jacket pocket. Leah turned to a woman beside her, who passed her a handful of white roses. She took a tentative step forward and dropped the flowers, one by one, on top of the coffin. Stepping back, she paused for a moment, raised her head and appeared to look straight at Blake. He darted sideways and pressed his face to the stone gatepost.

A couple of minutes passed before he risked taking another look. The mourners were walking, in dribs and drabs, towards the car park. Leah still stood beside the grave, her head bowed.

24

If it wasn't so insulting it'd be funny. The police arrest some crazy schizo, and try to pin the murders on him. When they announced that he'd been charged I felt a pang of jealousy.

I hate the thought of someone else getting the credit I deserve. Anyone with an iota of intelligence should be able to see this was the work of a brilliant mind.

They wheeled out that detective to grovel to the press. Sorry, but the psychologically challenged man charged with the murders was locked up in the madhouse at the time. Yes, I know, we should have checked first, but we're incompetent. I guess my little joke, laying my prey out in the crucifix position confused them. It doesn't take a lot.

Inspector Clueless. People like him, they're ordinary. Ordinary people lack imagination. They fear. They worry. About their families, their friends.

Don't get me wrong. I can understand why people have these fears. I have the emotional intelligence to work out what people are feeling and why. I'd be frightened too, if I was one of the herd.

Fenton is an ordinary man trying to do an extraordinary thing – catch me. I've already met his daughter. A little thing. It must be a big responsibility looking after a child. Children are such delicate creatures. They break so easily.

It's a diversion from my mission, but Inspector Clueless needs to be taught a lesson. A little something to make sure he'll never underestimate me again.

25

Blake couldn't explain how Vale got him to talk about the thing he never talked about. Maybe it was because she never asked him to tell her about the day his captors forced him to witness the ritual beheading of another hostage. She simply suggested he tell her something interesting about himself.

Her self-satisfied smile irked him. She looked far too comfortable leaning back in her expensive leather chair, her perfectly manicured fingers fluttering lightly on the dark green armrest, her legs crossed demurely at her ankles. He wanted to shock her. Shake that complacent look off her face.

'I'd met Earl Davis briefly a few days before they took us. He was working for an American charity, helping refugees from Syria in a small camp across the Iraqi border. I was there to write a series of articles on border activity.'

Blake paused, hoping for encouragement. He needed some sign that the psychologist was not only listening, but was genuinely interested in what he was saying. Vale obliged with an almost imperceptible nod and a sympathetic frown.

'Earl worked for a charity supplying water, food and medical equipment. I was staying at the camp for a couple of days. On the second night, they came to my tent. Two men dressed in black, both armed with Kalashnikov AK 47 assault rifles.'

Blake stood up and walked across the room. He rested his hands on the window sill, his back to Vale, and looked out at the cars, crawling bumper to bumper along High Holborn.

'I was blindfolded, thrown into the back of a truck and taken to a village on the Syrian side of the border. They put me in a hole. A hole dug under the floor of a village house. It took four days for me to stop shaking.

'On the fifth morning, they brought my usual breakfast of dry flatbread. They also brought Earl Davis. Until then I'd no idea they had taken him as well.'

Blake pivoted to his right, sat back on the window sill and dropped his gaze to the floor. Vale waited patiently. Eventually she prompted him with a question.

'Did you get to know him well?'

Blake walked slowly back to his chair and sat down. 'When you share a hole in the ground with another person for three weeks you get to know them very well, believe me. We had nothing to do except talk. We had nothing to cling to except each other. We'd run on the spot for ten minutes at a time for exercise. Even then we'd talk. Talk until we ran out of breath. I got to know more about Earl than I did about my closest friends and most of my family.'

The psychologist glanced at the clock mounted on the wall opposite her chair. She kept her head still, but her eyes shifted slightly. Blake took it personally.

'Sorry, I'm rambling,' he said, rising to his feet. 'I've used up my time and you're busy. I don't want to keep you.'

Vale stood up quickly. 'No, sit down. Please, sit down.' Blake did as she asked and studied the back of his hands.

'How did your captors treat you?'

'They looked after us, I suppose, but only because we were a commodity. I thought they were after a ransom, but it turned out they had different plans.' He stopped talking and clenched both his fists. His forehead glistened with sweat. 'Their leader called himself Ghazwan. One day he announced I had to die, to pay the price for Britain's foreign policy. He jammed the lethal end of a pistol against my temple. I'm not ashamed to admit that I wet myself.

'Earl spoke up for me when he could have stayed silent. He pleaded for my life. He tried to appeal to Ghazwan's better nature. The problem was the sick bastard didn't have one. He pressed the gun harder against my skull and pulled the trigger. It wasn't loaded. I collapsed anyway. Ghazwan placed the sole of his boot on the back of my head and ground my face into the dirt.'

Blake faltered and covered his face with his hands. This time the silence was too painful to be left unfilled. 'I'm so sorry,' Vale said.

'I knew this would be hard. I thought I could do it, but . . .' Blake's voice trailed off.

Vale lifted her electronic tablet off her desk and tapped her diary icon.

'Same time next week? Or I can do sooner if you'd prefer.'

Blake shook his head. 'I'll call when I'm ready.'

26

The new, larger incident room buzzed with a controlled excitement. Fenton stood in the doorway and studied his team. At the far end of the room, four civilian support workers sat in a row taking telephone calls from members of the public, simultaneously logging any information they considered useful on their computers.

In the centre, two intelligence analysts scoured national crime databases for past murders, attempted murders or violent assaults that might be linked to the case. It was a longshot, but Fenton was determined to throw everything at the inquiry. When a third body turned up, and past experience told him that was probably going to be soon, he'd start blaming himself. That was a dark, familiar place. He didn't want a return visit if he could help it.

He walked to the front of the room where Detective Constable Ince sat on the corner of a desk close to a large whiteboard, flicking through a pile of that morning's national newspapers.

A few still featured the murder hunt on their front pages,

but most had moved the story on, focusing on I, Killer's growing social media following. The tabloids were having a field day. Fenton picked up a couple and read the headlines with dismay: *Instagram Killer Is Online Thriller* and *Social Media Frenzy Over Twitter Ripper*.

'How is it you've time to read that crap?' he snapped at Ince.

The detective jumped up, a startled look on his pale face. 'Sorry, sir,' he said. 'I thought it'd be a good thing to keep up with the press coverage of the case.'

Fenton glanced down at the broadsheet newspaper Ince had been reading. He was glad to see that some sections of the press were treating the story seriously. The headline, across a lengthy double page article read: *If Murder Was A Click Away, Would You Look?* Underneath, a subheading made the paper's view on the subject clear. *Killer's Growing Celebrity Highlights Sinister Side Of Social Media.*

Fenton grunted his agreement, but was still seething over the tabloid coverage and took it out on Ince. 'We've got a press office full of men and women who are paid to keep tabs on the press. Let them do their job and you concentrate on doing yours.'

At that moment Daly walked in carrying three coffees on a cardboard tray. 'Thanks for joining us, Detective Sergeant. I was wondering when you were going to show your face.'

Daly shot Ince a questioning look. Her boss didn't usually resort to sarcasm. 'Actually, boss, I did get here a while ago, but thought I'd nip out and get us all a coffee.'

She placed the tray on the desk and handed Fenton his drink. He nodded his thanks, the coffee hot against the tips of his fingers through the plastic cup. Taking a sip, he turned and scanned the whiteboard. Mugshots of the two victims looked accusingly back at him, the dates, times and locations of their murders printed in black marker pen beneath the photographs.

The bottom half of the board was tellingly bare, except for a single image of a long, serrated hunting knife, which the pathologist was pretty sure would be similar, if not identical, to the weapon used by the killer to cut his victim's throats.

Fenton took one last look at the faces of the victims and turned around to address Daly and Ince. 'We haven't been able to gather any forensic evidence. The killer has been careful to not leave any DNA at the scene, no skin cells, no hairs, no clothing fibres, nothing. This may be simple good fortune. Or it could be the result of meticulous planning. My guess is it's probably a bit of both as well as being partly due to the fact that neither of his victims had the opportunity to engage him in a struggle before they were killed.'

Daly glanced across at Ince. We're going to need a bigger team, sir,' she said. 'Preferably detectives with plenty of experience.' She looked pointedly at Ince again. He didn't rise to the bait.

'That's already sorted,' Fenton said. 'We're bringing in more officers. You're going to be paired up. I want you and Ince to work together.'

Daly swore under her breath and the detective constable straightened in his seat on hearing his name. 'Excellent decision sir,' he said. Daly shot him a look and mouthed 'arse-licker'.

Fenton watched the pair leave the room and checked his watch. He was considering having a word with the intelligence analysts before going home, when Partington walked in.

'There you are,' he said. 'I'm glad I caught you. Detective Chief Superintendent Bell asked me to prepare a press release announcing that a psychological profiler is being brought in. I thought I'd let you know, out of courtesy, what we were doing.'

Fenton scanned the room. Everyone was hard at work. He kept his voice low. 'Fuck courtesy,' he said. 'I'm the senior investigating officer and the content of all press releases should be run past me as a matter of course.'

Partington took a moment to adjust his tie. 'That's what I'm doing now. I emailed you a copy of the press release earlier. As you didn't respond I assumed you hadn't seen it. Of course, it won't go out until you approve it.'

Fenton raised an apologetic hand: 'Right, thanks. Sorry about that. It's been a long day. I thought you were telling me that the press release had already gone out.'

The press officer smiled: 'No worries.' He turned to go, but Fenton wasn't done.

'One more thing,' he said. 'Is there nothing we can do online to at least try to counter this fascination with images of murder victims? It's annoying the shit out of me that so many people find a killer's handiwork entertaining.'

Partington shook his head. 'I know what you mean. But the internet is a lawless environment. Right now children can access hard porn, terrorists can post videos of their crimes, cyber bullies are driving teenagers to suicide and there is nothing anyone can do about it. The best way to shut down I, Killer's disgusting fan club is to catch him.'

27

Detective Constable Ralph Ince sat at a white plastic table outside a coffee shop on High Holborn and pretended to read the sports pages of *The Times*. A black baseball cap covered his cropped hair, the peak pulled low. Every now and then his eyes flicked from the newspaper to the door of a Victorian town house twenty yards to his left.

Ince loved surveillance jobs. Secretly watching people going about their business gave him a thrill. It started at secondary school. He found it hard to make friends, and would spend his lunchbreak trailing random people around the town centre, making a game of finding out what they were buying and trying to work out what they did for a living. He loved the power of seeing without being seen.

The brass handle of the door rattled and Ince raised his head a couple of inches, tugging his cap down. His target emerged on to the brown stone doorstep and hesitated before stepping on to the pavement. Ince lifted his expensive cup of coffee to his lips and concentrated on blowing the froth as Adam Blake passed by, heading east along High Holborn.

Ince allowed himself a smile of satisfaction. Surveillance was one of the reasons he'd been determined to get out of uniform as soon as possible. The other thing he loved about spying on people was you didn't have to be on duty to do it.

He'd spend most of his days off following people he considered interesting, or suspicious. Sometimes they'd be total strangers he didn't like the look of. On other occasions, they'd be people he'd come across investigating a case and decided to check out even if his superiors thought they were innocent. He took another sip of coffee and wiped the froth off his upper lip with a swipe of his thumb. Why people paid good money for shit like this he couldn't understand. Still, if the best place to stake someone out is a scummy coffee shop, then you have to order a scummy coffee.

He folded the newspaper and pushed it to the other side of the table. Growing up at school he'd hated sport. Especially team games. He never could kick a ball straight, or catch one, and his classmates never hesitated to tell him that he sucked.

He always did his best work alone. Like today. Blake's alibi had checked out, but Ince believed his bosses had been wrong to rule him out as a suspect. He'd devoted his day off to an unofficial surveillance mission and his hunch had been proved right.

Blake spent the morning sneaking around the City of London Cemetery and Crematorium spying on Lauren Bishop's funeral. That wasn't normal. In Ince's mind, it smacked of guilt. He hadn't been a detective for long and he'd be the first to admit he had a lot to learn, but he'd heard of several cases of killers attending their victims' funerals.

From the cemetery, Blake had walked to Stratford, where he'd caught a bus to Holborn. He climbed the stairs to the top deck in search of a seat, while Ince hid in the huddle of passengers standing near the exit doors. The journey to Holborn took thirty minutes. He followed Blake straight to the town house and the brass plate screwed next to the door revealed the purpose of his visit. If that's not suspicious then I'm Jack the Ripper, Ince thought.

He reached for his cup, but changed his mind. He didn't need to pretend to like coffee any more. He took his cap off and ran his fingers over the bristles on his head. After spending an hour or so researching Blake on the internet, he'd become even more convinced that the journalist needed to be watched closely.

Anyone held hostage by a bunch of fanatics before being forced to witness a friend's head being cut from his shoulders is going to have issues. Ince also spent time watching the video of the beheading on the internet. He'd watched it over and over again. The footage was grainy and you couldn't really see the gory details. But Blake had been right there, on the spot, watching the hooded knifeman go to work on his friend's neck.

28

Marta tried her best to hide her delight when her boss arrived home early and told her she could take the rest of the evening off. She didn't want Tess to see how desperate she was to get away from the house for a few hours.

The two of them had been getting on so well since the incident at the school, and she didn't want to do anything that might jeopardise their improving, but still fragile, relationship. She'd put the progress down to their agreement not to tell Tess's father about the stranger. The intimacy of a shared secret.

She initially declined the offer of a night off, knowing full well that Tess's father would insist. When he recruited his daughter to his cause, both of them declaring that she deserved the treat of an extra evening out, Marta agreed, surprising herself with her ability to conjure up the perfect mix of gratitude and reluctance.

An hour later, she was sitting at a table in a pub in Finsbury Park, drinking vodka and coke with half a dozen Romanian friends. The Eagle didn't have a lot going for it. The building's modern exterior promised more than it delivered. Inside, the décor was stuck in the 1990s.

The rust-coloured walls, which had originally been bright orange, clashed with a threadbare, heavily stained, green carpet. The whole place reeked of stale beer and stale bodies and an unusually high percentage of regular customers had a tendency towards violence after a few drinks. There were two good reasons Marta spent time in the pub whenever she got the opportunity. First, the drinks were cheap. Second, most of the Romanians living in that part of north London loved to hang out there. She could be herself, speak her native language and truly relax. Even so, she couldn't drop her guard completely. None of her friends knew she worked as a nanny for a senior policeman, or that she was living a lie. They all thought she earned her money waiting on tables at a pizza restaurant.

Marta sipped her drink and looked around the table. Her friends – she considered them friends though she couldn't allow herself to get too close to them – were all in their early twenties.

She watched the two single women and two couples talking animatedly, their voices raised enough to be heard above the clamour of the crowded bar and smiled to herself. Like her, they were fighting to survive, to build a future. Despite that, or maybe because of it, when the opportunity came along they loved getting drunk and having a good time.

As she downed the last of her vodka, a familiar figure weaved through the crowd and approached the table. She considered Dorinel Macek tall, dark and not quite handsome. His eyes were too close together, his nose appeared off centre and his mouth too wide. Still, there was something about him women found appealing. Marta included.

Macek squeezed on to the bench and handed her a large vodka and coke. 'Seems like I have come here in time. You are having not much fun without me.'

Marta knew he'd lived in London since his early teens. She couldn't understand why he struggled with the language. The last time they had talked she asked him for an explanation. He threw his head back and laughed out loud.

'I knew you were not just a pretty face,' he told her. 'You also have a good brain, no? Me, I am a pretty face only.' She laughed too, but didn't believe a word of it.

She raised her glass to him. 'Thank you for this, but if you think I need you around to have a good time then you are crazy.'

Macek tried to look hurt, but his eyes smiled. The more Marta tried to keep him at arm's length, the more he worked to wear her down. 'I only wonder why a girl like you is not all the time smiling. I think I will make you a happy person, if you give me a chance.'

Macek liked her a lot. You didn't have to be a genius to work that out. She liked him too and found his persistence flattering, but she was unsure about allowing their relationship to move past flirting. He had already asked her out twice and both times she had knocked him back. He'd handled rejection well and refused to give up.

Marta lifted her glass to her lips, but didn't take a sip. They were packed so tightly around the table she could feel the warmth of his thigh against her leg. If she had too much to drink she might end up doing something she regretted. Her life was complicated enough. In an ideal world, she would love to be Macek's girlfriend, but she owed it to her mother and sister to be disciplined. To focus on keeping her job.

She tilted her head and leant towards him until she could feel his breath on her lips. Being disciplined didn't rule out having a good time and she didn't need to get drunk to enjoy flirting.

'I know how to have a good time, Dorinel,' she whispered. 'I also know you could probably make me happy. But should I give you a chance? I'll have to think about that.'

Macek moved his face even closer to hers. She thought he was going to kiss her. At that moment, she wanted him to. 'What is wrong?' he said. 'You look, how do you say? Like a bunny caught in the headlights.' Marta sat back and laughed. Macek joined in. The rest of the evening went better than Marta could have hoped. Macek paid her plenty of attention, but made a big effort not to pressure her.

At closing time, everyone was moving on to a club nearby, but Marta declined. She wanted to go home and get some sleep. Macek hid his disappointment and offered to escort her home.

The ferocity of her refusal surprised him. 'No, you go on with the others. I don't need a bodyguard.' Marta's heart raced. Her mind conjured up a chain of events that would end in disaster. Dorinel wondering how she could afford to rent a room in Islington. Him asking questions and discovering her lies. Mr Fenton finding out that she had never even been to Latvia, had never worked with children.

The thought of not having money to send home twisted her stomach. She blinked back tears. 'You go on with others. Enjoy yourself.'

Macek raised both hands in surrender, turned and made his way east along the Seven Sisters Road. Their friends were waiting two hundred yards away, standing patiently in the neon glow of a kebab shop.

Marta waited a few seconds to gather her thoughts before walking in the opposite direction towards Finsbury Park Tube station.

29

The last Victoria Line service to King's Cross left Finsbury Park at twenty minutes past midnight. Marta leapt on to the train, narrowly avoiding the sliding doors. The carriage stunk of stale beer and fresh vomit. The only other passengers, two men dressed in jeans and T-shirts, sat side by side. The smaller of the pair slumped forward in his seat, put his head between his knees and spat something unpleasant on to the floor. His friend laughed and slapped him hard on the back. Marta took a seat at the opposite end of the carriage.

After changing to the Northern Line at King's Cross, she spent the short journey to Angel wondering if Dorinel would ever speak to her again.

On leaving the station, Marta crossed the A1 and walked briskly up White Lion Street. The road was well lit and there were still plenty of people out and about.

After ten minutes, she turned right into Penton Street. She estimated it would take her at least another ten, maybe even fifteen minutes, to reach her destination. Marta cursed herself loudly for choosing to wear three-inch heels. They looked good, but every ligament, muscle and joint in her feet was protesting loudly.

She was seriously considering taking the shoes off, when a noise behind her made her glance over her shoulder. A tall figure headed her way, eating up the distance between them. Marta scanned the other side of the street desperate to spot somebody else.

As she came level with a length of black railing in front of a row of five terraced homes, she opened the gate of the second house, swung it shut behind her and climbed the half a dozen steps to the front door. She made a show of struggling to find her key, before pulling one out of her jacket pocket. Taking her time, she lifted it towards the lock, waiting for the stranger to pass.

Her hand shook as the figure drew level with the gate. She held her breath, pretended to struggle to find the right key and listened to the footsteps fade into the night. Panic evaporated like sweat from her skin and she chided herself for letting her imagination get the better of her.

Marta returned to the pavement and decided to change her route. Earlier, she'd passed the entrance to an alley she'd used several times to get to Tess's school. Running between an office building and a terrace of homes, it led directly to Risinghill Street, cutting her journey by a good ten minutes.

She walked down Penton Street, retracing her steps, until she reached the narrow entrance.

30

*S*he darts into the narrow passageway, counting her steps in her head. At fifty-five she sees the welcome glow of a street light.

She lengthens her stride. One of her heels snags on a crack in the pavement and she stumbles, scrapes a knee on the wall. Steadying herself, she looks up to see the silhouette of a man standing at the exit. He stretches out a gloved hand and beckons her. When she doesn't move, he calls out to her.

'You shouldn't be out on your own,' he says.

The street light behind the stranger forms a halo around his head. She takes a small step back. He takes a big step forward.

'Don't be frightened,' he says. 'I'm a police officer.'

Marta's chest is burning. She's been holding her breath. 'You are police?'

The stranger nods and takes another step. 'There are dozens of us out on patrol tonight. You must have heard the warnings. Now where is it you're going?'

Marta finds her voice. 'I'm on my way back to Risinghill Street.'

The police officer laughs. 'We're virtually there, aren't we?'

NOW YOU SEE

He moves aside and gestures for her to pass. She steps forward, he grabs her neck and slams her against the wall. She cries out, her legs fold and she slides on to the floor. 'Please no,' she sobs 'Smile for the camera' he says. She blinks up at the mobile phone.

She doesn't see the hand whip towards her, a black handled blade gripped by gloved fingers.

31

Fenton always tried to eat breakfast with Tess, even on days when he wasn't able to take her to school. It gave them a chance to talk about things that were important to her, and often a complete mystery to him. He was trying his best to be a mum, as well as a dad, but felt he was failing miserably. More often than not he found himself resorting to nodding, laughing and agreeing thoughtfully in all the right places.

He'd been up since 6 a.m. that morning and had prepared them both scrambled egg and smoked salmon on toast. He slid the plate in front of her with a flourish and a loud 'Ta-da!'

Tess eyed him suspiciously. 'My birthday's months away,' she said.

Fenton put his plate on the table opposite his daughter, sat down and pulled a mock-hurt face. 'Just treating my best girl.' Tess grinned at him and tucked in. The grin warmed his heart and he made a mental note to cook her special breakfasts more often.

Marta had been primed to take Tess to school today because Fenton needed to get into the office early. The onerous task of writing a detailed report on the Ellis Taylor fiasco awaited him, and he wanted to get it out of the way.

It wasn't going to be easy to explain why they had charged Taylor with two murders he couldn't have committed, without pointing the finger at Detective Chief Superintendent Bell. Of course, the fool was to blame. He'd been desperate to solve the cases and suck up to the media, but Fenton couldn't say that. No way. As much as he might want to. Stitching up his boss wouldn't go down well. Watch each other's backs. The unwritten rule. The thing was, Fenton knew damn well that he couldn't trust Bell to watch his. He washed a forkful of scrambled egg down with his coffee. 'Is Marta up yet?'

Tess nibbled the edge of a bit of burnt crust. 'Dunno, Dad. Haven't seen her yet.'

Fenton stood and dropped another slice of bread into the toaster. He was hunting down a jar of marmalade when his mobile rang. He checked the screen and sighed. Daly didn't make social calls. He shrugged an apology to Tess and answered it.

'Sorry, sir, but I thought you'd want to know as soon as possible. There's been another I, Killer internet posting.'

Fenton's stomach tightened. 'Shit,' he said.

'It's on the image-sharing site Flickr. A close up of a woman's face. She's looking up at the camera and I'd guess she's pleading for mercy. It's been up since five a.m. and has already had several thousand views. These sickos must be constantly searching for new I, Killer posts.'

'Unbelievable,' Fenton said, more to himself than to Daly. 'Just a headshot?'

'That's right. With a message, of course.'

'And the message is . . .'

'If you hunt the hunter, you risk becoming the prey.'

Fenton rolled his eyes at Tess and walked quickly out of the kitchen into the hallway, closing the door behind him. 'What the hell is that all about?' he said, not actually expecting an explanation. 'No photo of a body, no report of a body found?'

'Not so far,' Daly said. 'But the pattern suggests . . .'

Fenton shook his head. In a city like London, teeming with nine million people, predators will always find a victim. 'I'll be thirty minutes.'

He ended the call, ran upstairs to his bedroom and grabbed a jacket from the wardrobe. Marta hadn't shown her face. Probably suffering after her night out, he thought. She needed to get a move on if she was going to get Tess to school on time.

He walked to her bedroom door and knocked softly. No response. He grabbed the handle and thought about going in, but a natural reluctance to invade a young woman's private space held him back. He was still thinking about it when Tess appeared beaming at the top of the stairs

'Don't worry, Dad. We've got plenty of time to get to school.'

Fenton backed away from the door and returned his daughter's smile. 'All right, darling,' he said, bending down to kiss her forehead. 'Have a great day. I'm probably going to be home late tonight, sorry.'

Tess gave a 'whatever' shrug. 'What's new, Dad? I don't think you've ever not been late back from work.'

Fenton checked his watch and headed downstairs. Stepping outside, he put his hands on his hips and tried to remember how far up the street he'd parked his car. Vehicles of all shapes and sizes lined both sides of the narrow road. He shivered, the cool morning air damp against his skin. He spotted the Ford Focus about fifty yards away, and as he neared it something caught his eye. The front of the vehicle faced away from him, but through the rear window he could see what appeared to be a cardboard box on the bonnet. Bloody vandals, he thought, breaking into a jog. As he drew level with the car's boot, he got a clearer view and slowed to a walk. The standard brown packing box had been placed upside down, close to the windscreen. Fenton gripped it and slid his fingers underneath. The lid flaps felt loose and slightly sticky. He lifted the box, and stared at the object left on the bonnet.

He turned away, grabbed the handle of the passenger door, bent over and vomited his breakfast into the gutter. Wiping his mouth with the sleeve of his jacket, he raised his head and looked back at the severed head, the blue eyes open and as lifeless as marble.

32

The beheading of Marta Blagar ignited a media frenzy that spread like wildfire.

Within an hour of Fenton's discovery, the killer had added fuel to the flames by posting a second picture. Blake sat on the edge of his bed, his laptop on his knees, and stared, mesmerised, at the look on the young woman's face the moment it dawned on her that she was about to die.

In the 'after' photograph, a thick layer of blood caked the jagged edge of her neck. Blake swallowed hard and fought the urge to look away from the screen. The facial expression appeared strangely serene, the skin translucent and alabaster pale. From both eyes, dark red trails ran down the cheeks like tears of blood.

Blake slammed the laptop shut, stood up and undressed, dropping his clothes in a pile on the bed. Slipping on a pair of shorts, a vest and trainers, he headed for the running machine. He switched it on and started jogging.

As usual, the electronic hum of the treadmill helped him

block out the world and think. He'd been doing a lot of thinking lately.

Since his last session with Vale, Blake had been feeling calmer and less burdened. The beheading of the Romanian nanny had changed something else. As he'd stared at the photograph on his laptop something had shifted deep inside his chest. Of course, the image sickened him. It threatened to unearth too many buried horrors. But, more than anything, it had forced him to think more about Lauren. About her lying on her back, the wound across her neck gaping like a second mouth.

He was sweating heavily now. The beads of perspiration running down his cheeks camouflaged his tears. He grabbed his vest, lifted the material to his face and wiped his eyes. For the first time in a long time he felt driven. Right or wrong, he wasn't going to stand by and do nothing. Never again. He slammed a hand down on the treadmill's red stop button and picked up his mobile.

Leah answered the call straightaway. 'What?' she said.

Blake didn't think much of her phone manners, but decided it'd be wise not to voice his opinion. 'How are you?'

She let out a short sigh. 'How do you think I am?'

After their last conversation Blake had hoped for a warmer response. 'Please, Leah. We need to speak. It's important.'

'What's the problem? You sound out of breath.'

'There's no problem. We need to talk, but not over the phone.'

She sighed again. 'What's so important?'

'What do you think? It's about Lauren.'

Leah fell silent for a moment. 'All right,' she said. 'Come over.'

It took Blake thirty minutes to walk to the Docklands. It would've been a ten-minute journey on the Underground, but he still couldn't face descending into the tunnels. He walked along the Mile End Road, taking in the sights, smells and sounds of a vibrant Muslim street market before turning into White Horse Lane. By the time he crossed the congested Commercial Road, he could see the London's mini-Manhattan in the distance. Canary Wharf's silver steel and glass skyscrapers jabbed aggressively at the grey clouds lurking over the Isle of Dogs.

When Blake arrived, he found Leah waiting for him on her doorstep, dressed casually in black skinny jeans and a pastel green jumper. She led him down the hall, pointed to the sofa and asked if he wanted a tea or coffee. He declined both. Leah sat in a tan leather chair directly opposite him, perching on the edge of the seat. She didn't look particularly happy to see him.

'I've been thinking about what you said. About us starting our own investigation into Lauren's murder.'

She waved a dismissive hand. 'I remember. You needed time.'

'What makes you think I can do any better than the police?'

'I don't think you can do any worse. I desperately want to do this and I'd hoped you would too. You know how to ask the right questions and who to ask.'

She waited for him to respond. He stayed silent. She

dropped her head for a second then lifted it and looked at him. 'I've seen the news. That poor woman.'

Blake shook his head. He wasn't there to talk about that. 'The thing is, I can't stop thinking that if I hadn't driven Lauren away she'd probably still be alive.'

Leah eyed him sympathetically. 'Don't torture yourself. I've decided that if you won't do it, I'm going to find someone who will,' she said. 'The police aren't getting anywhere. If nothing comes of it, then at least I've tried. I don't understand why you're not as desperate as me to catch this man. Lauren talked about you all the time you know.'

'She walked out.'

'She couldn't stand to see you wasting your life. She said you were too comfortable being miserable.'

The words hit Blake like a slap in the face. 'She said that?'

'She desperately wanted to help you, but said you wouldn't help yourself. Wouldn't even consider therapy. You need to stop feeling sorry for yourself, get off your arse and do something.'

Blake smiled. For some reason, her anger amused him. 'Thanks for the advice,' he said. He stood up and paced to the other side of the room. 'Actually, I've started seeing a therapist. The psychologist they referred me to when I first got back.'

He could tell that the announcement had caught Leah off guard. She glared at him, her eyes wide. Eventually she forced a smile. 'That's good. Really good. I'm glad. I really hope it works out for you.'

Blake nodded, relieved that she hadn't berated him for not taking this step when he was with her sister. 'It has helped,' he said. 'A bit. But, to tell you the truth, I'm not sure whether I'm going back.'

For a drawn-out, awkward moment they looked at each other in silence, both unsure what to say next. Leah spoke first.

'I think you should carry on with it. That kind of therapy can be incredibly effective.'

Blake held Leah's gaze as he spoke. 'You know they made me watch as they hacked off my friend's head?'

He knew Leah had probably read the newspaper reports, but she recoiled at the words, a look of horror on her face. Blake laughed softly at her discomfort. 'Don't worry,' he said. 'I'm not going to burden you with the gory details. I just want to explain. I've never been able to get what happened that day out of my mind, the terror on Earl's face. Since Lauren's murder things have changed. It's her face I see now before I fall asleep. She was a good person.'

Leah swallowed hard. Blake hoped she was starting to understand why he struggled with emotion, that her sister had fallen for him, hard and fast, at a time when he wasn't ready to catch her.

'I'm pleased you feel we can talk like this,' she said.

Blake took a deep breath. For more than a year now he'd been battling an overwhelming sense of helplessness. That feeling had been replaced by something he couldn't put a name to. Something powerful.

'I won't take any money,' he said.

Leah stood up quickly, her cheeks flushing pink. 'Are you saying what I think you're saying?'

'I'm going to do it, but I won't need paying.'

'You'll need cash for expenses, surely?' Leah didn't want to stop talking in case he changed his mind again. 'Let me pay your expenses. Anyway, I expect you to do a professional job. A proper job.'

Blake nodded, more to himself than to Leah. 'Let's see how it goes. I'll have to do some research first.'

Leah blinked hard, but couldn't stop tears rolling down her face. 'We can do this. I know we can. It has to be on a professional basis though. I'd want regular reports.'

'I can't promise anything,' Blake said. 'If the police can't track down this killer there's no reason to believe it's going to be easy.'

He stood up and Leah stepped forward and hugged him tight. He felt the dampness of her cheek against his neck and pulled her a little closer.

'Thank you,' she whispered. 'We can do this.'

33

I think Fenton got the message. Loud and clear. Don't mess with the big boys. Don't hunt the hunter. Don't fuck with me.

It was easier to take the head off than I imagined it would be. It helped watching those videos on the internet. A handy way to pick up a few tips on technique. I'm so talented at this killing business it's frightening. Sometimes I scare myself.

The girl radiated fear. It flowed out of her. There was a moment when the penny dropped and she knew that she was living the last few moments of her life. That's where the power of the internet comes in. Why the camera is mightier than the knife. I get to share that special moment.

I'm trending on Twitter and going viral on Facebook. Everything is going perfectly to plan. Plenty of people are denouncing me as evil, that's no surprise. But they're still drawn, still clicking, still looking.

The media coverage is stirring up fear across the city. Warnings about walking the streets alone at night, more appeals for information. It's priceless really. When panic spreads through a herd, the chaos makes it easier for a predator to pick off the weak. When people lose their heads, they're more likely to lose their heads.

The only negative thing about the press coverage is the way the papers refer to me as evil. That's such a simplistic, naive view. Branding me evil is downright stupid. It can't be evil to be true to yourself. It's in my blood, my sweat. Are soldiers who kill when they're ordered to evil? Is a father, or mother, who kills to protect their children evil? Is a wife, or husband, who puts their terminally ill partner out of their misery evil?

I don't believe in God or the devil. I don't believe in atheism. I definitely don't believe in humanity.

Evil, like beauty, is in the eye of the beholder.

34

Detective Chief Superintendent Bell squinted across the desk as he tried to smile, but only succeeded in looking as if he was suffering from a bad case of trapped wind. Fenton put it down to nerves. The reason sat opposite them both, her body ramrod straight, her arms folded across her chest.

Assistant Commissioner Patricia Hall had commandeered Bell's office for the morning meeting and Fenton could feel his boss's discomfort at having to temporarily surrender his personal seat of power.

'We have a situation which is running out of control and we can't allow this to go on,' Hall said, her voice low and forceful. The assistant commissioner's grey hair was cropped short. She had a wiry frame and wore a permanent expression of disapproval that reminded Fenton of his old headmistress.

'We can't have people being beheaded on the streets of London. The fact that the victim was an employee of the man leading the investigation only makes matters worse.'

Bell shifted on his chair like a fat worm wriggling on a hook. 'We're doing everything possible,' he said. 'We're doing our best, throwing everything we can at trying to catch this man and I'm confident we'll get a breakthrough soon.'

The assistant commissioner threw him a look of disdain. 'Your best is obviously nowhere near good enough. This killer is fast becoming some kind of twisted celebrity and we're becoming a laughing stock. I'm informed one enterprising trader is even selling T-shirts with I, Killer printed on the front in blood red, and he's selling a fair few by all accounts.'

'That's sick,' Bell said.

For the first time in a long time, Fenton found himself in full agreement with his boss.

The assistant commissioner had no intention of letting up. 'Why haven't we been able to trace the source of these posts?'

Bell nodded sagely, a tactic he often used when he felt out of his depth. 'I believe the DCI can fill us in on that,' he said.

Fenton kept his expression neutral. His boss was a master at passing the buck. 'I'm no expert, but I'm told there's all sorts of software you can use to prevent detection. Even something as simple as moving around to use different public wi-fi services will make you hard to track down.'

Hall frowned. 'You're saying nothing can be done?'

'No, I'm not saying that. We have officers out visiting wi-fi spots in cafés, restaurants, hotels, libraries even, but it's time-consuming legwork. I'd be lying if I said it wasn't a longshot.'

Hall summoned something resembling a sympathetic smile. 'And how are you coping with everything?' she said. 'It must have been traumatic, finding that poor woman's head. Don't forget we have counselling services for officers who feel they need help with that kind of thing. If you haven't already done so, I recommend you make an appointment.'

Fenton had the distinct impression that she didn't really care whether he'd suffered trauma or not. She was simply saying what she thought she ought to say, expertly repeating responses learnt at the numerous senior management courses she'd attended while climbing the career ladder.

'I can handle it,' he said. 'I'm focused on doing my job.' It was a lie and an unconvincing lie at that. He hadn't slept for more than thirty hours. Every time he closed his eyes he saw Marta's head on the bonnet of his car. He'd spent the last two nights outside his daughter's bedroom, listening to her crying herself to sleep. He was exhausted and still suffering from shock. But he wasn't going to admit it. This wasn't the time to show weakness.

Bell opened his mouth to speak, but Fenton shut him down with a look. 'The killer has changed his pattern to make a point and that could turn out to be his downfall. Unlike the first two victims, Marta, I mean Miss Blagar, was selected to specifically get at me. The killer wanted to demonstrate his superiority. His ego is making him take more risks.

He's been so careful up to now. To carry out a decapitation he must have had much more contact with the body. This gives us a better chance of finding some forensic evidence that's going to help us track him down.'

The assistant commissioner raised an eyebrow. 'So, you don't feel at all responsible?'

'Responsible for?'

'For goading the killer during your last press conference. For getting under his skin, making him strike out at someone in your household.'

Before Fenton could respond, Bell put the boot in. 'I must agree with the assistant commissioner.'

'Of course you must,' Fenton snapped. 'You're a natural born arse-licker.'

Bell's face reddened as he started to protest, but the assistant commissioner silenced his spluttering with a wave of a hand.

'That kind of language is unprofessional,' she said. 'Personal insults will get us nowhere. We have a killer terrorising the city and we're starting to look as if we couldn't catch a cold in the Arctic.'

'I couldn't agree more,' Bell said. 'The press is having a field day at our expense. What I was trying to say before you started throwing insults around was that your deliberate baiting of the killer back-fired big time. I had a complaint from the media office that you didn't run your statement past them. If you had they would have advised you to tone it down.'

'I don't give a shit about managing the press. All I care about is catching this killer.' Fenton waited for another ticking off, but instead Hall and Bell simply exchanged an uncomfortable glance. An uneasy feeling stirred in Fenton's gut.

'We all want this case wrapped up as soon as possible,' Hall said. 'We're increasing the size of the investigation team again and we believe the addition of a psychologist will prove important. Belinda Vale will study the case files to provide a detailed profile of the killer. This type of work has been pioneered by the FBI and has proved invaluable.'

Fenton didn't look convinced. 'Surely it doesn't take a genius to come up with suggestions about the personality of a cold-blooded murderer. I can tell you now, he's definitely a psychopath. He's probably in his mid-twenties, fit and athletic. More than likely he lives in London, has a good job. In his spare time he's an evil bastard who loves killing people and gets off on the feel of his blade penetrating their skin and the sight of blood draining from their bodies. And, of course, he was abused or traumatised, or both, as a child, so it's not really his fault that he grew up like this is it?'

Fenton forced himself to stop talking. Anger was his natural response to threat. At the same time as satisfying his bloodlust, the killer had threatened both Fenton and his daughter. He'd wanted to make the point that getting to Tess would be easy.

Hall exchanged looks with Bell again. 'I have been reviewing the case with Chief Superintendent Bell and we are both wondering why you haven't pulled Adam Blake in for additional questioning.'

'He has a cast-iron alibi. The landlord of the South Pole pub has confirmed that Blake was there all night on the evening of Lauren Bishop's murder.'

Hall lifted a bony hand. 'We all know what happened to Blake. Pure coincidence? We're going to pull him. Question him again. Double-check the alibi.'

Fenton wasn't used to being told how to do his job. It pissed him off big time. Especially when the person issuing the instructions was right. 'I'll get my team on to it,' he said.

Hall looked momentarily taken aback, as if she'd expected more resistance, hoped for it even. She glanced down at a sheet of paper on the desk in front of her. Fenton guessed she was consulting notes she'd made prior to the meeting, and that added to his growing unease. In his experience, if a superior officer brought a script in a meeting, it almost always meant they were about to break bad news.

She looked up at Fenton and cleared her throat with two short, sharp coughs. 'This unpleasant business has been difficult for you, and I know you'd want to make your family, your daughter, your priority. After an internal review of the murder investigations and an assessment of your position, it has been decided to remove you as senior investigating officer.'

Fenton said nothing. His brain struggled to process what he'd heard. He looked to Bell for some kind of support, but his boss avoided his gaze. Hall cleared her throat again. 'It's been decided that you should take compassionate leave,' she said. 'The length of that leave, which starts right now, has yet to be decided. Of course, you will remain on full pay. I stress, this is not a disciplinary action, rather a measure to give you the time and space to recover from the trauma you suffered and to care for your daughter.'

Fenton stiffened, the look of surprise on his face changing to disbelief. 'You've got to be joking. This is crazy. It doesn't make sense. Taking me off the case is going to set the investigation back. You're playing right into the killer's hands.'

Hall looked down at her notes again. 'I'm sorry,' she said. 'It's done. You're officially on compassionate leave. You'd be wise to make the most of it. Rest and recover, spend some quality time with your daughter. We all know what she's been through. Losing her mother to cancer, and now this. She's going to need her father.'

Fenton turned accusingly to Bell. 'What have you got to say? I assume you knew this was coming.'

'Having considered everything very carefully, I have to agree with Assistant Commissioner Hall.'

'I bet you fucking do.'

Hall clenched her jaw so tightly the blood drained from her unlipsticked lips. 'I'm aware this is not what you expected to hear, so I'm prepared to cut you some slack. This time. But there's no leeway on this one, I'm afraid. You're out. It's been decided.'

Fenton shook his head in frustration. How high did this balls-up go? If no higher than Hall, then maybe he had a chance to challenge it. 'This is going to stall the investigation at a time when we need to rev it up,' he said. 'What the hell do you think the press are going to make of it? They're going to go to town on it. It's admitting failure. Who's going to take my place? Nobody on the team has the experience to run an investigation. This is my case.'

Hall shrugged her narrow shoulders. 'It's not as if you've made much progress. Quite the opposite in fact. The papers are already baying for blood. It might be viewed as a good thing that we're shuffling the pack. Trying something new. A press release will be put out explaining that you are being replaced because of personal reasons. That won't be hard to justify after what happened. The killer has targeted you and your family. That makes it personal. It wouldn't be right for you to be involved in the investigation. Surely you can see that?'

Fenton couldn't see it. He didn't even want to look in its direction. What he did want to do was to catch the man who'd killed Marta. Evil had come too close to his daughter. They're right about one thing at least, he told himself. Damn right it's personal.

'This is a big mistake,' Fenton said. 'There's a good chance that my press statement may have forced the killer into making his first error. It bruised his ego. Changing his selection process meant he probably had to hang around, watching my house for days, tracking Marta's movements. He had to follow her then lie in wait for her. There's a good chance someone saw him, or that he was caught on CCTV somewhere. I've got people studying footage from cameras in the area right now. This could be our chance.'

Hall nodded her agreement. 'That's all true,' she said. 'Rest assured, your replacement, an experienced senior investigating officer from another division, has already been fully briefed. I repeat what I said earlier. You're out. At least until this case is over. There's no going back.' Hall stood up and raised both her hands to signal that she'd had the final word.

The instant the door closed behind her, Bell stood up, walked around his desk and reclaimed his chair. He puffed out his chest, relieved to be back on the power side of the desk 'I'm sorry, but there was nothing I could do,' he said. 'The decision to replace you has been approved at the highest level. I couldn't do anything to stop it, even if I wanted to. I had no choice but to go along with it.'

Fenton's shoulders drooped and he hung his head. Bell was a snivelling tosser, but there was nothing to be gained from telling him something he already knew. Hurling abuse at the toad-faced bastard might well offer a distraction from the guilt he felt about Marta, but that relief would be fleeting. A young woman had been murdered, mutilated, simply to send him a message. Teach him a lesson. An innocent life snuffed out. He wondered why she had thought it necessary to lie to him. The poor girl had never even been to Latvia.

Tess hadn't attended school since Marta's murder. She'd barely ventured out of her bedroom. The family liaison officer watching over her while he was out, and the uniformed officers standing guard outside their front door were supposed to reassure her. Instead, they only added to her anxiety. He'd go back, comfort her when she cried and try to answer her questions. He no longer had an investigation to run, a team to lead.

Fenton stood and walked slowly to the door. As his fingers slipped around the chrome handle he turned back to face Bell. 'You're making a big mistake,' he said.

35

Blake stood facing the northern perimeter of the western section of Victoria Park. Directly in front of him was Gore Gate, the entrance from Gore Road. To the right of the gate he could see the spot where Lauren's body had been found in dense undergrowth between two mature plane trees.

The late-afternoon sun hung low, casting long shadows across the park, the crispness of the air giving a false impression of purity. Blake tucked his hands in his jacket pockets and recalled the news reports on the murder. The police believed Lauren had been killed shortly before dusk.

He imagined her enjoying the softness of twilight as she walked unsuspectingly towards her death. With that image firmly in his mind, he turned and walked towards the centre of the park. The light was dimming fast and he guessed he probably had no more than twenty minutes before the park rangers ushered the stragglers out and locked the gates.

Apart from a couple of cyclists heading west, the half-dozen people Blake could see were using the time to exercise their dogs before returning to their tower blocks. Coming his way, a scrawny black youth in a grey tracksuit was being taken for a walk by powerful looking black and tan dog, with a head the size and shape of a rugby ball. Neither the youth nor the dog gave Blake a second glance.

After five minutes, the path veered east towards a modern, redbrick building with a few wooden tables outside the front entrance. Above the glass, in bold red script on a white sign, were the words Vic's Café. To the left of the sign, a small, black security camera pointed its lens in Blake's direction. The tables had been cleared and wiped clean and inside the café looked empty, but he stepped off the path and walked to the door. He pushed his face close to the glass and peered in. He could see another group of tables, but these ones were topped with red-and-white-chequered tablecloths.

Blake raised his right fist and rapped his knuckles on the glass. There was no sound or movement inside. He was considering whether there would be any point in knocking again when someone tapped him on the shoulder. He spun around, his right fist still clenched.

'Steady on, mate, no need for that. We've stopped serving. We're closed. Banging on the door won't do you no good. There's plenty of takeaways nearby if you're hungry.'

Blake found himself looking down at a pair of dark hooded eyes and an aquiline nose, jammed between a shiny bald pate and a bushy beard. In his late thirties, the man stood at least three inches shorter than Blake and probably two stone heavier. Most of that extra weight padded his torso between his chest and his waist.

Blake unclenched his fist and stuck his hand back in his jacket pocket. 'I'm not looking for something to eat. I want a word with the boss. It's important.'

'You're speaking to the boss, mate. The owner, the manager and the chef. The only thing I don't do is wait on the tables or clean the toilets. I got people to do that. That's what the minimum wage is for. Anyway, what's important to you ain't necessarily important to someone else. You get me? Now this park is going to be shut in about fifteen minutes. The gates locked. We've got to get a move on, like, pronto.'

Blake stepped away from the door and pointed up at the sign. 'I take it you're Vic?'

The café owner scratched his beard, turned and walked towards the eastern boundary of the park. Blake followed and found himself having to jog every now and then to keep up. 'I'm not Vic,' the café owner said over a powerful shoulder. 'The name's Perry. Perry Lee. I called the place Vic's Café cos it's in Victoria Park. See what I did there?'

Blake didn't answer. He didn't think an answer was expected. 'I'm making inquiries into the murder of Lauren Bishop and I wanted to speak to you about your security camera.'

Perry Lee stopped and looked up at Blake. 'I've been through all this before, mate,' he said. 'Weeks ago. Why've I gotta go through it all again? Who are you anyway? You ain't no copper, I know that.'

Blake nodded and smiled, eager to put the man at ease and get him talking. 'Is it that obvious?'

The café owner walked on. He might have smiled back, but it was hard for Blake to tell through the facial hair. 'I can spot a plainclothes copper a mile off, don't worry about that. They always look like a cross between an accountant and a nightclub bouncer. And that's just the women. You get me?'

Blake said nothing. He concentrated on keeping up. The sun had slipped below the horizon and the light was fading fast. They were heading for the park's Crown Gate. Blake estimated they'd reach it in about ten minutes.

'I could tell you were no copper right off. You're tall enough, and ugly enough, I'll grant you that. But you got an edge coppers don't have.'

'I'll take that as a compliment, shall I?'

'Take it how you want. Don't matter to me. But if you ain't no copper what are you doing poking your nose into this murder? And who are you anyway? You know my name. Rude not to introduce yourself, I always think.'

Blake decided he had no reason to lie. 'My name is Adam Blake. I've been asked by the victim's family to look into the case. A bit of extra manpower. Help the police along if I can. That's all.'

Lee gave Blake a sideways look designed to let him know that he wasn't fooled. 'Like I said. I've been through it all before with the detective who came to see me on the day the body was found. Young bloke. Younger than me. Ince, I think. He seemed to know what he was doing.'

Blake nodded. 'I was trying to follow the route the victim took as she walked through the park and I noticed the security camera above your door. I wanted to check that the police had asked to have a look at the footage.'

The café owner stopped again and pointed a stubby finger in the direction of Gore Gate. 'That's where they found the body,' he said. 'Hidden in the bushes there. A bloody mess apparently. They closed the park for a whole day near enough. My takings hit the sodding floor that week.'

Blake wanted to focus on the security camera. 'I know the park has its own CCTV cameras, but I take it the one above your café's door is your own?'

'That's right, mate. There's CCTV at the main gates, but most of the small entrances to the park aren't covered. I gotta have my own protection ain't I? I'd be stupid not to. There's a lot of dodgy people about. The gear's a bit pricy, but it's worth the investment. My camera catches everyone who comes in the café, and everyone who passes by. It's a digital camera, but I've set it up to convert the footage on to a DVD. I keep them a week then record over them. I ain't got a camera inside the café. Like I said, they're not cheap.'

They'd started walking again, and were no more than a couple of hundred yards from the gate. 'I got me van parked out there and I gotta get home quick. I got someone waiting for me and she's tasty. You get me? I ain't got no more time to waste.'

'I get you,' Blake said. 'You say you gave the police a copy of the footage from your camera?'

'I already said I did, didn't I? The day after the murder the park was closed, but they let me and the other business owners in, cos we got stuff to do, yeah? I checked the DVD out, you know, but didn't see nothing at first because I didn't know what the woman looked like, did I? It wasn't until I saw her picture on the news that I realised she was on there.'

Blake grabbed the café owner's right elbow. 'You're saying Lauren Bishop was on the camera footage?'

'Get the fuck off me,' Lee snarled, wrenching his arm free. 'I told the detective she was on it. She came into the café just before closing time.' It was a cool night, but Blake's skin flushed with the rush of an adrenaline surge. 'You gave the police a DVD of the footage from your camera showing the murder victim entering your café on the day she was killed?'

'Yeah, that's what I'm saying. Like I said, Detective Ince was his name. Young bloke, but he knew what he was doing. Good job too. The park was swarming with cops, but nobody came to ask about my camera. At that stage I hadn't seen the television and didn't know the woman was on the footage, you get me? It was lucky this Ince was on the ball. He turned up, asked me a couple of questions and took the DVD. I half expected them to get back to me, but they never did.'

Blake said nothing. He was too busy wondering. Wondering why the police hadn't released the footage of Lauren going into the café on the day she was killed as part of their appeal for witnesses. He was still thinking hard when they reached the park's Crown Gate and stepped out on to Grove Road.

Lee gestured at a plain white transit van parked nearby. 'That's my motor mate. I ain't got time to stand around yapping. I got a hot date, remember?'

Blake nodded. 'One thing before you go. Was Lauren Bishop with anyone when she went into the café?'

Lee shrugged and gave his beard a tug. 'I think she was followed in by a man, a tall geezer he was, but it was hard to tell if he was with her or not. Like I told that Detective Ince, you can't see much of his face because he was looking down. They're both on the footage, but I don't remember seeing either of them inside the café. It was a busy day.'

Blake dug deep into his jacket pocket and pulled out one of the business cards he used to hand out while working as a reporter. 'Thanks for talking to me,' he said. 'If you think of anything else, give me a call.'

Lee screwed up his face and looked at the card as if he'd been offered a dog turd. 'All right, mate, but I've told you everything I know.'

Blake watched Lee climb into his van, start the engine and pull off into the rush-hour traffic. He waited until the vehicle was out of sight before heading south towards Mile End Road.

It seemed possible that the killer had followed Lauren into the café, maybe charmed her enough to walk together towards Gore Gate, then produced a knife and forced her into the undergrowth. The police had found video footage of Lauren on the day she was killed. They'd chosen not to release it and to keep its existence secret. It didn't make sense.

36

Blake had half expected the police to come calling again. He recognised Ince from their last encounter. This time he was accompanied by an older detective, a woman who flashed her badge in Blake's face long enough for him to make out the name Daly.

Thirty minutes later he was sitting in the familiar white-washed interview room, sipping a lukewarm cup of coffee. Ince started off the interview going over old ground, asking Blake about his whereabouts on the night Lauren was murdered.

'We've been through this before,' Blake said wearily. 'I told you I was in the pub all evening. You film these interviews so why don't you watch the last one and leave me alone?'

Ince rested his hands on the table, and leant across. Blake caught a whiff of cheap aftershave. 'We don't believe you. We're going to double-check your alibi and we want to know exactly where you were when Edward Deere and Marta Blagar were murdered.'

Blake sighed. He struggled to concentrate on what Ince was saying because all he could think about was the security camera footage from Vic's Café. If the police knew about it why were they keeping it quiet? If they didn't know about it then why had Ince buried it? Whatever the answer, he had no intention of revealing his hand until he knew what was at stake.

Daly stepped away from the wall and let Ince know with a nod and flick of her ponytail that she was taking over.

'If you hunt the hunter, you risk becoming the prey. What does that mean to you Mr Blake?'

'The meaning is pretty self-evident, isn't it?'

Daly sat down and peered across the table. 'I'd like to know what you think it means.'

Blake kept his eyes fixed on the detective sergeant. 'Like thousands of other people, including you no doubt, I've seen the messages. I guess only the person who wrote them knows exactly what they mean.'

Daly took a moment to think before posing her next question. 'Considering what happened to you in Iraq, how did the photograph of the severed head make you feel?'

'I felt how any normal person would. Sick to my stomach.'

'Yet you chose to go on the internet and search for the picture.'

'I was curious.'

'What about the pictures of your former girlfriend? Did you search for those too?'

'I've learnt that it's better to confront these things. Avoidance does you no good.'

Daly managed a sympathetic smile. 'Sounds like something a therapist would say.' Blake stiffened in his seat. 'Don't worry Mr Blake. At this stage, your medical records are still confidential, but I'd be surprised if you weren't seeing a psychologist. PTSD can cause serious problems. We see it in the police force a lot. Anger issues, violent outbursts. Are you having problems controlling your temper?'

Blake shook his head.

'Did you get angry with Lauren Bishop? Did you want to punish her for walking out on you?'

'I cared about Lauren,' he said, his voice barely more than a whisper. 'I'd never hurt her.'

Daly nodded. 'That makes it worse, doesn't it? Harder to bear. The killer who murdered your former girlfriend has moved on to beheading people. Isn't that a strange coincidence?'

Blake jumped to his feet. The sudden movement sent his chair crashing to the floor. 'I need to go,' he said. 'I haven't done anything.'

Ince stepped forward, but Daly waved him back. 'Pick up the chair and sit down,' she said. 'We've still got a lot to talk about.'

37

Belinda Vale lived alone. It was better that way. She'd never dreamt that she would end up on her own two years after getting married, but she'd come to terms with it. Her ex-husband blamed the failure of their relationship on her obsession with work.

They didn't part as friends. The bitter insults, the sneering, hurt her more than she let on. She didn't want to give him power. You spend so much time straightening out the minds of your patients, you can't see how screwed up you are, he told her.

Her growing interest in the psychology of killers had been the last straw. He'd described the fascination as freaky, and as a parting shot he'd insisted that she needed to see a psychologist.

She opened the door of her fridge, picked up a half-empty bottle of white wine, maybe it was half full, she wasn't sure what mood she was in, and poured herself a large glass. On the way to her study she took a sip. The wine was sharp and cold, and made her wince. She put the glass down on the desk and opened up her laptop.

After the divorce had been finalised, she had bought a two-bedroom flat in the Barbican's Shakespeare Tower. Her practice was a lucrative business and helping people sort out their psychological problems was rewarding in other ways. In comparison, working on a freelance basis for the police profiling serial killers paid peanuts, but she knew she had a gift for it. Somehow, dealing with the details of violent death made her feel alive. The apartment's second bedroom was no more than a box room and after moving in she had immediately turned it into an office. Before sitting down, she switched off the light and closed the door. While profiling she preferred to sit in darkness, focusing all her attention on the screen of her laptop.

The desk was positioned in front of the room's small window and for a moment she took in the view of east London at night. In the darkness, the city pulsed with light, energy and life. Was the killer out there, she wondered? Probably. Serial murderers rarely strayed from their home turf. They preferred to feel comfortable in their killing zones. Without a doubt, there were other damaged minds out there too, people who'd thought about killing, imagined themselves doing it, struggling daily to hold back their rage.

Her fingers fluttered across the keyboard as she located the files containing New Scotland Yard's reports on the three murders. The prospect of putting herself inside the killer's mind filled her with dread and excitement in equal parts. Before she could start work on the profile, she had to find out as much detail as she could about the people selected to die, and how their lives ended. Who was killed and how would provide a valuable insight into the killer's desires and motivations.

She would also study copies of the I, Killer internet posts. To her they were a wonderful thing – a rare insight into the mind of a 'Pure Psychopath'. She reached out a trembling hand and clicked the first file.

At 5.30 a.m. Vale hauled herself out of bed, slipped on her silk dressing gown and hurried into the study. As she waited for the laptop to power up, she looked out the window at another grey morning breaking over the city. She'd finished the first draft of her profile at 2 a.m. and fallen asleep the instant her head had touched the pillow. Turning her attention back to the laptop's screen, she started to read through her work.

Serial killers are typically male and often claim first victims in mid-twenties to mid-thirties. No reason to believe this one is different. Method of killing and the decapitation involved in latest murder require high level speed, power and strength.

Although first and second murders appear to have impulsive element, in the killer's mind they will have had a definite purpose. The third involved careful selection and detailed planning. Am certain next one, and there will be a next one, will be organised rather than impulsive, and involve another beheading. Killer has evolved since the first kill. The clear escalation of violence is a search for identity. Beheading is now the dominant signature. Don't think the posing of bodies into crucifix position is significant. Unlikely to be a religious element to murders. Psychopaths have no need for gods. They worship only themselves.

Killer is building a big following on social media. Is addicted to the dark side of the human psyche, and is using internet posts to draw more followers in. Organised murderers are commonly intelligent and meticulous. They obsess over the details of their killings, wanting them to be 'just right'. They are often successful in their ordinary lives and have an inborn ability to blend in. Our killer may be a monster, but will not look like a monster.

Will have a good knowledge of forensic science and how to avoid leaving evidence at the crime scene. Serial killers often develop a fascination with police procedure and methods of detection. Victims so far: one man, two women. If pressed, I would predict next target will be female.

She turned away from the screen and gazed out of the window at the east London skyline. The first kill. The first time. A visceral thrill. The discovery of a pleasure so intense, so exquisite, everything else pales into insignificance. The second killing failed to live up to the first. A homeless man sleeping under a bridge. No challenge there. The next time sights must be set higher. A challenge to be risen to. A senior detective's household, a severed head. A demonstration of dominance, power, omnipotence.

She shifted away from the window and turned back to the laptop. Lifting her hands to her aching head, she gently massaged her temples before reading on.

Not all serial killers are psychopaths, but everything suggests that this one is. To cut a woman's head off as part of a cold, organised murder, rather than in a wild, uncontrolled rage, that takes a high level of psychopathy. That doesn't mean insanity, far from it. The brain is different. Brain scans have shown psychopaths have abnormalities in the prefrontal cortex of the brain, areas associated with impulse control, empathy and remorse. An estimated 1 in 100 people are psychopaths, but most don't turn out to be killers. The general consensus is that those that do are exposed to an environmental trigger. This can be a traumatic childhood, sexual or physical abuse, regularly witnessing violence.

Psychopaths despise authority figures because they crave control themselves. They are drawn to jobs that will give them power over others, and high status, such as lawyer, surgeon, civil servant, police officer.

Selecting Detective Chief Inspector Dan Fenton's nanny shows a desire to up the stakes, increase the thrill of the kill. There is common belief that serial killers take more and more risks because they want to be caught. This is false. The opposite is true. What actually happens is that they often have a superiority complex, sometimes even a God complex, and as a result believe they are invincible. They believe they will never get caught. This over-confidence can lead to mistakes and, in the end, to their capture.

She turned off her laptop, tucked it under her arm and allowed herself a wry smile. No matter how much she loved it, profiling could never be a substitute for hard, forensic evidence, for a confession, for catching the perpetrator in the act of murder. It was like explaining how, and why, a volcanic eruption had occurred, rather than predicting when it was going to happen.

38

'It's my fault she got killed, Dad. My fault.'

Fenton shook his head and reached out to console his sobbing daughter. 'No, Tess, it's nothing to do with you. It's just one of those terrible things. Sometimes, bad things happen to good people.' As the palm of Fenton's hand settled gently on the girl's head, she shied away, sat on the edge of her bed and pulled both hands up into the sleeves of her daisy print pyjamas.

'You mean like Mum?' she asked softly.

Fenton nodded and swallowed the lump in his throat. 'Exactly. She was a good person. The best.'

Two weeks had passed since Marta's murder. Every day since, Tess had cried herself to sleep. Were all the tears shed for Marta? Fenton doubted it. He'd confiscated Tess's mobile phone and banned her from using her laptop. The thought of a friend sending her a link to the photographs of Marta terrified him.

He stepped closer and sat beside her. She kept her head down, but shifted a few inches further along the bed. Fenton sighed. 'What happened to Marta was terrible. But you're not to blame. That doesn't make sense. I won't be going into work for a while because I want to make sure you're all right. Don't worry, darling, we'll catch the man who killed Marta. I promise.' He tried his best to sound as if he believed what he was saying. There was no doubt in his mind that taking him off the case had seriously compromised the investigation. For a start, his replacement, Detective Chief Inspector Norman Tobin, had a well-deserved reputation for being slow off the mark and even slower on the uptake. By the time he'd got up to speed, who knows how many more bodies would be out there?

Fenton had been told to stay away from the office, and strictly forbidden to contact anyone on the murder team. It made no sense. He'd got under the killer's skin. Rubbed him up the wrong way. There was a clear link between them now and that link could be exploited to lure the bastard in.

He edged closer to his daughter and wrapped an arm around her shoulders. This time she didn't shy away. Her frail body shuddered against his ribcage as tears spilled down her face.

'You don't understand what I'm trying to tell you,' she said. 'I'm scared it's my fault that Marta's dead. What if I could have saved her? We should have said something. It might actually by my fault. Actually, Dad.'

Fenton knew the pain of guilt and helplessness. He'd lived with it for months after his wife's death, and even now, on some days, the bad days, it would resurface. 'What do you mean, Tess? That's just not true. If anyone's to blame then it's me. The killer chose Marta because I was leading the team trying to catch him. He wanted to get at me. To show me how clever he is and how stupid I am.'

Tess shook her head, put both her hands on her father's ribs and pushed herself away. 'You're not listening. Please listen to me. We should have told you, I know that now, but it's too late. Marta said the best thing for everybody would be not to say anything. We agreed to keep quiet about it. It was our secret, but it all went wrong. We should have told you what happened. You could have saved her.'

Fenton frowned, stood up, turned and leant forward to face his daughter. He placed his hands under her elbows and gently lifted her to her feet.

'Told me what, Tess? What secret?'

'About the man after school.'

'What man?'

'It happened about two weeks ago. On a Monday, I think. Marta was late picking me up from school. I wandered off, to teach her a lesson really, to scare her. I was being horrible. It was before I liked her.'

'What man, Tess?'

'He seemed nice. He asked me if I was lost. He had a nice smile. We talked for a couple of minutes until Marta came.'

'Why keep it from me? I don't get it.'

Tess sniffed and wiped her nose with her pyjama sleeve. 'Marta was worried that you'd be angry about her being late. Frightened she'd lose her job. She didn't say it, but I knew that's what she was panicking about. I thought you'd be cross with me because I'd gone off on my own. We agreed not to say anything about it. We were friends after that, so I thought it was a good thing, you know, keeping the secret.'

Fenton couldn't make sense of what he was hearing. 'I don't understand,' he said. 'What's this got to do with Marta's death?'

Tess sniffed again. 'I don't know, but he talked about you. Said he knew you. He asked me to give you a message. What if he's the one who killed Marta? We should have told you.'

Fenton's gut twisted. He crouched down until his gaze was level with Tess's red-rimmed eyes. 'Can you remember what he said?'

Tess nodded. 'I think so. It wasn't horrible or anything. Something like, tell you to take care of the little things.'

'Are you certain, Tess? Those were his exact words?'

'I think so, yes . . . Tell him to look after the little things.'

Fenton dropped to his knees and gently gripped her shoulders. 'What did this man look like? Would you know him if you saw him again?'

Tess's bottom lip quivered. 'He was very tall, but he was wearing a hoodie and a cap, like a baseball cap, under the hood. It made it hard to see his face. He sounded kind though.'

Fenton pulled his daughter into a hug. 'Don't worry, darling, you're not to blame,' he whispered. She burrowed her head into his chest and he squeezed tighter.

He left a still sniffling Tess sitting cross-legged on her bed, reading her favourite book, *Charlotte's Web*. Her mother had given it to her a month before her death. Tess had read it so many times she could recite big chunks of it word-for-word.

Fenton made himself a coffee and sat at the kitchen table, the stranger's words bouncing around inside his head. Was this the man who beheaded Marta? His stomach churned. The only little thing that needed taking care of was Tess. It sounded like a harmless message, but felt like a serious threat.

He drained his cup, strode quickly into the hall and skipped downstairs. He had a sudden need for fresh air, and to reassure himself that the day shift uniforms had turned up. He stepped outside in time to witness the changing of the guard. A freckle-faced female constable acknowledged him with a nod as she took her place beside the front door. Fenton watched the night shift drive off. 'Where's your oppo?' he asked.

The constable smiled. It made her look even younger, far too young to be in uniform on the streets of London. 'Just me today, sir.' Fenton shook his head. 'I'm not going far. Just up the road for a few minutes.'

The sky, heavy with cloud and streaked several shades of grey, pressed down hard on the city. Fenton stuck his hands in his trouser pockets and walked east along Risinghill Street. The air was heavy with moisture, but not enough to form a mist.

Parked cars lined both sides of the road, except for a

section where his had been on the day he found Marta's head. That part of the street was still cordoned off with white tape, even though the forensic team had finished their work days before.

Fenton knew what he should do. It was the opposite of what he wanted to do. The right thing would be to telephone New Scotland Yard and tell the new senior investigating officer exactly what Tess had told him. All his life he'd done the right thing, but, for the first time, the lines were blurring. Right for whom? For the force, his bosses, for society? What about doing the right thing for himself and for his daughter? If he did the correct thing, Tess would be taken in and questioned for hours, maybe even days, until they squeezed every detail of the encounter out of her. She'd handle it. He had no doubt about that, she was tougher than she looked.

Still, she'd been through so much trauma, he didn't want to put her through more if he didn't have to. Wasn't as if she'd got a good look at the man's face, and there was no guarantee that the new senior investigating officer would draw the right conclusions, or do anything sensible with the new information. There was no hard evidence that the man near the school gates had been the killer, but gut feeling, and the threat implicit in the man's words, told Fenton all he needed to know.

He wanted the killer caught and caught soon. He also wanted to be the man to nail him. Wanted it more than anything. As things stood, that wasn't going to happen.

He was off the case officially, but what was stopping him

from going after the killer unofficially? Well, for one thing, he'd probably be kicked out of the force. Fifteen years of loyal service, and all pension benefits, down the drain. Fenton shrugged the thought away. Tess's safety was his priority. Nothing else mattered.

The knowledge that the man who'd spoken to his daughter might have been I, Killer sent a chill through his body and triggered a thought that had hovered in the back of his mind for days. The killer knew where he lived and had probably followed Marta and Tess to school on more than one occasion.

Like most senior police officers, Fenton's personal details, address and telephone numbers were kept off all the commercial and public databases available online. At the junction with Penton Street and Chapel market, Fenton spun one hundred and eighty degrees and started back the way he'd come. This time his stride was longer, his pace more urgent.

The killer must have found his personal details on the police computer system. He was either a computer geek who hacked into the network from a remote terminal, or a civilian support worker at New Scotland Yard. Or a police officer.

39

Fenton had his key in the lock of his front door when the press pack arrived. A convoy of four cars screeched to a halt at the kerb, each delivering a reporter and photographer on to the pavement.

A tall woman in a tan trouser suit got to Fenton first, thrusting a digital recorder in his face. 'What's the real reason you've been taken off the case?'

'No comment.'

'Is I, Killer targeting your family?'

'No comment.'

The other reporters gathered round, all waving recording devices. 'How did you feel when you found your nanny's head on your car?'

'Is this the end of your police career?'

'Is there a message you want to send to I, Killer.'

Fenton held up both hands and the journalists fell silent. 'All questions must go through our press office,' he said. 'I'm sure you know the telephone number.'

The woman in the trouser suit tried again. 'What would you like to say all the people out there who are sharing the I, Killer posts?'

From the back of the pack came a barrage of camera flashes. Fenton held up a hand to obscure his face, stepped back over the threshold, and slammed the door shut. He gripped the handle, his knuckles white. The sensible thing to do would be to ignore the last question, keep his mouth shut and let Partington handle the press.

He yanked the door open and stepped on to the doorstep. The reporters, chatting among themselves as they strolled to their cars, scrambled back, excited by the thought that they were about to get a spicy quote, a new angle to keep their news editors happy.

Fenton took a deep breath. 'Anyone who goes online to search out images of people about to be murdered and photographs of their mutilated bodies simply to satisfy some sort of twisted, morbid curiosity should be ashamed of themselves. They should take a moment to think about the victims, and their families, then go and take a long, hard look in the mirror.' The reporters surged forward, shouting over each other as they fired off new questions. Fenton stepped back and slammed the door shut.

He was sitting on the sofa, his head in his hands, when his mobile rang. He snatched it out of his pocket, thinking it could be Daly with important information before he remembered he'd been taken off the case.

Leah Bishop's voice was low and he had trouble hearing

what she was saying 'You'll have to speak up,' he said. 'Can you hear me?'

'Loud and clear, detective.'

For a second Fenton considered suggesting that she should call him Dan, but decided against it. 'I'm sorry, but I can't answer any questions about the investigation. You need to contact the incident room at New Scotland Yard.'

'That's not why I'm calling. It's about a friend. A friend who wants to speak to you.'

Fenton remembered giving his private number to Leah after the press conference and assuring her that she could ring him for updates. 'I'm sorry, Miss Bishop, but, like I said before, I'm no longer part of the team investigating your sister's murder.'

'I know all about that, but it's you my friend wants to talk to. It's important.'

He considered claiming the signal was poor and cutting her off, but curiosity got the better of him.

'Who is this friend?'

'It's someone I've asked to look into my sister's murder. All the murders. You know, a fresh mind examining the facts. It's not that I don't trust the police to do their job properly.'

I'm not sure I've got as much faith in them as you do, Fenton thought. 'Are you talking about a private investigator? Do they know what they're doing?'

'It's Adam Blake. He's not being paid. He wants to help.'

'Blake? You're kidding.'

'I've never been more serious.'

'You know he's still considered a suspect?'

'I do. He's been questioned again, and released. I trust him completely. He wants to talk to you. It's important. He says you'd be a great help, a valuable asset to have on board.'

'He does, does he? I'm glad somebody thinks so.' Fenton paused to weigh up the situation. This was an unexpected turn of events. By all accounts, Blake had been a formidable journalist. Maybe, with expert guidance, he could dig something up that could be useful.

'I need to think about this,' Fenton said. 'I'm not ruling it out, but I've got to tread carefully.'

'That's great. I'd be so grateful. We'd be so grateful, if you could spare the time to talk. I understand you're in an awkward position.'

Fenton had hoped that his suspension would be short-lived, but after his performance on the doorstep that was unlikely. 'I'll let you know, one way or the other, in a couple of hours,' he said, pressing the 'end call' button without waiting for a response.

He liked Leah Bishop, she seemed intelligent and trustworthy. Blake was clearly as sharp as a razor, but harder to read than hieroglyphics. He gave off a dangerous energy that reminded Fenton of some of the more volatile criminals he'd dealt with over the years. But you never know, Fenton thought. Maybe it could work.

40

There is nothing like death to make you feel alive. I was pretty attuned to my surroundings before, but now I'm seeing, hearing, smelling and feeling on a higher plane.

The world is obsessed with my exploits and now Inspector Clueless has been suspended. New Scotland Yard's finest investigator found himself up against a far superior intellect and crumbled.

Time is passing faster every day. I need to focus on my mission. I'm close now, but I don't want to rush. That's how mistakes are made.

Ninety-nine point nine per cent of the population couldn't do what I do. They don't have it in them. I see weak people all around me, living a life of ignorance and defeat. This is why my following increases day by day. Through the medium of the internet they can get a little taste of what it means to be me.

As you can tell, I'm in a philosophical mood. Maybe analytical is a better word. It's probably the news that the police have engaged a psychological profiler that's got me thinking this way.

What a joke. I know exactly what will be appearing in the report and it angers me that someone thinks they know what's going on inside my head.

What really gets to me is all the personal, family stuff this shrink is going to be guessing at. Falsely claiming an intimate knowledge of my thoughts and motivations to inflate her ego.

I can't abide the idea of someone with a few letters after their name judging me, judging Mother. I don't behead people because I lost my father. I'm not impelled to spill the blood of innocents because Mother did what she did.

I kill because I can.

41

Detective Constable Ralph Ince watched his target leave the Victorian town house in High Holborn.

Seven hours ago, he'd had no problem spotting the psychologist amid the commuters streaming out of Holborn Tube station. It took her four minutes to walk to her consulting rooms and he'd followed at a safe distance. Her first patient, a tall, elegant woman wrapped in a black leather coat, arrived at two minutes to nine.

Since then, a steady stream of patients had arrived and departed. To ease the boredom, he'd changed his surveillance position every couple of hours, alternating between a bus shelter and the doorway of a pharmacy. Fortunately, both positions were close to a café selling iced doughnuts and cola.

Ince crossed the road and followed the psychologist back towards the Tube station. He slipped into the tide of pedestrians, positioning himself on the fringe of a small group of Japanese tourists dressed as if they were expecting a blizzard. Every few strides he was able to catch a glimpse of the back of Vale's head, or her black high heels and slim ankles. She was a decent bit of stuff. No doubt about that. She'd be loaded too, Ince thought. Why her patients were willing to pay a small fortune to have her mess about with their minds he'd never know. They needed to get their bloody heads examined.

At the entrance to the Tube station, he stopped and watched her descend the stairs and approach the ticket barriers. Satisfied she was set on catching a Central Line train and heading home, he started walking back the way he had come. His car was parked nearby and there was no need for him to follow her. He already knew her address. He'd got all the information he needed from the police database.

Like all the other officers at New Scotland Yard, he had access to the computer network, but he wasn't supposed to use it to fish for personal information, especially if his inquiries were not connected to an official investigation. Improper use of the force computer system was considered a serious offence. The thing is, they'd have to catch him first and he knew how to cover his tracks.

Ince crossed the road and went into the Corner Café. The woman behind the counter saw him approaching and smiled. She'd served him at least four times that day.

By the time he arrived at the counter she had already placed an iced doughnut in a paper bag. He nodded a greeting and handed her a ten pound note.

'Make that two doughnuts and a bottle of water please, love,' he said.

She raised her eyebrows and stretched her smile. 'No cola this time?'

'Just water. One of the litre bottles.'

As she turned to pluck the mineral water from a low shelf, Ince took the chance to appraise her figure. Not bad, he told himself. Not bad at all. If he wasn't so busy he'd seriously consider taking her out. She obviously fancied him something rotten. He dropped the change into his jacket pocket and grabbed the doughnuts and water. Pausing at the door he looked back, flashing the woman a wink. He could still hear her laughing as he climbed into his car. The drive through the centre of the city was slow. Twilight fell and the sky glowed purple. Ince looked in the rear-view mirror and smiled at himself. It had been a good day so far. He'd arranged with Daly that he'd go to Victoria Park and re-interview some of the people they'd questioned after the murder of Lauren Bishop. The plan was that the detective sergeant would stay at the Yard and plough through the paperwork in the hope of turning up something they'd missed the first time around.

Ince had his own plan. Going over old ground with council officials and park traders would be a waste of his valuable time. He'd woken up that morning with a strong feeling that somebody needed to keep an eye on Vale. He alone knew, because of the extra surveillance work he put in on his days off, that she was treating Adam Blake. He couldn't explain it, but something about that made him feel uneasy.

Ince had half expected Blake to turn up for another

therapy session, but there had been no sign of him. He allowed himself another smile at the thought of his boss being booted off the case. Thank God the top brass weren't totally stupid. Fenton was well past his sell-by date. Time for him to make way for new talent.

By the time Ince pulled up on the east side of the Barbican's Shakespeare Tower, the sky was black and moonless. He counted five storeys and shifted his focus to the corner of the building where he knew Vale's flat was located. The light was on in one of the rooms. Ince guessed it was the living area. He fiddled with the lever under his seat and slid back to give himself more leg room. The police pool car was uncomfortable and as draughty as hell. But it was bland and unlikely to attract attention, making it perfect for the job in hand.

He picked the bag of doughnuts off the passenger seat and took one out. Holding it delicately between his thumb and forefinger, he took a large bite before placing it on his lap. The sugar hit his bloodstream almost immediately and he licked bits of icing off his lips. He needed to exercise control and ration his food. He was there for the night. If you're going to do a job, then do it properly. No messing about. Remembering that he'd thrown the water on the backseat, he shoved an arm back and rummaged around until his fingers closed around the plastic bottle. He unscrewed the top, opened the driver's door a fraction and poured more than two thirds of the water into the gutter. Even as a young boy he'd never liked drinking the stuff.

Everybody told him it was tasteless, but they were wrong. It tasted disgusting. He'd bought it because the bottle would come in handy later when he needed a piss.

The window next to Vale's living area lit up, catching Ince's attention. It was either a bedroom, or the bathroom. He opened the glove compartment and took out a small but powerful pair of binoculars. He fiddled with the focus control until he could clearly see the psychologist reaching into a wardrobe and taking out what looked like a silk dressing gown. She put the gown on the bed and reached both hands behind her back to unzip her dress.

Ince's breathing quickened. Without taking his eyes from the binoculars, he picked up the doughnut and licked the icing.

42

Blake took a slug of warm beer and greeted Fenton with a curt nod. It had been his suggestion that they should meet in the Star. An old haunt of his, he knew the Fleet Street pub would be free from the menace of piped music. A table in the cellar bar would have the added advantage of rendering mobile phones completely useless.

Fenton slid on to the chair opposite Blake, cupping a half-full whisky glass in his hands. 'What's this about?' he said.

Blake's mouth curved with the threat of a smile. He was happy to dispense with social niceties. 'I take it Leah has already explained what's going on?'

'She has, but I want to hear it from you.'

Blake paused before responding and took a look around. He hadn't been in the Star for more than a year. It hadn't changed. In fact, it had probably been much the same for a couple of centuries. The lighting was weak, the tables randomly patterned with woodworm holes and the room smelled strongly of spilt beer, stale sweat and testosterone. It was early, but the place was already filling up.

'Leah wants me to look into her sister's murder,' he said. 'I refused to consider it at first. Thought it'd be better to leave it to the police. But she is very persistent when she wants to be.'

Fenton found Blake's casual use of Leah's first name irritating. 'What exactly did your former girlfriend's sister do to change your mind?'

'She convinced me that asking a few questions couldn't do any harm. That anything I could do to help catch this man would be a bonus. After thinking about it carefully, I agreed.'

Fenton took a sip of whisky and studied the man sitting opposite. Tall and lean, and in his early thirties, Blake wore jeans, a white T-shirt and a brown, needle-cord jacket. His dark hair accentuated an angular face. His eyes were close together, his stare like a hawk's. There was something unpredictable about him. Fenton wondered whether he'd always been that way.

'My feeling is that your first thought, the one about leaving it to the police, was spot on,' Fenton said. 'The new senior investigation officer still considers you a suspect, especially since the beheading.'

Blake stared into his beer. 'What about the old senior investigation officer? What do you think?'

Fenton picked up his whisky and took another sip. 'My gut tells me that they are wasting time and resources trying to link you to these crimes. On the other hand, either this escalation to a beheading is pure coincidence, or someone is deliberately trying to make life difficult for you.'

Blake said nothing and Fenton used the silence to think. If the beheading was designed to point the finger at Blake, then maybe he and his team had been wrong-footed from the start.

'Do you think it's possible that the killer selected Lauren because she was your ex-girlfriend? That her murder wasn't random at all?'

Blake's expression didn't change, but Fenton felt him tense. 'That makes no sense. I can't think of any reason anyone would target me. Anyway, what about the second victim? Edward Deere has no link to Lauren or to me.'

Fenton had no answer. 'You're right. The murder of Deere doesn't fit in, but maybe we shouldn't rule anything out.' He still wasn't sure about joining forces with Blake, but he was willing to listen. 'What have you got?'

Blake pushed his glass to one side and leant forward. 'I've already made a few inquiries. Went to Victoria Park to speak to a few people about the day Lauren was murdered. I found out something weird. Something that doesn't make sense. Leah thought maybe you could explain it.'

Fenton sighed. Everybody thinks they're a bloody detective. Too many crime dramas on television. 'She did? So, where is she? I thought she was going to be here.'

'Something must have come up,' Blake said. 'She'll get here when she can.'

Fenton nodded, more to himself than to Blake. 'I can't hang around for long. I've got a daughter at home being looked after by a female police constable she doesn't know. She won't go to bed until I'm back.'

Blake made a face as if he'd tasted something unpleasant. 'What I don't understand is if you had security camera footage showing Lauren going into a café on the day she was killed, why didn't you use it in the appeals for information?'

Fenton shook his head slowly. 'What do you mean?'

'The security camera film of Lauren, and possibly the killer, going into Vic's Café. It doesn't make sense not to make it public.'

'I don't know what you're talking about.'

'You were in charge of the investigation, weren't you?'

'You know I was.'

Blake took a moment to consider whether there were any circumstances in which the senior investigating officer in a murder hunt wouldn't be told about the discovery of such important evidence. The answer was no. 'The café owner is certain Lauren was on the film.'

Fenton shifted forward to the edge of his seat. 'You've seen it? The footage.'

'No. It was handed to one of your team. Detective Ince.'

'Ince took the film?'

'That's what I was told.'

'And you believe it?'

'Why would anyone lie about it? The café owner, a Perry Lee, said he thought the police hadn't noticed his security camera. He installed it himself. It's not part of the park's CCTV system. He thought your team had cocked up until Ince arrived and demanded the previous day's footage. Lee checks the film at the end of every day, but he had no idea Lauren was on there until he saw her picture on the news bulletins and recognised her. I assumed you knew all about the footage and had taken a decision not to release it.'

Fenton considered what he'd heard. He found himself thinking the unthinkable. Why would Ince withhold vital evidence? To protect somebody. Maybe even himself? That wasn't possible. Was it?

The pause in the conversation gave Blake the chance to put two and two together. 'If this Ince is hiding or has destroyed the footage, then he's got to be a suspect.' As the significance of what he'd said dawned on him, Blake clenched his right fist. 'Shit,' he said. 'It could be a fucking cop.'

43

Fenton raised a hand. 'Calm down,' he said. 'Let's not jump the gun. We've got to think about this carefully. Not rush into doing anything stupid.'

'What's there to think about? Ince is hiding evidence that could have led you to the killer. Especially if the killer is on film as well. Are you saying Ince can't be the killer?'

Fenton drained his glass. The heat of the alcohol burned his throat. 'What I'm saying is we have to tread carefully. We're not in possession of any hard evidence yet. If the killer is someone who works inside New Scotland Yard then the last thing we should do is report our suspicions officially. That could mean the killer, whoever it is, would know we're on to him. He could go to ground, cover his tracks. Make a run for it even.'

Blake could see the sense in what Fenton was saying, but the prospect of taking things slowly troubled him. 'While we're pissing around someone else is going to get killed. We've got to do something and we've got to do it quickly.'

'*We* don't do anything. I'm a senior police officer. I won't be one for long if I start interfering in a murder investigation. I daren't even think about taking a close look at Ince, checking his background, his private life. I couldn't do any of that, or advise anyone else to do it, without getting into a heap of trouble. Do you understand what I'm saying?'

Blake frowned. 'Do you think I'm stupid?'

'I think you're a bit touchy.'

Blake wasn't sure what to make of Fenton. He'd earned himself a reputation as a hotshot detective, and at thirty-four was the Met's youngest senior investigating officer, but he was coming across as irritatingly cautious. He appeared to be an honest, decent citizen, but Blake didn't trust him. He'd only known him for twenty minutes and Blake didn't trust people he'd known for twenty years.

'If, theoretically, Ince is the killer,' Blake said, 'then he has access to all the investigation documents. He's always going to be several steps ahead of the police.'

Fenton nodded. 'He'd also have access to the Yard's computer databases. I think that's how the killer found out my address and targeted my daughter's nanny.'

'How old is she? Your daughter.'

'Tess is eleven.'

'How is she?'

'How do you think she is?'

Blake didn't know how to respond, so he said nothing. The two men were staring at each other across the table when Leah arrived.

'I hate awkward silences,' she said, dragging a stool from

a neighbouring table and sitting down in one seamless movement. 'They can be really, what's the word? Really awkward.' She smiled. Fenton smiled back. Blake didn't. He got up and shouldered his way to the bar. By the time he returned to the table, carrying a pint in one hand and a white wine and a whisky in the other, Fenton had brought Leah up to speed. 'I can't believe you've got a suspect already,' she said. 'I knew you two would make a great team.'

Blake dished out the drinks and sat down. 'While I was at the bar I had an idea,' he said. 'If the detective here agrees, I think we can nail this thing.' Fenton gave a non-committal nod, inviting Blake to go on.

'It seems that even if this Detective Ince is innocent, the killer is still someone inside the Yard. He almost certainly has the ability to break through computer security, giving him unlimited access to police databases. I know someone with a talent for getting into networks they're not supposed to get into. With a bit of cooperation from the detective here, they'll be able to hack into the Yard's system, have a good rummage around and tell us who's been accessing information they shouldn't.'

Fenton laughed, but the sound was humourless. 'You want me to help some dodgy geek hack into the Yard's computer network? You're crazy.'

'It's the only way we're going to speed things up. We need to catch this killer before he decapitates someone else.' Fenton flinched. He closed his eyes as he tried to blot out the image of Marta's bloodied, severed head.

Blake sensed he'd hit a nerve and pressed his advantage. 'This person has worked for a couple of newspapers on major investigations. He owes me a favour and he's good. He could probably hack into the system without help, given time. But we haven't got time, have we? If you give us your password he'll be in and out in a few hours. He can cover his tracks. He's done it before and never been caught.'

Fenton turned to Leah, hoping she'd back him up. She shrugged. 'If this is what it takes to catch Lauren's killer. To stop him taking another life. Isn't it worth it?'

'Of course I want him caught. But I also want a job to go back to when this is all over. I like being a detective.'

Blake and Leah exchanged a glance that made Fenton feel like an outsider. 'The only illegal thing we're asking you to do is supply us with your password. We can make sure nobody ever finds out. Any advice, expertise you're willing to share, then sure, I'll take it on board. We don't have to broadcast that either. Any dirty work that needs doing, you can leave that to me.'

Fenton believed Blake, especially his promise that he'd be up for any dirty work. The thought crossed his mind that deep down he had already made a decision. Why else would he have agreed to the meeting? He wanted a chance to finish the job he had started. To put the killer behind bars. Not because that's where he deserved to be. Not because it was his duty. He needed to do it for Tess.

Across the table, Blake shifted impatiently on his seat. For a moment, Fenton considered stretching out his silence to see how long it took before Blake blew. He picked up his whisky, took a sip and smacked his lips in appreciation.

'There is one thing I haven't told you,' he said. 'It's possible the killer has spoken to my daughter. At her school gates, a few days before Marta was murdered.'

Blake and Leah exchanged a look of incredulity. 'Are you serious?' Blake said. 'Please tell me you're kidding.'

'Do you think I'd joke about this?'

'In that case why can't we just show her a picture of Ince?'

'She says she can't remember anything about the man except that he was tall. Tess is small for her age. She'd probably describe any man as tall. Anyway, he made sure she didn't get a good look at his face. Wore a hoodie, and baseball cap under it for good measure. He gave her a message for me, but I think the real message was that he could get to her whenever he wanted. That I couldn't keep her safe.' Leah reached across the table, placed her hand on Fenton's wrist and squeezed.

Blake shook his head in disbelief. 'What the fuck is the matter with you? There is a good chance that a killer has threatened your daughter and you're wasting time wondering whether giving us your password is the right thing to do.'

44

Blake walked briskly along Victoria Embankment, heading towards Westminster Bridge. On his left, the mud brown Thames rolled by. A blue passenger ferry churned a trail of froth as it moved upriver to Hampton Court. He was in a hurry. The person he was meeting wouldn't hang about if he was late. Jimmy Mouseman never stayed in one place for long.

Jimmy was a hacker for hire. He earned his living hacking into emails, Facebook pages and mobile phone messages. You name it, he hacked it. As long as you made it worth his while. It was a cold afternoon, the clouds low and threatening. Blake zipped his jacket tight and turned up the collar to protect himself from the wind blowing off the water. As he passed Cleopatra's Needle, he took advantage of a red traffic light to cross the road, jogged past Embankment Tube station and took a right into Northumberland Avenue. At the top of the hill, he crossed the Strand into Trafalgar Square.

Blake considered the place to be the heart of the city and,

as always, it was heaving with people. Stepping inside the square's low boundary wall he turned right. Mouseman was where he said he would be, stretched out on a stone bench seat, his legs crossed, his arms folded, and the oversized hood of his grey top pulled over his face to his chin.

Blake approached stealthily, grabbed the man's ankles and swung his legs off the bench. The hacker grabbed the edge of the bench to stop himself sliding off and let loose a torrent of swear words. Blake sat down beside him and gave him a nudge with his elbow.

'Caught you napping did I, Jimmy? You must be losing it. I thought you prided yourself on being on the ball. Ahead of the game.'

Mouseman pulled his hood up until his eyes were visible and gave Blake a look that threatened to freeze his blood. 'That was uncalled for, mate. Bloody rude as hell. Yer at least a minute late and bloody lucky I'm still here. You wanna do some business then get on wiv it. I ain't hanging around this shithole much longer.'

Blake had written a feature article on the murky world of hackers and Mouseman had agreed to be interviewed, anonymously of course. People like him lived under the radar, permanently off the grid. Mouseman wasn't his real name and Blake was sure the appalling cockney accent was fake.

'Calm down, Jimmy. Can't you take a joke these days? I've got a job for you. A big one. I'll make it worth your while.'

Mouseman jumped to his feet, tucked his hands in the

pockets of his hoodie and scanned a group of Japanese tourists milling around the lion statues guarding the base of Nelson's Column. The hacker stood as tall as Blake, but under his baggy sportswear he carried a lot of surplus weight.

'Look, mate, you got a couple of minutes if yer lucky. I got a go soon as. The place is too open. Too many cameras. Too many watchers. It's making me nervous.'

Blake took a moment to consider his approach. He didn't want to scare Mouseman off. The hacker made most of his money working for the tabloid press, dodgy lawyers and the odd internet fraudster. In the interview he'd given Blake, he had claimed that he'd never let a client down, and boasted that he'd never been caught. Hacking into New Scotland Yard's heavily protected computer system would be a significant step up. A bigger risk. Likely to bring a heap of trouble down on his hooded head if it went wrong.

'The thing is, Jimmy, we need you to get into the Yard's system. Have a look around, follow a few trails, see if anybody's been poking about in places they shouldn't have. We've got one name in particular we want you to look at.'

When Blake stopped speaking, Mouseman turned slowly to face him and yanked his hood back, exposing chubby cheeks and an uneven blond fringe. 'You're fucking kidding me, right?' he said.

'I'm deadly serious, Jimmy. This is important. And it's going to be easier than you think. I've got a password for you.'

Mouseman's eyes widened. Blake had come up with the magic word.

'You did say password?'

'I did. It'll make it easier, and safer for you.'

'I know what it'll do. What's this story about anyway?'

'I'm not doing a story Jimmy. I don't work for the papers any more. This is bigger than any story. Believe me.'

Mouseman was thinking so hard Blake could feel it. Thinking that maybe it'd be worth the risk. If it was that important he was in a powerful negotiating position.

'Five thousand pounds,' he said.

Something about the greedy gleam in his eye made Blake's skin crawl. 'Five hundred. That's the budget for this job. This is important. Life and death. You can use your dubious talent to do some good for once. Think about it.'

Mouseman used both his hands to pull his hood back over his head and stared into space. After a few seconds, he gave an apologetic shrug. 'Thought about it. Gonna pass on the opportunity to do good. Doing good never got nobody nowhere. Find some other mug.'

Blake hadn't allowed himself to consider the possibility of being turned down. He didn't have a Plan B. As the hacker turned away, he reached out an arm, grabbed his left shoulder and spun him around. In one swift, forceful movement, he grasped two handfuls of hoodie material and slammed Mouseman on to the bench.

Tightening the material around the hacker's fat neck, he forced his head down slowly until one side of his face was pressed against the cold stone. His eyes were closed tight, his face contorted in pain. Blake could feel him trembling.

He bent forward, placing his mouth close to Mouseman's ear.

'You're going to do this thing for me because it's the right thing to do. You're going to do it and when you've done it I'm going to give you five hundred pounds. You're going to be happy with the fee and overjoyed that you've helped your fellow human beings. Is that clear?'

Mouseman opened his eyes and Blake relaxed his grip a fraction to allow him to nod. 'Good. That's the right answer. I knew you'd see it my way in the end. Like I said before, this is important. Important to me. Life and death. Do you understand, life and death?'

Mouseman nodded again. A tiny clear droplet slid from his left eye socket, over his nose and dripped on to the bench. Blake wasn't sure if it was sweat or a tear.

45

'So, tell me why this was so urgent,' Belinda Vale asked. She sat directly opposite Blake, her legs together at the knees and crossed neatly at the ankles. Her hands rested on her lap, clutching an unopened notebook.

Blake avoided the question. He looked around the consulting room as if seeing it for the first time. 'This place must cost a fortune to rent. No wonder your fees are extortionate.'

The psychologist resisted the temptation to smile. Always best to keep things professional. She said nothing, but tilted her head, inviting Blake to keep talking.

'Thanks for fitting me in at such short notice.'

Vale accepted the thank you with a nod and tried again. 'Why did you need to see me so desperately?'

'Because I'm worried. No, not worried, scared.'

'About what? I thought you'd been feeling better.'

Blake squirmed in his seat, lifted a hand and rubbed the back of his neck. 'I was. I am. But stuff I'd locked away. It's running loose now.'

Vale opened the notebook and started writing. Blake leant forward. He was curious to know what he'd said that was so interesting, but he was too far away to read it. She closed the book, lifted the pen to her mouth and tapped her bottom lip.

'Letting all these emotions out is the first step to getting back to how you were before you were traumatised.'

Blake shook his head, hard. 'These feelings aren't good and they're not going away. They keep going around in my head, getting stronger and stronger.'

'What sort of feelings?'

'You tell me, you're the psychologist.'

'Anger would be natural. The suppression of anger is bad.'

Blake gave a humourless laugh. 'Anger's natural? What about rage? All-consuming, blinding rage?'

Vale suspected there was more going on than the simple release of pent-up emotions. 'I guess you've been following the news,' she said. 'The murders.'

'It'd be hard to miss.'

Blake did his best to keep the tone of his voice casual, but he wasn't fooling anybody.

'It's not a good idea to project your feelings about Iraq on to something else.'

Blake stared blankly into space, his jaw muscles twitching. 'I know what evil looks like,' he said.

Vale resisted the urge to argue. She started scribbling in her notebook again, but only because she needed time to think. Mixing her therapeutic work with her criminal profiling wouldn't be a good idea, but they were drifting together and she felt powerless to stop them colliding.

'The nature of evil, and whether it exists or not, is a complex debate. Let's not go there. What I am concerned about is the effect this killer is having on you. I know it's hard, but I suggest you avoid the news coverage of the investigation as much as possible and focus on accepting what happened to you in Iraq.'

Blake rubbed the back of his neck again. 'This is like going to see a doctor, right? Or going to a priest and confessing?'

'I'm not sure what you mean.'

'Well, I can be sure that anything I say here is confidential, right? You can't repeat it to anyone. The police, or anyone?'

Vale stiffened in her seat. 'You're worrying me now,' she said. 'If you tell me anything that I feel poses a real threat to another person then confidentiality goes out of the window.'

Blake shook his head and smiled. 'It's nothing like that. I simply want to know exactly where we stand on what gets said here. It's not easy telling a stranger your secrets. These murders are resurrecting emotions I thought were dead and buried.'

Vale wondered whether she should admit to being the profiler on the murder hunt, but decided it would serve no purpose other than complicate the relationship between patient and therapist. 'That is bound to be the case and it's why you should avoid any temptation to view the images of the victims posted on social media.'

Blake winced at the mention of the photographs. 'I think about Lauren, how I let her down, all the time.'

Vale lifted her pen, but decided against making a note. The issues surrounding Blake's therapy and her profiling were starting to get inextricably tangled.

'Let's get back to this anger you talked about. I'm concerned that you may be linking the murders to what happened to your friend in Iraq,' she said.

Blake shrugged, took a deep breath and exhaled slowly. 'This isn't about Iraq. That's done with. This is about Lauren.'

Vale lifted her pen again and this time scribbled a short note. The session wasn't going the way she expected. 'You're angry with Lauren?'

Blake didn't answer. Vale tried again. 'With yourself?'

Blake stayed silent, but looked away.

'Guilt can manifest itself as anger.'

'I didn't love her enough. Not properly. I couldn't.'

Vale nodded. 'PTSD can do that to a person. Emotional detachment.'

'But I didn't want to be detached. I needed her. She was a kind, beautiful, loving person. I couldn't give her what she wanted and she left. Now she's dead.'

'Do you feel responsible for her death?'

Blake turned back to face Vale and shrugged. 'I feel guilty about not being able to love her in the way she deserved. I was too damaged to love anyone, then.'

Vale usually distrusted intuition as a therapy tool, but she had a strong feeling that there was another dimension to this guilt. 'Is there someone else you have feelings for?' Blake didn't answer. He stared back at her, his silence saying more than words.

Vale closed her notebook. 'I know you might not think it, but you are making progress. The fact that you understand what happened between you and Lauren and are able to talk about it suggests you are ready to free up your emotions, give yourself permission to feel.'

Blake shook his head. 'The only thing I want right now is to see the monster who murdered Lauren locked up with no hope of getting out. I'm worried that if the police don't get their act together soon the evil bastard will go to ground.'

Vale wanted to steer Blake back to his anger issues, but couldn't help being drawn in. 'That's not going to happen.'

Blake swivelled slightly in his seat, and gave the psychologist a sideways look. 'Of course,' he said. 'You'll know something about the mind of a killer. At least your certainty about him killing again suggests you do.'

'We shouldn't be discussing this,' Vale said, 'but this killer won't be able to stop even if he wants to. His social media following is growing and that acclaim will drive him on. He loves the attention. He won't be able to give that up. He's in the grip of an addiction.'

'Shit,' Blake said. 'Where did that come from?'

Vale gave him a sheepish smile. 'Sorry about that. I got a bit carried away. But, believe me, I, Killer will murder again and soon. It's as inevitable as death.'

46

Fenton knocked softly on his daughter's bedroom door and popped his head in the room.

Tess was sitting on her bed propped up between two enormous fluffy pillows, her favourite book on her lap. She tore her eyes away from the page, an expression of mild irritation on her face.

Fenton gave her a thumbs-up sign. 'Dinner's ready,' he said. 'Your favourite.'

Tess wrinkled her nose and gave him a curious look. 'You don't know what my favourite is.'

Fenton feigned a hurt expression. 'I bet I do. Come see.'

Tess slid off the bed, carefully placed the book on her dressing table and followed him to the kitchen. On the pine table were two pizza delivery boxes.

Fenton smiled to himself as Tess jumped on to her chair, her eyes shining in anticipation. 'When I called the order in I asked them to cut yours into slices so you can use your fingers.'

Tess pulled back the lid. 'Extra cheese and pepperoni,' she

squealed. She picked up a wedge and took a bite as Fenton sat down opposite her and attacked his pizza with a knife and fork. After devouring half, Tess put her slice down and eyed her dad suspiciously.

'You don't like people eating with their fingers,' she said. 'What's going on?'

Fenton tried to smile, but the chunk of dough and cheese in his mouth made it impossible. He swallowed it quickly. 'I thought you deserved a treat, that's all.'

Her response was not what he'd expected. She shoved her plate away and sat back with a frown. 'I don't want another nanny,' she said. 'I don't need one. I'm not a baby.'

Fenton put his knife and fork down. 'It's nothing to do with that,' he said. 'Come on, eat up. I'm expecting a visitor in half an hour so I want to tidy up.'

Tess's frown deepened. She crossed her arms across her chest and her bottom lip quivered. 'It's a new nanny, isn't it?'

Fenton shook his head. 'I promise. It's work.'

Reassured, Tess turned her attention back to devouring her pizza. She managed four slices before reluctantly admitting defeat and retreating to her bedroom. Fenton cleared the table, wrapped the leftovers in tin foil and put them in the fridge.

The sound of the doorbell startled him. He scanned the flat and realised he hadn't got round to tidying. A pile of washed clothes sat heaped in a plastic basket on the kitchen floor waiting to be folded and put away. Scooping them up, he stuffed them back in the tumble dryer.

He hurried downstairs and opened the door. 'Sorry I'm late,' Leah said with a smile and stepped inside. She was dressed casually, but smartly, in tailored trousers and a sweater.

Fenton decided against offering his hand to shake, or leaning in for an exchange of continental kissing. 'Don't worry,' he said, stepping to one side to give her space to pass. Before following her, he glanced at the two uniforms on guard duty. Both men acknowledged him with a nod.

Upstairs Fenton gestured for Leah to make herself comfortable on the sofa and asked if she wanted a coffee. Leah shook her head. 'I'm fine, thanks. You said you had a few questions about Lauren?'

Fenton sat in an armchair opposite her, happy that she was eager to get straight down to business. 'If I'm going to be any use to Blake, I thought it'd be handy to fill in a few gaps. As you know, it seems your sister walked across the park with her killer. I was wondering whether that suggests she'd met him before. Was she particularly cautious about that sort of thing?'

Leah took a moment to think. 'Lauren was a free spirit. Very open, very friendly. If someone had spoken to her, passed the time of day with her, she would have responded in a friendly manner and not thought twice about walking with them, if they happened to be going the same way. Not in a public place like Victoria Park. Having said that, she wasn't stupid, or reckless. If she had felt there was anything dodgy going on she would have been careful. She was pretty good at reading people and sizing up situations.'

'Did your sister ever mention anything about being watched or followed in the weeks before her murder?'

Leah frowned. 'She never said anything to me. What are you suggesting? I thought it was simply a case of her being in the wrong place at the wrong time?'

'I'm not suggesting anything. I'm exploring possibilities. People who do what this killer is doing are usually Grade A psychopaths. More often than not, they carefully select their victims, usually for a reason that exists only in their twisted minds, and stalk them for days, even weeks. In some cases, they make a point of getting to know their victims socially. They almost all have an uncanny ability to put people at ease. If you get to meet them several times, and you know what to look for, you can often pick up that there's something off about them. Something not quite right.'

Leah's eyes filled with tears, but she blinked them back. 'Could I have some water, please?'

Fenton darted into the kitchen and returned with a tumbler he'd filled to the top. He handed it to Leah and she took a small sip.

'I know talking about this can't be easy for you.'

Leah took another drink and sighed. 'Lauren and I had a difficult relationship. In some ways, I think we were too alike and in others so different. Our parents died in a car crash in France seven years ago. After that we drifted apart. We only started to get close again after she left Blake.'

Fenton hadn't expected Leah to bare her soul and was at a loss at how to respond. He played safe and nodded sagely at her. She took the hint and changed the subject. 'I thought maybe I'd get to meet your daughter tonight. It must have been horrible for her, and you, of course, you know, what happened to her nanny.'

'Tess is in her room. You know what eleven-year-old girls are like. Last time I checked, she was reading.'

'That's pretty impressive.' Leah said. 'I'd expect most children of her age to be glued to their computer screens or smart phones.'

Fenton leant back in the chair and felt his body relax. Leah was easy to talk to. 'You know, Marta was the first nanny Tess liked. The fifth since her mother died. She gave the others such a hard time. I think she felt they were employed to replace her mum and wasn't having any of it.'

'What was your wife's name?'

'Josephine. I called her Josie.'

'She got sick?'

'Cancer. Once we had the diagnosis it took her quickly.'

'That's so sad. I'm sorry.'

Fenton smiled ruefully. This was the last thing he had expected to talk about. For the past year and a half, he'd had to be strong. For Tess. He'd done it by trying his best to pretend it had never happened. Saying the words out loud, for the first time in a long time, felt less traumatic than he'd expected. 'Coffee?' he asked. 'Or I could open some wine?'

'Coffee would be good.'

Leah followed him into the kitchen and sat at the table. Neither of them spoke while Fenton made the drinks, but it was a comfortable silence. As he handed Leah her coffee Tess walked in. She stared silently at Leah, not bothering to hide her disapproval.

'Hi, Tess,' Fenton said. 'I've been telling Leah all about you. We're having coffee, but I could do you a hot chocolate if you'd like?'

Tess ignored him, went to the sink and half filled a glass with water. On her way back to her room, she hesitated and looked over her shoulder.

'If you're a new nanny then you're wasting your time,' she said. 'I'm old enough to look after myself now.'

'No, I'm not a nanny,' Leah said, laughing softly. 'But it's nice to meet you anyway.'

The girl switched her gaze to her father. 'Is this a date or something?'

'It's not a date, don't be silly,' he said. 'Leah and I are working together. It's a work meeting.' Tess gave him a weary look and walked out, closing the door behind her.

'I'm sorry about that,' Fenton said. 'She's a great girl really. She's struggling a bit, that's all. She hasn't been to school since Marta was killed. The truth is I'm thinking about sending her to stay with my parents in Devon for a while. Just until the killer is caught.'

Leah picked up her coffee and took a drink. 'I understand that you're worried about her safety, but after what happened I'd be surprised if she wouldn't rather be with her father.'

'Maybe you're right,' he said. 'I just want to do the best thing for Tess. I know I've made mistakes recently. Josie was a remarkable woman. The void her death has left is impossible to fill.'

'Being a single parent is hard. You're doing your best, anyone can see that.'

'What if my best is not good enough?'

Leah didn't have an answer and Fenton decided to move the conversation back to the investigation. 'Can I ask you a bit more about your sister?'

'Feel free.'

'How long was she in a relationship with Blake?'

'Nearly a year, I think.'

'What did she say about her relationship ending? Why did she leave him?'

Leah thought for a moment before replying. She was a bit puzzled about the way the conversation was going. 'It was complex. She loved him. That was obvious.'

'But she walked out on him.'

'She did. She didn't want to, but she felt she had no choice. Lauren saw the good in him. She wanted to help him. When it became clear he didn't want to help himself she gave up. He was lost. Like a kid lost in the dark woods. That's what she told me. She tried to guide him out, but got frightened about being dragged into the darkness herself.'

Leah paused, took another sip of coffee and frowned. 'What is this all about? I've asked Blake to take a fresh look at Lauren's murder and you've agreed to help. I don't understand these questions.'

'I just want to get it clear in my head why you picked

Blake. There are plenty of experienced investigators for hire in the city. I could even recommend a couple of former police officers who'd do a good job for you. I know Blake was a well-regarded journalist, but it's not the same thing.'

Leah shrugged. 'I believe he can do a good job. He's got the skills. Otherwise it'd simply be a waste of time. I did some research of my own and he had a reputation as a fearless reporter.'

'A bit too fearless if you ask me,' Fenton said. 'There's a fine line between bravery and stupidity. Hanging around the Iraq–Syria border armed with nothing more than a pen, notebook and smartphone could be considered foolish.'

Leah shook her head. 'He may be a bit reckless, but I don't think he's a bad person. He's honest. Says what he thinks. I like that about him. Are you having second thoughts?'

'I'm not. I simply want to understand who I'm working with and why.'

'Another reason I chose Blake was to do something for Lauren. To try to finish what she started. She always said he needed to get back to work. To focus his mind. I also believe he wants to do it for Lauren. Needs to, even. Does that answer your questions?'

'I suppose it does.'

Leah pulled her mobile from her pocket and tapped at the screen. 'I'm ordering a taxi to pick me up in ten minutes,' she said. 'That should be long enough for you to fill me in on the progress you've made.'

Fenton thought her use of the word progress a little opti-mistic, but he didn't say so. 'It's early days yet. I'm taking a fresh look at the three murders. Obviously, I haven't got access to the files any more, but I did bring some notes home with me and I've a pretty good memory for details.'

'What about this suspect Blake has already come up with? The detective who took the café's security camera footage?'

'I think calling him a suspect is a bit strong,' Fenton said. 'We've only got the café owner's word for it. If it is true, we can't afford to let Ince know that we know. If he gets a whiff of what we're up to he could destroy the footage. It's possible he's done that already. But keeping this to ourselves makes me uneasy. I've been suspended not sacked. I'm still a police officer. I could be accused of withholding evidence.'

'But nobody knows you're working with Blake. I'm not going to tell anybody.'

Fenton took a swig of coffee, pulled a face, then took another. 'Let's hope we can keep it that way. I like Blake, but he seems to have no qualms about breaking the law.'

'What do you mean?'

'He's arranged for that contact of his to take a look at the Yard's computer system to see if anyone's been accessing data they shouldn't have.'

Leah frowned, her perfectly plucked eyebrows almost meeting. 'That's a problem because . . .?'

'Because it's as illegal as hell and he's going to land us all in big trouble if he's caught.'

★ ★ ★

Fenton stood at the window sipping a cold beer as he watched Leah slide into the backseat of the taxi. He put the bottle down, covered his face with his hands and rubbed his eyes. He needed sleep, but knew it wouldn't come easy. Walking over to the sink he poured the remaining beer away. For a moment, he considered checking on Tess. Only for a moment. He didn't want a grilling about Leah.

Feeling cowardly, he tiptoed past her bedroom, but the sound of sobbing stopped him dead. He pushed the door open and walked in. Tess had yanked the duvet over her head. He pulled the cover back and gently wiped a tear from her cheek with his thumb. 'Don't cry,' he said.

'I don't want to go. Please don't make me, Daddy.'

'Hey, come on. What's this about?'

Tess sniffed loudly. 'I heard you. You're sending me away.'

Fenton bent down and kissed her softly on the top of her head. 'I think it might be a good idea for you to stay with Gran and Granddad for a while. You always love it when we visit.'

Tess rubbed her eyes hard with the back of her hand. 'I want to stay with you.'

'I know that, darling, but it's my job to keep you safe.'

'I'll feel much safer, I'll be much safer if I'm with you.'

Fenton pulled the duvet up to her shoulders, bent down and kissed her hot forehead. 'I want to do what's best for you. I'll think about it. Okay?' She replied with another sniff.

By the time he climbed into bed it was almost midnight.

His eyes ached, but he knew sleep was a long way off. Opening the drawer of his bedside table, he pulled out a sheet of paper, unfolded it and carefully smoothed it between his fingers.

Written on the paper, in a flowing elegant script, was Josie's last message to him. Fenton smiled to himself. He'd been lucky to have married an amazing woman. She knew what was coming and she knew it was coming soon, and she chose to write him a list of instructions. Josie had always loved writing lists.

Her last list was almost certainly the shortest. Three things, just three things he had to promise to do. Number one was the easiest. Take all of Josie's love and give Tess double. Number two. Make our daughter laugh at least once every day. He'd failed miserably on that one. Number three. When you're ready, find Tess a new mum. Fenton doubted that was ever going to happen, but he'd promised anyway.

He carefully folded the sheet of paper up, slipped it back in the drawer and switched off the light. Lying in the darkness, he tucked his hands behind his head. The likelihood of him sleeping was zero unless he stopped thinking about Josie.

He started mulling over the events of the last few days. He'd always been a stickler for following rules and regulations, doing everything by the book. That had been a big part of his success. Most big cases were broken by slow, steady police work. Each stage of a murder investigation, from initial door-to-door inquiries, to background checks on suspects, and the assessment of forensic evidence had to be done meticulously and in the right order.

One careful step at a time. That was how he led murder inquiries and, until now, it had worked for him. Somehow, he'd found himself banished from the Yard, entangled in an unofficial inquiry with a former journalist who didn't follow the rules. Hell, Blake didn't even acknowledge that a rule book existed. It wasn't too late to back out. To admit he'd made a mistake. So, what was stopping him?

Fenton closed his eyes in a feeble attempt to block unwanted thoughts. After a few seconds, he opened them again. As his vision adjusted to the darkness, he accepted the undeniable truth. More than anything, he wanted to be part of taking this killer down. The Yard had decided to deprive him of that privilege. He couldn't accept it. It was unacceptable. Evil had come to his doorstep. He wasn't going to sit around waiting for his replacement to get lucky.

Fenton's eyes closed again. This time they were heavy with tiredness. He rolled over on to his side, ready to embrace sleep; then his mobile rang. He reached over to the bedside table, snatched up the phone with one hand and switched on the lamp with the other.

'What the hell is it, Blake?' he said, wanting to shout but having to keep his voice down because he was worried about waking Tess. 'Do you know what time it is?'

'I do, but here's a tip for you, detective. If you haven't got a watch, take a look at the screen of your mobile. The time should always be on there.'

Fenton pushed himself up into a sitting position and swung his legs over the side of the bed. He'd told Leah that he liked Blake, and he'd been telling the truth, but sometimes the man could be downright annoying.

'I assume this is important.'

'Sorry to interrupt your beauty sleep,' Blake said. 'I know how much you need it.'

'What is it?'

'Detective Constable Ince.'

'What about him.'

'He's been a naughty boy. Accessing parts of the computer network way above his security level. Looking at stuff he shouldn't be looking at. Reading information about people he shouldn't be reading about.'

Fenton stood up and switched on the main light. 'Are you sure about this?'

'My contact is sure and I'm sure he knows what he's doing.'

'Shit,' Fenton said. 'How did Ince get into these files if he didn't have the right clearance? The security on the system is meant to be virtually impregnable.'

'I think the word "virtually" is the key to answering that question. According to my man, Ince must have specialist knowledge. A talent for all things techie that he's been keeping secret.'

'What files has he been looking at?'

Blake hesitated before answering. When he did speak it was clear he'd chosen his words carefully.

'I don't want to go into that sort of detail right now. Like computer systems, phones can be hacked into fairly easily, if you know what you're doing. Get back to your beauty sleep and we'll talk more in the morning. Somewhere out in the open maybe.'

'Where do you suggest? I don't want to leave Tess for too long.'

'I'll text you in the morning. Goodnight. Sleep tight.'

Fenton tossed his mobile on to the bed. There was no way he was going to sleep. He picked the phone up, went to Google and searched for I, Killer. One point seven million results in 0.89 seconds. Fuck.

He was fighting to stifle an urge to hurl his mobile at the wall when the third item on the results list caught his eye. *Breaking news on the BBC. New I, Killer post.* He opened the page. The bulletin was brief. *Serial killer sends internet followers chilling new post. Police say the message appeared on Twitter account set up one hour ago.*

My next victim has shown her childish face #IKiller.

Fenton read the news bulletin again. The killer wanted his followers to be ready for his next offering. Whetting their appetite . . . *her childish face*. Fear for Tess flamed in his chest.

47

The Regent's Canal is one of London's best-kept secrets. Stretching nine miles from Paddington in the west to the Limehouse Basin in the east, Blake thought of it as an oasis of calm in a city of troubles.

Sitting on a wooden bench facing the waterway, he tilted his face to the sky and let the autumn sun warm his skin. The four-mile walk along the towpath, from Victoria Park to the York Way canal bridge in south Islington, had given him plenty of time to think how best to handle Fenton.

The suspended detective would advise caution; suggest that, based on his vast experience, they shouldn't jump to conclusions. Blake had other ideas. He was in the mood to jump so high he'd need a parachute.

He nodded encouragement as a puffing, middle-aged man wearing unflattering, skin-tight Lycra pedalled by, and returned the smile of a woman in her mid-twenties jogging in the opposite direction. For almost a year, Blake had done all his running indoors. Watching a green and red narrowboat chug under the bridge, he allowed himself to consider joining the towpath joggers.

He turned at the sound of footsteps to see Fenton descending the slope. Wearing a dark suit, white shirt and black tie, the police officer looked like he was on his way to a funeral. 'Right on time,' Blake said. 'Nice of you to dress up for the occasion. If I'd known I'd have worn something smarter.' Fenton stopped behind the bench, took a white paper bag out of his jacket pocket and tossed it to Blake. 'Shut up and eat,' he said.

Blake opened the bag and pulled out a bagel filled with bacon and cream cheese. The bagel was still warm. He took a bite and licked his lips.

'How did you know I missed breakfast?'

'I guessed,' Fenton said, pulling another paper bag from his other pocket and taking out a similarly filled bagel. 'These are good. Trust me. Freshly baked every morning at a place around the corner.'

Blake took another bite and placed the remaining portion on the bench beside him. 'Very tasty, but where's the coffee I ordered?'

Fenton ignored the jibe. 'Let's get on with your report, shall we?'

Blake shook his head. 'Oh, no, let me stop you right there.' he said. 'Let's get this straight. I'm not reporting to you. The only person I report to is my client. I'm passing on information. Letting you know what's going on. I'm in charge of this investigation. You're advising. That's all.'

Fenton bit into his bagel and chewed over his response. 'I'm not sure your employer would totally agree with you, but let's not quibble over semantics. What's Ince been up to?'

Blake didn't dislike the detective. In a way, he had a lot of respect for him and his record, and was pleased to have him as a sounding board. But this was his investigation, and he was going to do it his way.

'Ince has been poking around your supposedly impregnable computer system like a pig rooting in shit.'

'It'd help if you could you be a bit more specific.'

'Obviously, he has access to the murder files because he's part of the investigating team.'

'Obviously.'

'But, according to my expert, he's been dipping into files his security clearance shouldn't allow him to access.'

'Such as?'

'Such as the personnel files of several of his fellow officers, containing their home addresses, phone numbers, next of kin, all that sort of stuff. He's also been dipping into files holding details of the murder victims' families, checking out a psychologist named Belinda Vale, and nosing around in the private files and documents of one particular senior officer.'

'I take it you mean me?'

'That's exactly who I mean.'

Fenton walked round to the front of the bench, considered sitting down next to Blake, but changed his mind. 'As suspicious as it sounds, none of this actually proves that Ince had anything to do with the murders.'

'How did I know you were going to say that?'

'It does prove that he's engaged in criminal activity – improper use of police databases – and he would certainly be booted off the force and face charges as a result, but we can't do anything about it because we'd be admitting that you and your hacker pal broke the law yourself. Computer hacking carries a maximum sentence of ten years in prison.'

Blake smiled. 'I like the way that, almost without hesitation, you switched the word "we" to "you" in that sentence about breaking the law.'

Fenton stepped back off the towpath to allow another cyclist space to pass. 'I hope your man knows what he's doing, that's all.'

'Don't worry,' Blake said. 'He's assured me he's covered his tracks, and our arses. As far as Ince goes, I get what you're saying but it's all pointing to him. We can't afford to pussyfoot around. We don't know when the killer is going to strike again.'

Fenton swallowed the last of his bagel, used the paper bag to wipe the grease off his fingers and stuffed it back into his jacket pocket. 'We have to make sure we've got enough to nail him before we move. If it is Ince, and he finds out we're on to him, he could do a disappearing act. We need solid evidence.'

No surprise there, Blake thought. 'What do you suggest?'

'Old-fashioned surveillance. Follow him, stake out his home. See what he gets up to in his spare time.'

Blake shook his head. 'That's it? All those years leading

murder investigations and that's the best you can come up with?'

'It works. Believe me, that basic stuff works. If there's no DNA to work with, no fingerprints, no CCTV footage, all the technology in the world is useless.'

'So, I watch him. What then?'

'The best scenario is that he leads you to a lock-up garage or some other storage space stuffed with evidence. Weapons, photographs, the laptop or smartphone he's been using to post his messages. The worst is that he's nothing more than a cyber snooper. While you're on surveillance duty I've got a friend or two at the Yard who I can call on to look into Ince's background.'

Blake got up from the bench, and took a step towards Fenton. 'I take it you've seen the new I, Killer message on Twitter?'

Fenton nodded. 'Of course I've seen it. Everybody's seen it.'

'He's warming up his followers. Telling them to be ready for his next show. What if I find someone is in imminent danger?'

'Then we act fast. I contact my colleagues and tell them what's been going on.'

'Even though that'll mean you'll probably have to earn a living as a supermarket security guard?'

'I'm not going to keep my head down and let someone die.'

Blake nodded. He knew Fenton was the kind of man who

always did the right thing in the end. That was one of his strengths. It was also his biggest weakness. 'One other thing,' he said. 'Before I declare this meeting over, do you know why Belinda Vale has a personnel file at the Yard?'

Fenton shrugged. 'She's a psychologist. Has her own practice, in Holborn, I think. She also works as a criminal profiler. From what I can recall she's a damn good one. I'd guess she's been called in to draw up a profile of the killer. What's it to you?'

Blake didn't like the thought of admitting that he'd been seeing a psychologist. They'd only talked a few times, after all. It crossed his mind that it would be less embarrassing to lie and that there was no reason Fenton needed to know the truth, but he decided to come clean anyway. What the hell, he told himself. Why should he care what anybody thought?

'I've been to see her a couple of times,' he said. 'To talk things through. I had no idea she was part of the murder investigation.'

Fenton sensed Blake's discomfort. 'A couple of officers I worked with had to retire early because of PTSD,' he said. 'One was shot trying to arrest a drug dealer. He almost lost a kidney. The other entered a house after a neighbour called to report hearing strange noises. He found two girls, four and six, dead on their beds. Their drug addict mother had strangled them both before killing herself with a heroin overdose. Both officers swear therapy helped.'

Blake knew that the point of the story was to show understanding and sympathy, but he didn't need either. 'All right, for now we'll do it your way,' he said. 'I'll keep a close eye on Ince and we'll see what happens. I'll be in touch in a day or so. Thanks for breakfast.'

He stepped on to the towpath and started walking back the way he'd come. He'd taken a couple of paces when Fenton called out for him to stop. 'One last thing,' the detective said. 'If it turns out that Ince is our man then you need to be careful. Don't go doing anything stupid.'

Blake considered making a smart remark about being touched that Fenton cared. Instead, he gave an almost imperceptible nod and carried on walking. When he reached the York Way tunnel he looked back. Fenton had disappeared.

The meeting had gone the way Blake had expected. He'd agreed to go along with Fenton's cautious approach in principle, but a strategy that involved hours of watching and waiting didn't suit his temperament. He believed in making things happen. Blake took a couple of deep breaths. He knew that London was one of Europe's most polluted cities, but, as he stood by the water in the late-autumn sun, the air smelled fresh, almost sweet. As he watched a blond teenager and his even blonder girlfriend share a joke as they paddled by in red plastic canoes, Blake felt more positive about life than he had in a long time. If an opportunity to make things happen came along, he'd grab it.

48

The bitch has overstepped the mark. Claiming to know me. The real me. Telling lies about me. Making assumptions about my childhood. Who the hell does she think she is?

She thinks she's something special. She definitely wants others to believe she is. She's that sort. To get what she wants she'll lie. Not little lies. Great big, dirty, fat, twisted lies. She'll repeat them with such conviction you won't dare challenge them.

I rarely get worked up about things. I prefer to be more considered in my response when people wrong me. Take my time, wait for the right moment, then slide the knife right in. I've undermined the confidence of a lot of tedious people. It's easily done. All of these victims were feeble. There, I said it. Hit the nail on the head without even thinking about it. They were all victims. Victims from the day they were born.

This woman has judged me to be no more than an inferior product of my childhood. Before I mastered the art of concealment, I had to deal with child psychologists. They came to the conclusion that I was different to other children because my parents didn't bond with me on an emotional level.

None of them could see the truth. I didn't bond with my parents because I was different from other children. What is psychology anyway? Lots of long words to fool you into believing it's scientific, but it's all talk. Talk about narcissism, paranoia, inferiority complexes, superiority complexes. Well, from what I can remember, all of the psychologists I came across suffered from at least one of those personality disorders.

By the time I was six I'd lost both my parents. I lived with eight sets of foster carers. I adapted to survive.

I am not the product of my past. I am the master of my present, the creator of my future. I am my own God.

What really gets me is that she hasn't said anything positive about me at all. She's not given me the credit I deserve. I don't torture my victims, not physically. I haven't killed any children. Not yet.

49

Tess sat at the kitchen table pretending to read. The family liaison officer stood at the sink rinsing out her mug. The soft-spoken constable, 'call me Helen', smiled over her shoulder. Tess smiled back, but impatience gnawed at her insides.

Humming softly to herself, Helen wandered off. Tess kept her head down and turned a page, her eyes sliding sideways to follow the constable into the bathroom. The lock rattled and Tess sprung off her seat.

She slipped her coat from the back of the chair and ran down the stairs. At the bottom, she turned right and let herself out into the back garden. She lifted the rusty latch and stepped into the alley.

Tess didn't like alleys. They were scary. She ran all the way to the end of the terrace and out on to Risinghill Street. After stopping for a moment to catch her breath, she walked purposefully along the road. She wanted to get back before her dad got home. Despite the sunshine, Tess shivered and zipped up her coat.

Her plan was to head in the direction of her school. She knew that would take her close to her destination. She couldn't go away without saying goodbye to Mummy. That wouldn't be right.

At the end of the street Tess stopped, her toes perched on the edge of the kerb. Marta always insisted that they crossed there because the traffic island meant they could stop halfway. She was about to cross when a car pulled up beside her. The driver leant over and opened the passenger door.

'Hello, Tess,' he said.

She frowned and stayed silent. How did he know her name? The man wore a dark jacket, a baseball cap and a friendly smile. 'Your daddy sent me to pick you up,' he said. 'He's worried about you.'

Tess shook her head. 'I'm going to the cemetery,' she announced and walked away. The car rolled slowly after her, the passenger door still open.

The driver's smile broadened. 'I know you are. Your daddy asked me to take you there. He's busy right now, but he said to tell you he'll meet you there later.'

Tess halted. She wanted to believe him, but knew he was lying. She knew not to accept lifts from strangers, especially this stranger. Her right leg started to tremble and tears pricked her eyes.

The man dug a mobile phone from his jacket pocket and stretched across the passenger seat. 'Here, you can call your dad if you want to check. Go on.'

Confused by the man's insistence, Tess reached out a shaking hand, hesitated, then pulled it back. That moment of hesitation was enough. Strong fingers curled around her tiny wrist and dragged her off her feet on to the passenger seat. The man leant over her, tugged the door shut and jammed his foot down.

As the car accelerated away he laughed softly. 'Strap yourself in,' he said. 'Daddy wouldn't want you to get hurt, would he?'

50

Blake arrived back at his flat in time to shower, dress and get to Westminster by midday. The demand for news updates on the hunt for the killer had become so unrelenting, New Scotland Yard's media team were holding daily press conferences.

He waved his old press card at a bright-eyed young woman behind the reception counter, his thumb strategically placed over the date of issue. Impersonating a newspaper reporter was, as far as he knew, not a criminal offence. Fraudulently gaining entry to the headquarters of the Metropolitan Police definitely was.

He rode the lift to the fifth floor in the company of a tall man in an expensive-looking light-grey suit. He looked familiar, but Blake couldn't recall where he'd seen him before.

The lift juddered to a halt and the doors slid open. Blake didn't move, allowing his lift buddy to exit first and stride down the corridor. The entrance to the media centre was directly opposite the lift. Blake pulled the door open and slipped in.

He'd been to a few press conferences at the Yard before, and the set-up was a familiar sight. The seating was laid out in ten rows of twelve. All but the last row had been already taken by reporters from newspapers, news agencies, news websites, television and radio.

In front of the seating, a raised podium was lit brightly with spotlights even though there was plenty of natural light from four large rectangular windows. On the podium were a long table, three microphones and three empty chairs.

Blake recognised a few faces among the reporters, but stood on his own at the back of the room. The event was due to start, the sense of anticipation palpable. The excited chatter dropped to a respectful murmur when three people arrived on the podium and sat facing the audience. Two of them took Blake by surprise. One was the man he shared the lift with, the other Belinda Vale. They sat on either side of a heavy-set, greying man wearing the world-weary expression of a senior detective.

The room fell silent as the younger man introduced himself as Ray Partington, a senior press officer. Blake remembered him as the man he'd watched comforting Leah when she broke down in front of the cameras. Self-assured and professional, he outlined the usual ground rules and introduced Detective Chief Inspector Norman Tobin as the man who had taken over the investigation.

'We also have an expert guest today,' Partington said. 'Psychologist Belinda Vale, the criminal profiler helping the investigation, has agreed to answer a few questions. The exact details of her profile of the killer will not be discussed. You'll appreciate the reason why, I'm sure. She has kindly agreed to answer general questions about serial killers. We'll kick off with a statement from DI Tobin.'

Blake watched Vale shield her eyes against the bright lights and wondered how much arm twisting she'd suffered before giving in. A dozen or so cameras flashed as Tobin cleared his throat, glanced down at the statement he was about to read, and dipped his head closer to the microphone.

'As the new senior investigating officer in this case, I want to assure the public that every effort is being made to apprehend the killer. Every available officer, both uniformed and plain-clothed, is working flat out to achieve this end.'

Tobin killed the atmosphere with his first few sentences. His round, florid face displayed even less enthusiasm than his monotone delivery. He droned on about how the public could be assured that any information received about the killer and his whereabouts would be treated in the strictest confidence.

'And finally,' he said, words that were greeted with a collective murmur of relief, 'I want to take this opportunity to repeat a general warning to the public to take precautions regarding their personal safety until an arrest is made. Women in particular should, when out late at night, make sure they are accompanied at all times. We don't want to stop people having a good time, but this is a situation where it is imperative that people use common sense.'

Partington jumped to his feet. 'Thank you for those wise

words. Unfortunately, DCI Tobin will not be taking any questions today. You'll of course appreciate he has a lot of work to do and won't be staying with us. I'll make sure you all get both a digital version and hard copy of his statement.'

The detective stood up and ambled through a door behind the podium. God help us, Blake thought. If Fenton's replacement is as good at hunting killers as he is at performing at press conferences, then they might as well award the killer the freedom of the city.

Partington shifted along the table and sat next to Vale. 'We're moving on now to our esteemed psychologist,' he said. 'She has kindly agreed to take a few questions, but, I repeat, they mustn't be about the specifics of her profile.'

While he was instructing the reporters that before asking a question they would be required to raise a hand and identify themselves, a female voice rang out from the front row.

'Isn't it the case that there is no real evidence that offender profiling has any value at all in this kind of investigation?'

Vale looked at Partington hoping that he might come to her rescue and steer the questioning back to the subject of serial killers. Instead he gave a nod, encouraging her to answer the question.

Blake was a long way from the podium, but he saw a trace of irritation flicker across the psychologist's face. 'Criminal profiling has its flaws,' she answered. 'But over the years it's been proved to be an extremely useful resource for officers trying to solve serial murders.'

The reporter came straight back at her with more of a

comment than a question. 'Yes, but isn't it a skill rather than a science? Something that's on trend, but not much use to anybody.'

Vale looked at Partington again and this time he stepped in. 'Before you get your answer, we need to know who you are.'

'Isabel Banks, chief reporter on the *Standard*.'

'Ms Banks,' Vale said. 'Profiling is not a new-fangled trend. It's a technique that has been developed and honed over the years. In fact, something very similar to profiling was used by detectives hunting Jack the Ripper as far back as 1888.'

Vale realised what she'd done as soon as the words slipped out of her mouth. Blake cringed in his seat. He knew what was coming.

'They never caught him either, did they?' Banks said. Laughter rippled around the room.

'Next question,' Partington snapped, determined to keep control of the situation. 'Let's keep to the subject, please.'

'Dave Richards, BBC London. This killer is building a huge social media following. Perhaps you can explain the psychology behind this phenomenon?'

Partington opened his mouth to intervene, but Vale stopped him with a wave of her hand. 'Good question, Mr Richards,' she said. 'I'm happy to answer because it's not about the killer, it's more to do with the basics of human nature.'

Encouraged, the BBC reporter fired off another question. 'Is the internet, social media, to blame? Do we need tighter controls?'

Vale shifted closer to her microphone. 'I'm not an internet expert, but I'm not sure it can be controlled. Social media isn't to blame. It's nothing more than a communication tool. How we choose to use that tool is a reflection of our nature.'

A hand shot up in the third row. The journalist didn't wait for Partington to invite him to ask his question. 'Tom Foxton, freelance,' he announced. 'Are you saying humans are inherently bad, naturally drawn to evil?'

Vale shook her head. 'We are capable of amazing acts of kindness, sensitivity, sacrifice and incredible creativity, but the human psyche also has a sinister side. The primitive part of the brain can make us capable of cruelty, torture, rape, murder and war. We're fascinated by death, but don't want to contemplate our own. It's no surprise to me that so many people are obsessed by these "before death" and "after death" images.'

Vale paused and Partington took the opportunity to move on to the next question, pointing at a flame-haired reporter in the front row. 'Bryony Noble, Reuters. I, Killer has become a celebrity psychopath. What about the moral position of his internet followers. Don't they share some of the blame for the murders?'

'Social media provides anonymity for those who want it. People can hide behind their screens and feel safe exploring parts of their psyche they have repressed without fear of being condemned by their communities. Being online takes away all the normal restraints of society. I, Killer is making murder a shared experience.'

Another hand shot up. Partington pointed at the woman,

nodding for her to go ahead. 'Tina Willis, Press Association. Some people believe that I, Killer's last message suggests that his next victim will be a child. Do you agree with this analysis?'

Vale closed her eyes. She'd been dreading this question, but she didn't feel it'd be right to dodge it completely. 'That kind of mind is capable of anything. There are no limits.'

For a brief moment, an eerie silence settled over the room. The freelance reporter broke it with another question. 'What about motivation? Is it sexual, or simply a lust for blood?'

'It can be both of those things, as well as many others,' Vale said, propping her elbows on the table and resting her chin on her hands. 'Sometimes they kill as revenge for a real or imagined slight, or simply for the thrill of it. It then becomes a thrill they need to replicate. It's often about empowerment. Power over another human being. The key is that after the first time they are driven to repeat the experience. Like drug addiction, all they can think about is the next high.'

She sat back as several reporters tried to get her attention, waving hands and shouting over each other in an unseemly scrum. She started speaking over them and they quickly fell silent. 'You may not be aware, but you are playing a big part in this whole thing. Serial killers can become almost as addicted to the attention they're getting in the media as they are to killing. They come to crave the notoriety. It becomes part of the game.'

Vale paused. This time the room stayed silent. She had the journalists' full attention. 'Maybe,' she said. 'If there's one thing you can take away from here today, it's that you should take care not to glamorise this kind of crime. I know you have a job to do, but please try to do it responsibly. Think about it.'

The plan might have been to keep her answers general, but she's definitely talking about the I, Killer posts, Blake thought. A low murmur of excitement filled the room. Everyone was thinking the same thing.

A blonde television reporter started to ask a question about police incompetence, but Partington closed her down. 'I'm afraid that's it, folks,' he said. 'We're out of time. Thank you for your cooperation.'

The press officer turned to his right to congratulate the psychologist on her performance, but she was already on her feet and striding off the podium.

Belinda Vale stepped into the lift and pressed the button for the underground car park. The growing unease she'd felt from the moment she walked on to the podium to face the assembled media had taught her a valuable lesson. She swore under her breath that she'd never again be persuaded to do something that she didn't want to do.

The lift door pinged open and she hurried out. Although there was still an hour to sunset, the car park was dark and poorly lit. She stopped for a moment as she tried to remember where she'd left her car, and set off again after spotting it wedged between a marked Metropolitan Police Range Rover and a brick wall.

The rapid click-clicking of her high heels echoed in her

ears. Inexplicably, the sound made her feel vulnerable. In her peripheral vision, a shadow moved. She took a sharp breath and increased her pace. She'd almost reached her car when she heard a definite footfall behind her and swung around, gripping her car keys in her hand like a weapon.

Blake held both hands up and stepped back. 'Whoa there,' he said. 'Take it easy.'

Vale let out a long breath. 'What the hell are you doing creeping up on me like that?'

'Sorry if I scared you,' Blake said taking another step back, his hands still raised. 'I looked in on the press conference and wanted a word.'

'I wasn't scared. You startled me, that's all.'

It was a lie, but Blake understood her embarrassment. 'I thought it might be interesting to see how the press is reacting to the case.'

'And was it?'

'Fairly. Those conferences can be difficult. You did well.'

Vale shook her head. 'You won't get me doing another one. Partington will have to find someone else to keep the press happy.'

'He's a pretty good operator,' Blake said. 'Knows his job.'

Vale gave Blake a long hard look. 'You wanted a word?' she said.

'Why didn't you tell me you were working on the I, Killer case?'

'It wasn't appropriate. I don't want to mix my therapy work with profiling. It would be unprofessional.'

'I suppose that makes sense,' Blake said. 'I'll let you get off home. I'll see you next week and I promise not to mention the murders.'

Vale watched and waited until Blake had reached the lift before opening her car door and sliding in behind the wheel. She started the engine and drove slowly towards the exit. By the time she reached the security barrier, she realised the unease she'd been feeling earlier hadn't gone. It was still there, bubbling under the surface.

At the same time, it dawned on her that she hadn't been completely truthful about the reason for her anxiety. She genuinely believed that criminal profilers shouldn't let themselves become tainted by the media coverage of a case, but the real problem was the image that flashed through her mind while she listened to Tobin read his statement.

She'd had a vision of the killer sitting on his sofa watching that evening's television news bulletins, fascinated by clips from the press conference, listening to psychologist Belinda Vale answer the reporters' questions. He'd love every second of it.

Vale believed she knew better than anyone how this killer viewed the world. By agreeing to appear at the press conference she'd put herself in the public eye. Worse than that, she'd put herself in the hunting ground.

51

Fenton sat on the sofa, his head in his hands, anger churning like molten rock in the pit of his stomach. Detective Sergeant Daly stood in the centre of the room, watching her boss warily as a female police constable searched Tess's room.

He'd returned home to blue lights flashing in the street, his flat full of grim-faced uniforms, and the news that Tess had gone. He clenched his fists, unclenched them and clenched them again.

In the two hours since his return, a witness had come forward to say she'd seen a child matching Tess's description getting into a car. If he harms her, Fenton promised himself, I swear I'll kill him and post pictures of his mutilated body all over the fucking internet.

Daly had never seen her boss consumed by fury before. 'Would you like a cup of tea, sir?'

'No, I don't want tea. I want my daughter.'

'We'll find her.'

Fenton stood up, the suddenness of the movement

startling his sergeant. 'How did she get out? This place was supposed to be under police guard.'

Daly nodded and pulled nervously at her ponytail. 'I'm told we had a uniform on the front door as usual but, because an FLO was with Tess, there was nobody round the back. We think she went into the garden and out into the alley.'

'What have we got on the car?'

'Colour and make, but no registration number unfortunately. We're doing everything we can. Pulling out all the stops.'

Fenton paced over to the window and stared out on to the street. He wanted to be out there, looking for Tess, bringing her home.

'I've got to ask you, boss,' Daly said. 'Is there any reason she'd go off like that?'

Fenton chewed his lip. 'I suggested she should stay with her grandparents for a while. That's all.'

'Is there any chance she was going to meet someone she'd been chatting with online?'

Fenton stood up and disappeared into the kitchen. Daly heard a cupboard open and shut before he re-emerged holding a pale-pink laptop and a mobile phone. 'I took these off her after Marta's murder.' He handed them to Daly. 'Get them checked out, but I don't think you'll find anything. No, I know who's got her and it's not some paedophile.'

'Who, boss?'

'Who do you think?'

'We don't know anything for sure yet. We need to keep an open mind.'

'You do that. I'm going to look for my daughter.' Fenton strode out of the room and sprinted down the stairs. He stepped on to the pavement, his head turning from right to left, his mouth dry, his heart drumming his ribcage. It would be dark soon. Tess had never liked the dark. His car was still in the police pound where the forensic team had left it, and deep down he knew that randomly scouring the streets of London on foot would be a futile exercise, but he had to do something. He stuck his hands in his trouser pockets and walked east along Risinghill Street towards Chapel Market. The air was so crisp he felt it crackle as he filled his lungs. Parked cars lined both sides of the road, except for a section where his had been on the day he found Marta's head. White tape still fluttered around that space.

At the junction with Chapel Market, he turned left into Penton Street. He frantically scanned the pavements and the passing traffic as he racked his brain for places Tess might have been taken. At the end of the road he pushed past a group of pedestrians waiting at a zebra crossing, dodged through the traffic and sprinted north towards Barnard Park.

Halfway up Copenhagen Street, and five minutes from the park, Fenton stopped and doubled over, his hands on his knees. He was still gasping for air when his mobile rang.

'We've got her, boss, she's fine,' Daly said. 'She just walked back up the street.'

His vision blurred. 'You're sure she's all right?'

'Yes, boss. I'm sure.'

Fenton's whole body shuddered with relief. His mobile

slipped from his sweaty fingers and clattered into the gutter. He dropped on to his knees, scooped it up and lifted it to his ear.

He could hear Daly shouting down the phone. 'Are you there, boss? What's going on?'

'I'm on my knees thanking God,' he said.

'I'll send a car to pick you up.'

Fenton used the short car journey to calm himself down. The last thing Tess needed was him ranting and raving at her. Daly stood waiting for him at the top of the stairs.

'She's in her bedroom,' she said. 'She's tired and we're letting her rest a little, but we're going to have to take her in soon. We need to question her and she probably should see a doctor.'

'You told me she was fine.'

'She has slight bruising to her right wrist. Otherwise she seems fine, but we have to make sure. You know the drill.'

Fenton sighed. 'Let me speak to her first,' he said. He strode across to her room and went in. Tess was standing by the window looking out into the street. She turned, burst into tears and ran to him. He dropped on one knee and hugged her tight.

'Did he hurt you?'

Tess shook her head. 'He scared me, but he didn't hurt me. He took me to the cemetery and helped me find Mummy's grave.'

Fenton took her hand, led her to the bed and sat her

down. He sat beside her and put an arm around her. 'Did he touch you? You can tell me.'

Tess shook her head again. 'He didn't. He left me for a while so I could talk to Mummy. When he came back he gave me flowers for her. He said he'd bought them, but I know he stole them from another grave.'

Fenton squeezed her ribs. She felt so tiny and helpless he almost cried. 'Was it the man you saw outside school?'

'It might have been. I don't know. I'm not sure,' Tess said. Fenton took a tissue from his pocket and handed it to her. She dabbed her eyes, then wiped her nose and gave it back. 'Are you angry with me?'

Fenton screwed the tissue up into a ball and put it back in his pocket. 'No, but why did you leave on your own like that?'

Tess bowed her head and gazed at her feet. 'I wanted to say goodbye to Mummy before I went away.'

Tears rolled down her cheeks and she wiped them away with a sleeve. Fenton bent down and kissed the top of her head. Her hair smelled of fresh apples.

52

Blake didn't have a clue how much the Metropolitan Police Service paid detective constables. If asked to guess, he'd say not a lot.

The flat Ince rented took up the first floor of an end of terrace house. It looked as if it had been left to rot since its construction in the early 1960s. Several tiles were missing from the roof and the window overlooking the street appeared to be in danger of falling out of its crumbling frame. The flat next door, a faded 'To Let' sign pinned to its pitted brickwork, looked in an even worse condition.

It was feeding time for locals in the east London suburb of Dagenham. The smell of a fresh batch of chicken sizzling in a deep-fat fryer oozed from the Tasty Dagger takeaway and slithered down the street.

Finding out where Ince lived hadn't been a problem. If you're going to pay someone to hack into the Yard's computer system you might as well get them to harvest some useful information while they're at it. Blake had given the hacker a long list of addresses he thought might come in handy.

A sharp chill fell like an icy shadow as the last of the daylight faded. Blake hunched his shoulders and pulled his coat closer. He didn't know whether Ince was in the flat, on duty, or enjoying a day out somewhere in the city. The prospect of hanging around all night, waiting for him to turn up, didn't appeal.

There must be a better way, Blake told himself. The technology existed. It would be easy to stick a tracking device on Ince's car and follow him around on Google maps. Installing spyware on his computer would be useful. Better still, getting hold of his smartphone would probably tell you everything the detective had been getting up to.

Blake scanned the street. The rush-hour traffic crawled bumper to bumper. He was wondering whether it would be a mistake to leave his post to fetch a coffee when a dark shape flitted across the flat's only window.

A second later, a light flickered on. Shit, Blake thought. Instinctively, he turned his back to the window and joined the queue for fried chicken. After studying the menu board for a couple of minutes, he turned and peered through the shop window. The light had been switched off and the curtains pulled. A familiar figure emerged from the side of the building. On reaching the pavement, Ince turned right towards Dagenham East Underground station.

Blake hurried out of the takeaway and followed, keeping a safe distance behind and staying on the opposite side of the road. Ince wore a dark-green puffer jacket, jeans, trainers and a black beanie hat. He wasn't going to work.

New Scotland Yard preferred its detectives suited and booted.

Fenton might well swear by old-fashioned leg work, but trailing Ince around the city could turn out to be one big waste of time, Blake thought. Maybe he was off to meet a friend, going out to eat, or simply planning to sink a few beers in his favourite pub. Having said that, there was always the possibility that he was on his way to remove victim number four's head from his or her shoulders.

As they neared the Tube station, Blake darted across the road, squeezing between the front bumper of a black cab and the back of a double-decker bus. For a second he lost sight of Ince, but soon picked up his beanie hat bobbing in the crowd.

Blake reached the staircase leading down into the station in time to see Ince walk through the ticket barrier. He stayed where he was and watched him step on to the escalator and descend to the District Line platform. There's a time to be cautious and a time to be bold, Blake reminded himself. He turned and walked back the way he'd come, stopping outside Ince's flat. Darkness had settled like a stain, but the busy road was well lit.

A narrow, dimmer street ran along the side of the building. Blake stayed close to the end wall until he reached the back. A high wooden fence sealed off a yard accessed by a high wooden gate. To the right of the gate stood two large green bins. A root around in Ince's rubbish would probably provide an interesting snapshot of his lifestyle. Blake had worked alongside more than one reporter who'd built a career on sifting through the bins of celebrities and politicians, but his sights were set on richer pickings.

Standing with his back to the gate, he pulled his mobile out of his pocket and tried to look as if he was in the middle of a serious text conversation. Four youths in matching tracksuit bottoms and hoodies were coming his way, heading towards the bustle of the main street.

Blake kept his eyes glued to his phone and stepped back to give them room to pass. As the taller of the youths drew level with him, he jabbed out an elbow knocking the phone out of Blake's hands. It hit the pavement with a crunch, a crack appearing across the screen.

'Sorry mate,' the youth said. 'Me arm slipped.' His friends high-fived each other, cackling like maniacs. Blake said nothing. He dropped on to one knee and picked up the phone. They don't know how lucky they are, he thought. He waited until the youths reached the main street before lifting the gate latch and stepping in.

The darkness was denser in the yard. He gave his eyes a few moments to adjust before examining the door. It was old and slightly too small for its frame. Perfect. Through the glass panel in the top half he could see the narrow stairway leading to Ince's flat. Blake considered his choices. He could find a small rock or large stone, take off his coat, roll it up and use it to muffle the sound of breaking glass. Simple, fast and effective, but Fenton had stressed that it would be a mistake to give Ince any reason to suspect they were on to him. Blake crouched to examine the lock. A basic model and covered in rust. Basic and rusty were good.

He opened his wallet and took out a bank card. He'd been shown this method of picking a lock by a burglar turned security adviser. The feature he'd written about how this repeat offender was a perfect example of a leopard changing his spots had sold well. Unfortunately, the change of career was temporary.

Blake pushed the plastic card into the gap above the lock and the doorjamb and slid it down. He felt the plastic slip in front of the bolt, twisted the handle and pushed. The bank card buckled and the bolt stayed in place. Blake swore. One more attempt, then I look for a rock, he told himself. He put the card in place again, felt the bolt give, twisted the handle harder, and he was in.

He closed the door behind him and put the damaged bank card in his pocket, making a mental note to order a replacement. His heart thudded. Fear or excitement, he wondered. Probably a bit of both.

At the top of the stairs he found himself in a small, square living area. A grey brick archway led to a tiny kitchen. On the other side of the room were two brown wooden doors. Blake assumed they were a bedroom and bathroom. He reached for the light switch, but changed his mind.

The gloom couldn't hide the fact that the inside of the flat matched its exterior. The place was a dump. Clothes and newspapers lay scattered across the two-seater sofa. Four coffee-stained mugs stood in a line on the carpet next to a laptop. Blake smiled to himself. The flat looked as if it had already been ransacked. Good news. It meant that he could have a thorough search without worrying about tidying up afterwards. Unwashed plates and cutlery filled the kitchen sink. The yellow rubber gloves tucked behind the taps looked as if they'd never been used. Blake slipped them on. Time to get to work.

He opened the two cupboards mounted on the wall opposite the sink. One was full of cans of soup, baked beans and tinned peaches, the other empty. The fridge contained an empty pizza box, three cans of cheap beer and an unopened pack of mini pork pies.

Blake guessed Ince didn't have many friends around for dinner. He pulled the fridge away from the wall. Nothing there except mould and dead insects.

Next stop the bedroom. Behind the door a pile of washed and unwashed clothes had been dumped on the floor. Blake looked under the mattress and examined the uncarpeted floor for a loose board. Beneath the bed he found a digital radio and a shoebox full of DVDs, mainly crime movies. His initial excitement had been replaced by frustration. He'd found no evidence that Ince was guilty of anything – except being a slob.

Against the wall, opposite the foot of the bed, stood a single pine wardrobe. Blake opened it. It was empty. Empty except for the newspaper cuttings and photographs covering the inside of the door. Blake took a sharp breath. The cuttings were all stories about the I, Killer murders and the subsequent social media frenzy. Some of the headlines had been circled with a red marker pen.

Above the cuttings, arranged in a line, were headshots of Lauren Bishop, Edward Deere, and Marta Blagar. Beneath the victims, Ince had stuck full length photographs of Belinda Vale on the steps leading to her Holborn consulting rooms and Blake apparently leaving the same building. Between the photographs a large red question mark had been scribbled on the door. Blake stared at the images and cuttings for a while before closing the door. He moved to leave the room, but changed his mind. Pulling the wardrobe door open, he tore off the photograph Ince had taken of him and slipped it into his pocket.

Returning to the living area, he nudged a couple of newspapers to one side and sat on the sofa with the laptop balanced on his knees. The photographs and cuttings were damning, but they needed more to nail Ince for the murders. He pressed the power button. Nothing happened. The battery was flat. He scanned the room, but couldn't see anything that resembled a charger.

Blake slid the laptop on to the sofa, stood up and went to the window overlooking the main road. He parted the curtains a fraction in the hope that the street lights would illuminate the room and caught sight of something that sent a chill through his bones: Ince walking back to the flat. He ducked away from the window and stood in the centre of the room, every muscle momentarily paralysed by panic. The sound of his heart hammering against his ribs snapped him out of it. Picking up the laptop, he put it on the floor where he'd found it and ran to the kitchen. Except for the missing rubber gloves, it looked undisturbed.

He estimated he had about a minute before Ince arrived. He ran back into the bedroom and pressed his face against the window pane. A sheer drop. No drainpipe to cling to. No way to clamber on to the roof. He heard the rattle of a key turning a lock. A single bead of sweat trickled down the left side of his face. He needed a weapon. Something heavy he could use to knock Ince out. Burglaries and violent crime were pretty common in Dagenham.

Blake left the bedroom and ducked into the bathroom, hoping to find a window that offered an escape route. There was no window, just a toilet, a grimy bath and a sink. He heard footsteps on the stairs and shut the bathroom door. I've really screwed up this time, he told himself. He looked up at the ceiling, his eyes resting on what looked like a loft hatch.

No time to think. Blake clambered on to the edge of the bath, stepped on to the sink, pushed the loft panel up and hauled himself into the roof space. He quickly slid the access panel back into place and rolled on top of it.

He could hear himself panting like a marathon runner. He tried to hold his breath, but after a second or two gasped for air. The sound of footsteps grew closer. People like to talk about two kinds of luck. Good luck and bad luck. Blake didn't believe in either of them, but lying face down in a policeman's loft he was willing to accept some of the good stuff if it came along.

53

Blake breathed in slowly, the air heavy with the sweet, sickly smell of decay. He let his vision adapt to the blackness before lifting his head to look around.

Thick cobwebs hung from the rafters like strips of dirty lace, and a small water tank stood flush against a flimsy-looking wall separating Ince's roof space from the neighbouring flat's loft. Blake shifted his weight to one side to relieve the pressure on his chest. His torso was spread across the access panel, his legs splayed slightly apart and resting on wooden joists. He strained his neck to keep his face a few inches above a thick clump of insulation.

He froze at the sound of the bathroom door opening and choked back a sudden urge to cough. The stiffening muscles in his legs and lower back cried out for relief, and he willed himself to keep still. Blake held his breath and listened. After a few seconds, he heard a trickling and splashing. The sound of a tap running was followed by the bang of a door slamming shut.

Blake released the air from his lungs as slowly and quietly

as he could. He put his hands on either side of the hatch, pushed himself up on to his knees and stretched his back. He thought he heard the sound of footsteps descending the stairs, but he was reluctant to believe it. Maybe there was such a thing as good luck after all.

After five minutes he stood up, crouching to avoid being draped in cobwebs. It occurred to Blake that the loft would be a pretty good hiding place. Positioning his feet carefully on the joists, he pulled up the insulation, one strip at a time. It wasn't until he lifted the final strip that he found something. The corpse of a mouse, its skull crushed in a trap baited with a bit of chocolate biscuit. Blake edged towards the water tank. He stuck his hand in the narrow gap between the tank and the party wall, half expecting a mousetrap to snap his fingers. Nothing there. He could see the plasterboard wall had a long crack running from the joists to the roof.

Stepping back to the hatch, he squatted and slid the panel slowly to one side. He'd found nothing to incriminate Ince, but had managed to avoid what at one point looked like almost certain discovery. Still, it'd be a good idea to keep this little escapade to myself, he thought. What Fenton doesn't know won't hurt him.

He gripped the edge of the hatch, lowered himself slowly, and pulled the panel back to allow it to fall into place as he dropped to the floor. He flexed his knees on touchdown, to keep the noise to a minimum, stood up, arched his back and stretched.

In the short moment between dropping and landing, he'd

had one single thought in his head. Get out of the flat as quickly as possible. But something held him back. He had a strange feeling he'd seen something important. Something that had gone astray on the journey from eyes to brain.

Blake replayed his search of the loft, but drew a blank. Dropping back down into his landing position, he took a look around, his eyes level with the rim of the bath. The toilet needed cleaning badly, inside and out. The waste pipe under the sink had sprung a slow leak where it curved back to the wall. The wicker bin in the corner was full of scrunched up tissues and toilet paper tubes, the vinyl flooring at the tap end of the bath badly scratched.

Blake prodded the plastic bath panel with his fingers. It flexed. Kneeling down, he pushed the top of the panel with his right hand, worked a finger into the gap that appeared at the bottom, and yanked hard. There was a screech as the edge scored the flooring. Blake pulled again and the panel slid out. Tucked between the bottom of the bath and the floorboards, wedged beneath the plughole pipe, lay a mobile phone. Behind it, pushed closer to the wall, something more sinister glinted in the darkness. He fought back an inexplicable urge to reach in and grab it. Instead, he pushed the bath panel back into place, making sure it didn't split or buckle.

Outside, as Blake walked towards the main street, he pulled the crumpled photograph from his pocket, tore it into pieces and dropped them into a litter bin. The rubber gloves followed. He took out his phone, dialled and clamped it to his ear.

Fenton answered immediately. 'It's late,' he said.

'We've hit the jackpot.'

'What?'

'We've got him.'

'What?'

'You heard.'

54

The weak have a fascination with the strong. The powerless have a fascination with the powerful. My followers are demanding more. They hunger to learn, to gorge on my infamy.

What would the delectable Belinda Vale make of the real story I wonder? She has no idea. She got the absent-father thing right. Good guess. The four-year-old me walked into the bedroom and found the bedsheets dripping blood. I found out later that the public gallery was packed at Mother's trial. Female killers are a rare breed. The court ordered psychiatric reports, but whether Mother was sane or not, it didn't matter in the end. They sent me some of her belongings, including family photographs, jewellery and a leather-bound prayer book. I don't remember ever seeing her pray.

My foster carers put them in an old shoebox, a memory box they called it, and let me keep it under my bed. I flushed the contents of the box down the toilet. Everything except for a newspaper cutting I found tucked in the prayer book.

Giving Fenton another fright was a masterstroke. It

amused me no end. The calibre of these senior police officers is depressingly poor. I enjoyed the trip to the cemetery. I hadn't planned to send her back unharmed. A graveyard would have been a great place to leave a body. But the girl and I have something in common.

What feeds the public's appetite for blood and gore? The answer came to me this morning in bed. The instant I opened my eyes it hit me, like a shaft of sunlight slicing through the clouds.

They want to be me. They want to do the things I can do, but know they are incapable. They admire my strength, my brains, my ability to plan, hunt and take life as casually as snuffing out a candle.

55

'We've got the bastard,' Norman Tobin said, rubbing his hands together. 'Caved in and started blubbing like a baby as soon as we pulled him.'

Belinda Vale raised a hand to her mouth to stifle a yawn. She'd been fast asleep when she'd got the call and uncertain whether she was awake, or dreaming, when they told her about the arrest. She took a shower, but skipped breakfast before leaving for Westminster. As the investigation's psychological profiler, she would be needed to offer guidance on the best approach to take during the long hours of interviewing ahead.

The identity of the killer had been a shock. She'd spent the twenty-minute drive trying to reconcile her knowledge of the man with the crimes he'd committed. 'Detective Constable Ince has admitted the murders?' she asked. 'He says he's the killer? I, Killer?'

Tobin stopped rubbing his hands and laid them flat on the desk. 'He hasn't actually said that, but he's coughed to a lot of other stuff, crumbled like a soggy biscuit. He knows what we found in his flat. The evidence is damning and he knows there's nowhere for him to go. Detective Sergeant Daly has been leading the initial questioning, but she's going to need suggestions from you about the best way to coax the important stuff out of him.'

'What exactly has he admitted?' Vale asked.

'Illegal use of the Yard's computer database, accessing the private details of fellow officers, and witnesses. It also seems that when off duty he's been carrying out private surveillance on various subjects. Following them around, sitting outside their homes, making detailed notes about their movements. He had photos of all three victims and had cut out newspaper articles about the murders.'

Vale had met Ince once, in the station canteen, and that encounter had been brief. As far as she could recall, he didn't fit her profile of the killer. Her first impression had been that he was a small-minded, not particularly imposing young man. Sometime down the line she was going to have to put her hand up and admit she'd got it wrong.

'Who are these people he's been watching?'

Tobin shifted uncomfortably in his seat. 'Well, in addition to the victims, he had a photograph of you pinned to his wardrobe door.'

'A picture of me?' Vale was wide awake now.

Tobin nodded. 'It seems he's been watching you for a while. Our computer guys say it looks like he illegally dipped into your personal file on two occasions, and later accessed DCI Fenton's details a couple of days before killing Marta Blagar.'

'Ince was stalking me?'

'He says it's all innocent. That he just likes observing people. It gives him a thrill. He claims he's tried to stop, but it's an addiction.'

Vale nodded. A classic voyeur, she thought. In layman's terms, Ince was a Peeping Tom. Although she knew of a few cases where voyeuristic behaviour had escalated to violent assaults, it was unusual. On the other hand, the collage of photographs and newspaper cuttings matched the obsessive nature of organised serial killers.

'What have you got that links him to the murders? Any trace of the I, Killer posts on his computer?'

'We've got everything we need,' Tobin said. He had a self-satisfied grin on his face that made Vale want to slap him. 'When our officers searched his flat they also found a knife, which I'm confident will turn out to be the murder weapon, and a mobile telephone. In the phone's album we found photographs, and even some video footage, of two of the victims, Edward Deere and Marta Blagar. They were the photographs that were posted on the internet. He'd stashed them behind the bath panel. The knife is being tested, but I've no doubt we're going to find blood and DNA that we can match to the victims.'

Vale wondered if Ince had targeted her because she was the profiler on the case. It made sense. She was happy that he was safely behind bars, but disappointed that her profile had been so far off the mark.

There was still a chance that checks into Ince's childhood

would throw up one or two match-ups with predictions she'd made, but if she was going to have a chance of rescuing her reputation she'd have to come up with a successful strategy for the interrogation. Before she could think about the direction the questioning should take there were a few things she needed to know.

'You say Ince is denying any involvement in the murders?'

'He can deny it all he wants,' Tobin said, still smirking. 'The knife and the phone are going to convict him. He knows that. He's confessed to all the other stuff. Misuse of the database and stalking. In fact, we can't stop him spilling his guts about stuff he's done before and since joining the force. I think it's a pathetic attempt to muddy the waters. By admitting some stuff he's trying to convince us that he's being honest. I've seen it all before.'

'What led you to Ince? I understand there was no forensic evidence to go on.'

Tobin's smirk stiffened. 'We acted on a tip-off, but we would have got there anyway. The investigation started to gather momentum from the moment I took over. We were closing in. It was only a matter of time.'

Vale raised her eyebrows. She wasn't convinced. 'Who tipped you off?'

'Someone who called the murder inquiry helpline. He wouldn't give his name even though our operator assured him it would never be made public if he didn't want it to be. In any event, we've got the bastard. We've done our job. He's going to be convicted, locked up and never let out.'

Vale allowed herself a smile. The fact that Ince was arrested as a result of an anonymous tip-off would be conveniently buried. The Yard was going to have a lot explaining to do once the arrest was made public. The media would pounce like sharks in a feeding frenzy on the revelation that the killer was one of the Yard's own. It would be an even bigger disaster if the murder team was unable to claim credit for his capture.

Her thoughts were interrupted by a sharp knock on the door. Without waiting for an invitation, Ray Partington walked in.

'Sorry, boss,' he said. 'But the papers have heard we've pulled someone for the murders and all hell is breaking loose. We're going to need to give them something soon. If they come up with Ince's name before we give it out, we open ourselves up to all sorts of accusations.'

Tobin raised a placatory hand. 'Take it easy, Ray,' he said. 'Slow down. Prepare a news release, you know, the usual stuff about someone being questioned. Throw them a bone to keep them at bay, but no names yet.'

Partington gave Vale a look that left her in no doubt that he considered the detective chief inspector a halfwit. She acknowledged him with an almost imperceptible nod.

'I take it you two already know each other,' Tobin said.

'Belinda had a starring role in one of my press conferences. Her profiling knowledge made quite an impression.'

Partington refocused his attention on Tobin. 'I've already prepared an initial release along the lines you've just suggested, but I'm here to stress that we're going to have to be more expansive pretty soon. This is one hell of a story, and the more accommodating we are to the press, the more we give them to work with, the more likely they are to go easy on you.'

Tobin frowned. 'What do you mean me? Why would they single me out? I was brought in to sort this inquiry out, and under my command we've caught the bastard.'

Partington caught Vale's eye. 'When I said you, what I meant was us. What worries me is that if the media are starved of juicy details about Ince they could focus on the performance of the investigating officers. They are likely, excuse the unfortunate phrase, to want heads to roll.'

Tobin's face reddened. Vale could see a vein pulsating across his left temple. 'Thank you for the advice,' he said, sounding the opposite of thankful. 'As always it's valued. Send out the initial press release as discussed. We'll talk about how to follow that up tomorrow morning. I am sure that, as always, you'll use your expertise to protect the reputation of the force and its officers. Please close the door on your way out.'

The curtness of the dismissal didn't seem to bother the press officer. He nodded at Vale before striding off. The vein on Tobin's left temple had stopped throbbing, but his face was still flushed. Vale had no medical training, but she was pretty sure Tobin needed to get his blood pressure checked.

Reverting to a strategy she used to calm agitated clients,

she lowered her voice a notch and spoke slowly. 'I appreciate you've a lot to deal with, but I want to get started on working out the best way to get Ince to open up about the killings. If he's being interviewed now, I'd like to drop into the observation room and take a look.'

Tobin checked his watch. 'I think they'll be taking a break soon and resuming in about half an hour. You can start then. The man's broken. He's a babbling wreck, but he's not speaking about the murders. We've got enough evidence to convict, but I'd rather not have to go to trial on this. It'd be a bloody circus.'

Vale took a moment to think. A confession would mean the police wouldn't have defence lawyers picking over their investigation, exposing every mistake, highlighting failures and demanding a detailed explanation of the evidence trail that led them to Ince. She was surprised that the detective constable was resisting admitting guilt. Once caught, organised serial killers usually relish talking about their crimes.

'It's likely that he needs a bit of time to accept that there's no way out for him,' she said. 'The chances are that when that happens you won't be able to stop him boasting about how clever he's been.'

Tobin laughed nervously. 'Let's hope so,' he said. He stood up and checked his watch again. 'We've got time to pick up a coffee on the way.'

By the time they reached the observation room, the interrogation had already restarted. Vale sat close to the viewing window, choosing an angle that gave her the best view of Ince's face. His eyes were red and swollen, his complexion ashen. Detective Sergeant Daly stood in front of him, her hands on her hips. 'I've told you everything,' Ince said, thumping his right fist hard on the table. 'I admit it all. What more do you want?'

Daly paused and looked across the room at her new partner, a straw-haired, pot-bellied detective standing with his back to the wall.

'Let's start with Lauren Bishop,' she said. 'Why her? Did you try it on? Did she knock you back? Laugh at you? I bet that pissed you off.'

'This is crazy,' Ince said. He slid his hands out and gripped the edge of the table until his knuckles turned white. 'You really think I killed her?'

'You were on the spot pretty quickly. Secured the area. Made sure the murder scene wasn't contaminated. Handy that, if you want to make sure it's clean, evidence-free.'

'I was doing my job that's all,' Ince said, a tremor in his voice.

Daly sat down and leant across the table. 'I suppose you were just doing your job when you hacked into the computer system to steal personal information. Were you doing your job when you carried out unauthorised surveillance on innocent members of the public?'

'We've been through this before.'

'We need to do it again.'

Ince released his grip on the table, lifted his hands to

261

his face and rubbed his eyes. 'I know it's wrong, but I can't help it. I've always liked watching people. It started when I was a teenager. It makes me feel good. I can't really explain it.'

'Go on. Give it a try. You get a kick out of it. It's a sex thing then?'

Ince blushed and shook his head. 'It's not like that, no. Well, maybe sometimes. It depends who I'm watching. But it's not all about that. I'm good at it. Really good. I like watching people knowing that they don't know I'm watching. It's a compulsion. I think it's the main reason I joined the police. The chance to do surveillance. Watch people for a living. I admit I need help.'

Turning to her pot-bellied colleague, Daly mouthed the word 'pervert'. He grimaced in mock disgust. The detective leant back in her seat and drummed her fingers on the table as she considered her next question.

'When did this, er, this compulsion change?'

'I don't know what you mean.'

'I think you do.'

'Nothing's changed.'

Daly shook her head slowly. 'When did you move from watching people to stalking people, to killing people? Move on to cutting their throats, to hacking their heads off?'

Ince clasped his hands firmly over his ears. 'Why are you saying this? It's not right. I don't understand. This is madness.'

Daly sighed. 'There's no point lying. We found the phone

under the bath. The photographs, the newspaper cuttings, video footage and the murder weapon too. We've got you. There's no way out of this. It'll be easier all round if you stop pretending. It's not going to get you anywhere.'

Ince slumped forward and banged his forehead on the table. Daly watched his shoulders heaving and waited for him to stop snivelling. After a couple of minutes, he sat up straight and looked his interrogator directly in the eyes. 'This is fucking wrong,' he said, his voice suddenly deeper and more forceful. 'Believe me you're making a big mistake. Listen carefully, because after this I'm not saying anything else until I get a lawyer. Not a word. I don't kill people. For the benefit of the recording device I'll say it one more time. I don't kill people.'

The change in Ince's demeanour threw Daly off balance. The detective sergeant slowly circled the table as she gathered her thoughts. After a couple of circuits, she sat opposite Ince and crossed her arms.

'We've checked your shift pattern over the last few weeks. It's interesting to say the least. You were working on the day Lauren Bishop was killed and on the scene in super quick time. At the times Edward Deere and Marta Blagar died you were off duty. So far, you've not been able to tell us where you were and what you were doing when they were murdered. That doesn't look good.'

Ince crossed his arms, mirroring Daly's body language, and said nothing. The detective unfolded her arms and rested her palms on her lap. Ince immediately did the same.

Vale noticed Daly colouring up. Ince's body language game was doing what he'd intended it to do.

'You had video footage of two victims and the murder weapon in your flat.'

Ince stayed silent.

Daly turned and looked straight at the two-way mirror and shrugged. 'Okay then,' she said. 'We're going to take another break.'

Two police constables entered the room to escort Ince back to his cell. He held his head high as he rose to his feet, happy that he'd scored a minor victory.

Tobin had observed the whole exchange in silence. 'The little shit,' he snapped. 'What the hell is he playing at?'

Vale took a moment to consider what she'd seen. 'He doesn't fit the typical psychopath pattern. All that whinging and poor me stuff is unusual. Still, that switch to defiance, and the body mirroring, that's more typical. The suddenness of the change itself is interesting. Was he acting? Which is the real Ince?'

'I don't bloody know,' Tobin snapped. 'You're the bloody psychologist.'

Vale was momentarily taken aback. Tobin was desperate for a confession. She was there to give advice on the best way to get it. 'He's playing a game right now. It's a game that keeps him in control and he likes that. It's all about power and control. You need to get as much information as you can about his childhood and get him to talk about it. Bring him back to those times when he felt weak and powerless. I bet there were plenty of them. That's when he'll crack.'

Tobin put his hands on the arms of his chair and pushed himself slowly to his feet. 'He bloody better.'

56

The walk to Leah Bishop's flat gave Blake plenty of time to think. The killer was safely behind bars. The first job he'd had in more than a year was over. It felt good. Now he'd need something else to keep him out of trouble.

Blake turned into Millennium Drive and looked up at the apartment block where Leah lived. It was a smart address, offering a view over the Thames towards north Greenwich. Leah had called him the night before with an invitation to meet up for a lunchtime celebration of a job well done.

He took the lift to the second floor to find Leah waiting for him at her front door, a warm smile on her face. She reached out, grabbed his hand and pulled him into the flat. 'I can't believe you got him so quickly. I didn't really think it was possible. Lauren would be so proud.'

Her grip was firmer, her skin warmer, than he'd imagined. He couldn't think of anything to say, so he said nothing. She gave him a curious look and dragged him into the living room, where Fenton sat in a leather armchair cradling a steaming mug of coffee.

Blake let go of Leah's hand. 'Detective Chief Inspector Fenton,' he said. 'I thought you'd be back behind your big desk in Westminster by now.'

It was obvious from the surprise on Fenton's face that he hadn't been expecting another guest. 'Well, if it isn't my partner in crime.'

Leah gestured for Blake to take a seat and offered to get him a coffee. He sat on the sofa, but said no to a drink. Leah sat next to him, close enough to touch. She smelled fresh, like sweet rain.

'I wanted you both here to thank you for what you've done,' she said. 'Lauren's killer is locked up and who's to say how many lives you've saved by stopping him. It's such a shame that you've not been able to take any credit. I'm still not sure why.'

Blake looked at Fenton, inviting him to explain. The detective laughed: 'It's not possible because our friend here broke every rule in the book, along with several laws. He illegally entered Ince's flat, carried out an illegal search, and probably contaminated important evidence.'

Blake shrugged. 'If we'd done it your way I'd still be walking the streets following Ince around, ducking in and out of shop doorways to avoid being seen. At least we got him. Nobody else is going to get hurt.'

'That's true,' Leah said. 'It's sickening that those pictures are still out there though, still being drooled over. The internet is like Frankenstein's monster. Out of control.'

Fenton took a sip of his coffee. 'I'm happy the killer has

been caught. But the reckless way he went about it goes against the grain.' He pointed across the room at Blake, who stared at the finger with disgust. 'If it ever got out we'd all be in deep shit,' Fenton said. 'It would probably seriously endanger the case against Ince. His defence counsel could claim that the evidence found in the flat should be inadmissible. They could even suggest that Blake had planted it.'

Blake and Leah exchanged glances. Neither of them had considered that possibility. Leah broke the uncomfortable silence. 'There's no reason it should come to that. We are the only people who know what happened. We did what needed to be done.'

Leah's support made Blake feel good. 'That's right,' he said. 'We got the result we wanted. I took a risk and it paid off. There's no point in beating yourself up over what might have happened. You're still squeaky clean. You'll be back at the Yard in no time.'

Fenton didn't look convinced. He stood up. 'Sorry, Leah, but I've got to go,' he said. 'Tess is waiting for me. They're pulling the twenty-four-hour guard on the flat tonight.'

He walked into the kitchen. Leah and Blake heard the tap running as he washed up the mug. When he returned Leah followed him to the front door. Blake took the opportunity to take a good look around. The flat was expensively furnished and impeccably clean.

The front door banged shut and Leah returned. She sat down in the armchair Fenton had vacated. 'I don't know why you two can't get along. You make a great team. You've got such different skills.'

'We were lucky, that's all. Very lucky.'

Leah smiled with a look that said she appreciated his modesty. 'I meant what I said earlier. Lauren would be proud of you.'

Blake thought for a moment. Leah had been right. Taking on the case had been a turning point. 'What now though?'

Leah walked over to the sofa and sat down again. This time she was so close he could feel the warmth of her thigh against his.

'Are you asking my advice?' she said.

'I suppose I am.'

'Do what you're good at.'

Blake nodded. He understood what she was saying, but her proximity, her energy, shifted his train of thought.

'Can I ask you a question?' he said.

'Go right ahead.'

'Is there something going on between you and Fenton?'

She looked him directly in the eyes. 'Would you mind if there was?'

'There is then?'

She shifted a fraction to the side and leant away from him. 'No, there's nothing going on. Why would you think that?'

Blake sighed, the hollow feeling in his stomach fading. 'I didn't really think he was your type. Mr Sensible. Lives life by the rulebook.'

Leah smiled. 'And the negatives are?'

Blake could think of plenty, but he didn't want to keep talking about the detective. 'Is there anyone?' he said.

Leah dropped her gaze, then lifted her chin to look at Blake again. 'Maybe, but there's been too much going on.'

Blake had taken the plunge and was determined to carry on. 'What about us?'

Leah paused for a moment. 'Don't misunderstand me,' she said. 'Grief can do strange things to people. You're confused, not thinking straight. I'm not Lauren. I'm not a substitute.'

Blake was confused. He was confused about why she made him feel this way. Made him say stupid things. 'You may look similar, but you're nothing like Lauren. She was caring, gentle.'

'And I'm not?'

'You're you. Come on. I mean you're different that's all.'

Leah stood up and disappeared into the kitchen. Blake stayed where he was, listening to cupboard doors and drawers being opened and shut. After a few minutes, she returned, her arms folded across her chest.

'There's something I can't get past,' she said. 'It's something I can't just push aside and I don't know if that will ever change.'

Blake didn't want to hear it, but he knew she needed to say it. 'Tell me.'

A sad smile crossed her face. 'It's simple. You're my dead sister's former boyfriend.'

57

Childhood trauma, parental rejection, emotional starvation: these words are spewed out so condescendingly it makes me sick.

I wanted people to love me. I gave them ample opportunity. When they failed to see how special I am, I moved on. Well, it would be more accurate to say I was moved on. Usually at their insistence.

When I could, I'd leave them a parting gift. It started small. The first, a favourite ornament. A tiny crystal swan given pride of place on the mantelpiece. Grinding it under my heel and kicking the glass fragments beneath the sofa made me feel good.

On the day I left my seventh foster home, I decided to up the ante.

The family's ten-week-old kitten fitted perfectly in the microwave. Ten minutes on the highest setting did the job. The couple decided not to report me. They were scared I'd come back and do something even worse. I learnt an important lesson that day. I learnt about the power of being feared.

I hit the jackpot with my next placement. The weird thing is, I didn't even have to try to make them like me. They took to me immediately. I responded in a way which surprised everybody. I started to behave well. My new foster parents were delighted. One day after school, all smiles and glances, they sat me down, and explained that their prayers had been answered.

I'd done it. I'd passed the test. I'd fooled the suckers. They adopted me. In exchange for pretending to love them they gave me something that opened up the world to me. They gave me a new name.

Without it I wouldn't be where I am today. Like a snake, I shook off my skin, and slithered out of my past into my future.

58

Blake switched on the television and slumped on the sofa. He needed something to keep his mind off Leah. He reached for the remote and flicked through the channels on autopilot, not really registering what he was seeing.

Leah had made it clear that she couldn't contemplate a relationship with her sister's ex. Not now. Maybe never. Blake understood, of course he did, but that didn't mean he was ready to stop hoping.

On the television, a newsreader announced that a Metropolitan Police detective constable had been charged with the I, Killer murders and remanded in custody. A mugshot of Ralph Ince filled the screen.

The follow-up story focused on the reaction across social media. The correspondent's blonde curls bobbed as she reported breathlessly that the news that I, Killer had been arrested had exploded across Twitter, Instagram and Facebook, with the image of Detective Constable Ralph Ince being shared, viewed and 'liked' hundreds of thousands of times.

Blake switched the television off. He'd heard enough and

needed to pay a visit to the late-night grocery around the corner. Outside, the cloudless night carried a hint of the winter to come. He reached the store entrance just as his neighbour walked out clutching a six-pack of lager. Blake stepped aside to let the man pass, but he stopped and rested the lager on his beer belly.

He looked up at Blake and grinned, revealing a mouthful of tiny crooked teeth. 'Me and the missus have noticed you're doing a lot less running on that machine of yours. I'm not the sort of bloke who holds a grudge, so thanks and all that.'

Blake gritted his teeth. The old man always rubbed him up the wrong way. Blake couldn't explain it, but knew it was unreasonable. 'No problem,' he said. 'I'm doing more of my running outside these days.'

The neighbour smiled again. 'Good decision, mate. Much better for you. Also, I won't have to complain to the landlord and get him to kick your arse.'

Blake bit down on his bottom lip and shouldered his way into the shop, resisting the temptation to break the news that he was the landlord and was seriously thinking about getting a new tenant.

As usual, the air in the grocery store carried the scent of decay, but it always looked clean. Blake wandered around for ten minutes before buying a steak and kidney pie that would be edible after a few minutes in the microwave. He spent another five minutes talking football with a spotty youth at the till before walking back to his flat.

He was fetching a cold beer to complement the pie's

unsubtle flavours when his mobile rang. He didn't recognise the number, but answered it anyway. At first, he didn't recognise the caller's name either.

'I think you've got the wrong number.'

'No, mate, listen to me. It's Perry, Perry Lee. The owner of Vic's Café in Victoria Park. You get me?'

Blake remembered. The smooth, shiny head and bushy beard. 'Yeah, of course. How can I help?'

'I think it's me that can help you. You asked me to give you a bell if I remembered anything new about the day that woman was murdered.'

'Right.'

'I ain't remembered nothing. But I got something else for you.'

Blake wondered if Lee had been drinking. 'You're confusing me. What's going on?'

'It's that detective killer. I saw his photograph on the news. The detective that's been charged.'

Blake still wasn't sure what Lee was driving at and he was losing patience. Hunger always shortened his fuse. 'Yeah, I watch the news too,' he said.

Lee laughed. It was an unpleasant snorting sound. 'No, mate. You're not getting me. That Detective Ince who's the killer ain't the Detective Ince who came to me café. He don't look nothing like the one who took me security camera footage. Now do you get me?'

Blake's pulse started to race. 'You're sure about this. You know what you're saying?'

'Are you listening to me, mate, or what? That Ince on the television is not the detective who took the camera footage. He said he was Detective Ince, but he don't look nothing like him. You get me?'

Blake wanted Lee off the phone. He needed to speak to Fenton. 'I get you,' he said, and terminated the call.

59

Belinda Vale sat at her desk in her consulting room and read through her notes one last time. She'd been working on an interview strategy for four hours. Her eyes were tired and her head ached.

Her private therapy work had ended at 5 p.m. and after an hour's break for a light meal at a nearby Italian restaurant she'd returned to the office to concentrate on the I, Killer investigation. She'd reached the conclusion that Ince's apparent emotional distress, and refusal to admit to the murders, was a game, a mind game, a way for him to continue exerting control over the situation.

Checks into Ince's background had uncovered a surprisingly positive story. The only child of a single mother, he grew up on a rough estate in Barnet, north London, spent a few years in care. As a teenager, he'd kept out of trouble, except for one arrest for stealing beer from a supermarket. He was let off with a caution, and from that day set his sights on joining the police.

Vale closed her eyes and rubbed her eyelids with her

fingertips. He didn't fit her profile, or the typical profile of a serial killer. Maybe Ince was just an exception? One thing she had to admit, his performance under interrogation demonstrated a special talent for blending in, for deceiving. Behind that almost boyish mask of innocence and confusion lay a skilled manipulator.

She grabbed her pen again and added a final paragraph to her interview plan.

Appeal to Ince's ego. Expose the secret narcissist. Hint at admiration for his achievements. Praise his organisational skills and daring. Phrase a few questions in a way that highlights the media interest in the case, and the public's fascination with his internet posts. Eventually, he won't be able to resist taking the credit and will tell everyone who will listen what a genius he is.

Vale looked at the clock on the wall opposite her desk. If she left now, she'd be home by 10.30 p.m. Her headache was easing off. With luck, a good night's sleep would see her restored to full health. She'd email DCI Tobin a copy of her interview advice first thing.

She didn't often drive to work, but her office came with its own parking space, which came in handy when she knew she'd be staying late. Putting her notes and her mobile phone into her leather briefcase, she switched off her office light and descended the stone steps that led to the back of the building.

60

Blake strode down Ludgate Hill, his breath curling like wisps of smoke from his lips, the huge, illuminated dome of St Paul's Cathedral dominating the skyline behind him. Dodging the traffic, he crossed Farringdon Street, Perry Lee's words repeating in his head like a mantra. 'He wasn't the Detective Ince who took the security camera footage. Didn't look nothing like him.'

Halfway up Fleet Street, he turned into Wine Office Court and ducked into the Star. The bar was packed. Fenton was already waiting for him, seated at a rickety, dark wood table supping a pint of beer. Blake pushed his way through the crowd and slipped into the seat opposite Fenton, where a full pint waited for him. Without saying a word, he picked up the glass and took a long swig. When he'd finished, he wiped his lips with the back of his hand. 'I needed that,' he said.

Fenton got straight down to business. 'Do you think this Perry Lee is telling the truth?'

Blake shrugged. 'He's got no reason to make this stuff

up. Like I told you, he saw the mugshot on the television and realised it wasn't the detective who came to his café.'

'You know what this means?'

'It means we've got a big problem.'

Fenton sized up the nearest group of drinkers, to make sure he wasn't going to be overheard. 'It means that there's a good chance that Ince isn't the killer. It means that the police have got the wrong man. We gave them the wrong man.'

Blake took another sip of beer and mulled over the possibilities. 'What if Ince had an accomplice? Maybe the murders are the work of two men.'

Fenton shook his head. 'It's highly unlikely. Serial killers rarely work that way. They're lone wolves.'

Blake knew Fenton was right. 'But what about the knife? And the phone?'

'Think about it,' Fenton said. 'There's only one explanation.'

Blake already knew the answer. It'd been lurking in the back of his mind since Lee called him, but he'd pushed it away. 'He was set up.'

Fenton nodded, picked up his glass and drained it. 'You've got it. Top marks.'

Both men stared at each other as the significance of the situation sunk in. 'There's one thing I don't understand,' Blake said. 'How did the killer know we'd find the stuff he planted?'

'He didn't know. He probably had a plan to lead the police

to Ince, but because the café owner told you about the camera footage, we were ahead of the game. Well, we thought we were.'

Blake had to admit it made sense. With his help, the killer had struck lucky. 'What now?' he said. 'What happens if we go to the police with this? Tell them everything?'

Fenton had been asking himself the same question. 'They're not going to take our word for it, that's for sure. They'll need to speak to Perry Lee. Interview you about breaking into Ince's flat. Speak to me about working on the case with you.'

'So, I'll be charged with burglary and you'll be kicked off the force?'

Fenton lifted his empty glass, stared into it for a few seconds and put it back on the table. 'That's about it,' he said.

Blake downed the last of his beer and stood up. 'Do you want another?' Fenton shook his head. Blake edged his way through the crowd towards the bar. He was gone a good ten minutes. When he returned, he was carrying two pints. He put one on the table in front of Fenton. The detective said nothing, but nodded his thanks.

'I've been thinking,' Blake said.

'Why doesn't that surprise me?'

'I was wondering how the killer planted the evidence in the flat.'

'He probably did what you did. In through the back door. It can't be that difficult if you managed it.'

Blake ignored the insult. He was too busy thinking. 'Maybe there is a way to sort out this mess.'

'Such as?'

'Catch the real killer.'

Fenton shook his head. 'It wouldn't be right to keep this information from the police. If the killer's still out there it wouldn't be ethical to keep this to ourselves. He could be ready to kill again.'

'You said yourself that even if we give the police everything we've got they're unlikely to believe us until they've completed a thorough investigation. Going it alone could mean the killer is off the streets before he kills again. Surely, that would be justification enough?'

Fenton gave Blake a curious look. 'I agree that if we genuinely believed we could find the killer quicker than the police, then maybe that would be the way to go.'

Blake smiled for the first time since he took Perry Lee's call.

'I take it you've got an idea?' Fenton asked.

'Damn right I have.'

61

*B*elinda Vale opens the door to a blast of cold air. She steps into the darkness, turns, closes the door and locks it.

She walks quickly to her car, sighing as she slides behind the wheel. Pulling her seatbelt across her body, she starts the engine, switches on the headlights and reverses in a gentle arc. A grinding noise causes her to stop. She tries again. The grinding is even louder.

Banging the palms of her hands on the steering wheel in frustration, she climbs out of the car to check the back of the vehicle. The nearside tyre is flat. A six-inch gash in the rubber.

'For fuck's sake,' she shouts. She stands in the dark for a few seconds, taking deep breaths. Pulling her mobile phone out of her jacket pocket, she decides it's too cold and too dark to wait outside. She walks back to the door, unlocks it and steps inside. As she turns to shut the door it swings inward, smashing into her shoulder, spinning her around.

She staggers, breaks her fall with outstretched arms. Something snaps in her right wrist, but she ignores the pain, scrambles up and runs to the stairs.

Halfway up she misses her footing and sprawls face down. A hand grasps her left ankle. She cries out, more in fear than pain, and looks over her shoulder. She recognises him immediately. With that recognition comes two thoughts. One. My profile was right all along. He's a perfect match. Two. I'm going to die.

He has her ankle in his right hand and a mobile phone in his left. He aims the camera lens at her face. 'I'm going to make you a star,' he says.

62

Walking along Cannon Street, heading east, Blake was oblivious to the glittering beauty of the city at night. He had only one thing on his mind. If he was right, they had a chance to unmask the real killer. He'd explained his plan to Fenton and they agreed to give it a try. Tomorrow couldn't come quick enough.

The last Tube trains had long gone, but the heart of London never stops beating. The streets were still busy with revellers looking for another late bar. Blake turned up Old Broad Street, Perry Lee's words still ringing in his head.

Ahead, a large crowd milled around the junction with London Wall, the air thick with voices. Blake thought about taking a diversion down Great Winchester Street, but curiosity got the better of him. Edging through the mêlée, he reached a single line of police tape stretched across the road. Two police constables and one police community support officer, all of them wearing stab vests, were doing their best to stop people breaching the fragile barrier.

Several members of the public were yelling about having

last trains to catch, and every so often one plucked up the courage to duck under the tape and sprint across the road towards Liverpool Street station.

Blake caught the eye of the youngest police constable and offered a sympathetic smile. Relieved to see a friendly face, the young man wandered over.

'Looks to me like you could with a bit more manpower,' Blake ventured.

The police officer nodded. 'It's always the same nowadays. The thin blue line is so thin it's bloody anorexic.'

It wasn't funny, but Blake laughed. Everybody felt good when their attempts at wit were appreciated. Even policemen. The officer smiled and Blake took his opportunity. 'What's going on up there?' he asked, nodding into the distance where an impressive display of flashing blue lights lit up the darkness.

The constable looked uneasy and took a step back.

Blake wasn't about to give up. 'I don't suppose the top brass bother to let you know what's going on. Get you and your mates to do all the hard work, but tell you nothing.'

The constable frowned. He didn't like the suggestion that he was so far down the pecking order his superiors would treat him with disdain. Blake decided to change tack and rely on flattery. He'd always found that the younger police officers responded well to a bit of admiration. They join up as idealists. After a few years of daily exposure to the worst elements of society they turn into cynics.

'Anyway, as far as I'm concerned, you guys at the cutting

edge do a great job. That's what I think. I love all that police drama stuff on the TV. Can't get enough of it.'

The constable looked over his shoulder to make sure his colleagues were coping and stepped closer. 'All I can tell you is there has been an incident at the roundabout near the Barbican. We'll open the road as soon as we can.'

Blake turned away. It had been worth a try, he thought. He started to head back the way he'd come when an uneasy murmur rippled through the crowd. Everyone was staring, dumbfounded, at the screens of their mobile phones.

A gangly teenager in a furry hoodie waved his screen in his girlfriend's face. She squealed and pushed the phone away. The disgust on her face filled Blake with dread. He pulled out his mobile and googled I, Killer. Blake's heart rate surged at the sight of a Reuters newsflash. *I, Killer beheading on YouTube.* Hands trembling, he navigated to the YouTube trending page. The video topped the list and had already clocked up 223,557 views. He pressed the screen.

Vale sits on what looks like her office chair. Her hands are tied behind her back, her mouth gagged with grey duct tape. A large rectangular piece of card is taped to her chest. Written on it in capital letters are the words I MESS WITH MINDS. A man walks into shot and stands behind her. His face is obscured by a black, full-face motorcycle helmet. He puts his right hand on Vale's head and lifts his left, holding a black handled hunting knife to her neck. With a nod to the camera, he starts.

Blake's throat tightened, he turned away from the screen and gasped for breath. Legs buckling, he staggered across the pavement, sat down on the kerb and threw up in the gutter. He wiped his mouth with his sleeve and looked at his phone again. The video had been replaced by a still image of a head impaled on a stake at the edge of a roundabout.

Blake released his hold on the mobile and let it fall into the vomit.

63

Fenton waved his warrant card at the security guard and waited for her to raise the car park barrier. He flicked off the headlights, turned up the heating and drummed his fingers on the steering wheel while she called through to reception to report his arrival. The sun had not yet risen and a layer of morning frost framed his windscreen.

The red pole lifted with a clunk and Fenton drove to his usual parking space. He'd been awake, but still in bed, when Assistant Commissioner Patricia Hall called. He'd done his best to sound surprised when she told him that Ince couldn't be the killer. There had been no need to fake shock when he heard Belinda Vale's fate.

He stepped into the lift and pressed the button for the fourth floor. Hall had wanted to see him as soon as possible. He'd made it clear that he wouldn't consider leaving Tess on her own unless the twenty-four-hour guard was restored. Hall immediately arranged for a patrol car to blue-light its way to his home.

Fenton wondered what could be so urgent. He thought

it highly unlikely that Hall wanted to reinstate him. If she'd found out about his involvement with Blake's investigation he could kiss his career goodbye.

One thing he knew for certain. The murder of Belinda Vale would have set off alarm bells all the way up to Whitehall, even as high as Downing Street. The killer was making fools out of everybody. The door to the assistant commissioner's office was open. Fenton stepped in. Hall sat at her desk, her hands steepled beneath her chin, her brow furrowed. 'Close the door and sit down,' she said. 'I haven't got a lot of time. I've a media conference to attend in a couple of hours and I need to prepare.'

Fenton sympathised. The press would be scenting blood. 'Why am I here?'

Hall peered over her glasses across the desk. She looked a decade older than when he last saw her. Her face greyer than her hair, her eyes dull.

'You're here because I need you,' she said. 'DCI Tobin is standing down. He has no choice. A simple case of go before you're pushed. I'll be announcing at the press conference that I'll be taking personal control of the investigation.'

By the expression on her face, Fenton guessed she hadn't volunteered for the job. I bet she's still in pain from all that arm twisting, he thought. It made sense though. Putting an assistant commissioner in charge was one way of showing the press and the public that the force was determined to sort this mess out once and for all. The big drawback was that Hall had no significant experience investigating murder cases.

She smiled wryly, as if she'd read his thoughts and agreed with them. 'We're not bringing you back to the team. We can't be seen to be going backwards. But it's been decided that you should act as a consultant. Someone who I can talk the case over with, if and when I deem it necessary.'

For a brief moment Fenton considered telling her about Blake, his anonymous call to the murder helpline, and their new line of investigation. But he said nothing. If he was going to put his career in jeopardy it'd be better to do it from a position of strength.

It'd be easier to admit what he'd been up to if he could hand over the killer at the same time. Hall read his silence as reluctance. She put her hands flat on the desk and pushed herself up in her seat. 'I want your help because I value your ability. You know why we took you off the case and that it had nothing to do with your performance. Even so, I had a hard time persuading colleagues to let you back anywhere near this investigation. Don't let me down.'

'Don't get me wrong,' Fenton said. 'I'm happy to help, but how exactly is it going to work?'

Hall sighed, her thin frame sagging in her chair. 'You don't have to come into the office. It might be better if you didn't. We don't want the press making something negative out of this. I'll keep you up to date with what's going on and when I need advice I'll call. As simple as that.'

'What's happening with Ince?'

Hall screwed up her face. 'Detective Constable Ince will be kicked off the force. He'll be charged with improper use of our databases, and maybe even with stalking. It seems he was set up for no reason other than to make us a laughing stock.'

Fenton shook his head. 'There's more to it than that. The killer arranged this whole thing as a demonstration of his cleverness. I doubt he ever intended Ince to be convicted of the murder. He'd hate the thought of anyone else getting the credit for what he'd done. He thinks he's some kind of genius and wants everyone else to believe it.'

Hall picked up a pen, scribbled a note and sneered. 'So even though he's a psychopath who loves nothing better than hacking off his victims' heads, he's really quite a sensitive little shit.'

Fenton gave her a moment to calm down. He had a good idea what she was going through. Pressure from the press. Pressure from her superiors. Pressure from politicians. Stress like that takes its toll. 'Putting on a gory public display at a busy roundabout in central London is pretty risky. Surely the killer was caught on CCTV?'

Hall said nothing. Instead she adjusted the angle of her computer screen so both she and Fenton could see it and clicked on a video file. The footage showed a steady stream of cars, and the distorted glare of headlights, snaking around the roundabout.

Fenton could see nothing untoward. He leant forward in his seat and looked across at Hall. She raised a bony finger and pointed it at the screen. 'There,' she said. A single head-light came into view approaching at speed along High

Holborn. As the motorcycle neared, Fenton could see the rider wore a full-face helmet. Fixed to the back of the motorcycle was what looked like a pizza delivery box, strapped to the box a short wooden stake.

They both watched in silence as the rider pulled up beside the roundabout and dismounted. The killer quickly, but calmly, used his bodyweight to twist the wooden pole into the ground. He lifted the head from the pizza box and unceremoniously rammed it on to the stake, before getting back on the motorbike and riding off. From start to finish, the whole thing had taken six and a half minutes.

Fenton sat back in his chair. 'No one wondered what was going on? Nobody challenged him?'

Hall shrugged. 'I don't suppose anyone realised what was happening until he'd gone.' She balled her bony hands and rubbed her eyes. 'The killer must have broken into Ince's flat and planted the phone and murder weapon behind the bath panel. I'm guessing it was him who made the call to the murder helpline.'

Fenton nodded. 'You're probably right,' he said. You're definitely wrong, he thought. 'The killer selected Marta Blagar to teach me a lesson because he didn't like what I said about him. It's possible he chose Vale because her psychological profile wasn't to his liking. Ince is out of the frame, but it's still likely that the killer is someone close to the operation. Vale's profile has never been made public. Only someone connected to the investigation would have access to it.'

Hall steepled her hands. 'There's no definite evidence that the killer has seen the profile, but I've asked for a list of everybody who has had access to it. I'm also sending a forensic team back to Ince's flat. We know someone broke into the place to plant the evidence, right?'

Walking back to the lift, Fenton considered calling Blake to warn him that the police were about to descend on Dagenham, but decided against it. He'd be meeting him in a couple of hours anyway. They were still one step ahead of the police investigation. A small step.

64

Blake followed the lettings agent through the door and up the stairs. The layout matched the flat next door. The rooms seemed bigger because they were sparsely furnished and free of clutter.

The agent, who had introduced himself as Ricky Dean, wore a cheap grey suit and had such bad acne his face resembled a pizza. He waved an arm with a flourish towards the living room window.

'You got a lovely view of old Dagenham there, mate. All the hustle and bustle of east London. Check it out. Take your time. I ain't in a hurry to get back to the office.'

Blake wandered across to the window. The view consisted of a fried-chicken shop, a couple of vacant retail units and an off-licence protected by a security grille.

He hadn't slept the previous night. He'd climbed into bed with his laptop and scoured the news websites for stories about Belinda Vale's murder. The papers had all picked up that the psychologist had been working on the I, Killer case, and several suggested that everyone working on the investigation should be considered possible targets. The sessions with Vale had stopped him going over the edge after the loss of Lauren. Now she had been taken too.

Blake walked over to the bedroom and pushed the door open with his right foot to avoid leaving fingerprints on the handle. The room was empty. The rotting floorboards exposed. 'I think I've seen all I need to see Ricky,' he said. 'What's the rent on this place?'

Ricky tapped the keys of his mobile phone and waited for the information to appear on the screen. 'We're asking for five hundred and fifty pounds a month. I reckon if you offer four hundred and seventy five it'll be accepted.'

'The money won't be a problem, but I have a question about the previous tenant. You said he moved out a couple of weeks ago. How come the place looks as if it hasn't been lived in for months?'

Ricky grinned and bounced on the balls of his feet. 'Yeah, that was a bit weird. We let it out to this guy for three months, but I don't think he stayed here more than a few nights, if that. Maybe he was using it as a shag pad. Lucky sod.'

Blake walked towards the stairs, nodding slowly. 'Do you remember his name?'

Ricky stared into space as he tried to remember, the cogs moving so slowly you could hear them squeak. 'Something like Friar, I think. We've got all the paperwork at the office anyway.'

Blake put a hand to his stomach and grimaced. 'Would it be okay to use the bathroom? I think I've got a bit of a bug.'

'Knock yourself out, mate. It's going to be your place soon, anyway.'

Blake bolted the door behind him and checked out the ceiling. The loft hatch was where he'd hoped it'd be. 'Sorry Ricky,' he shouted. 'I may be some time.'

He ran the hot-water tap and flushed the toilet, stepped on the edge of the bath and put one foot on the sink. The dimensions of the room were exactly the same as the flat next door. Blake slid the loft hatch to one side and hauled himself into the roof space. He stood up and rested a hand on a low rafter to steady himself. Once his vision adjusted to the darkness, Blake slowly edged his way towards the water tank and dividing wall, taking care to place his feet on the wooden joists. When he reached the tank, Blake dropped on to one knee and took a close look at the dividing wall.

On the other side, he'd seen what appeared to be a hair-line crack running vertically from the top to the bottom of the partition. Even in the dark Blake could see that someone had used a serrated blade, maybe even a small hacksaw, to slice through the plaster board.

It would be easy for someone to swing the cut section out like a door, enter Ince's loft, and wedge it back into place on their return. Blake clenched his right fist and punched the air. Returning to the hatch, he pulled the panel back into place as he lowered himself into the bathroom. He flushed the toilet again and washed his hands, wiping them dry on his jacket, unbolted the door and pulled it open. Ricky stumbled on to the threshold.

'Are you all right, mate?' he spluttered, his face burning with embarrassment. 'I was worried about you. You were in there a while and I realised there wouldn't be any toilet paper or nothing.'

Blake smiled. 'I'm much better. A touch of gut-rot that's all. Let's get back to your office and tie this deal up, shall we?'

Ricky glanced at the toilet, twitching his nose like a sniffer dog. 'All right,' he said and headed for the stairs.

65

The walk back to the lettings agency took them ten minutes. Following Ricky through the glass door, Blake saw Fenton showing his warrant card to a plump woman with a bob of blonde hair.

Fenton turned and beckoned Blake over. 'This is my colleague, Adam Blake. I'm sorry he couldn't be honest with you this morning, but as I've explained we're investigating a very complex and serious crime.'

Spotting the name badge on the woman's left lapel, Blake stepped forward, smiled easily and offered her his hand. 'We're very grateful for your help, Janice,' he said. 'My apologies for posing as a potential customer, but it had to be done.'

Janice took his hand and squeezed rather than shook it. 'You could have come to me as the manager and explained the situation.'

Blake widened his smile. 'Like I said, I am sorry, but there are legal difficulties around this investigation that would have made that awkward.' He looked at Fenton hoping for support and received a baffled expression in return.

'Have you still got the previous tenant's paperwork?' Blake said.

'Of course. It's all on computer nowadays.'

'That includes proof of identity?'

'That's right. It's a new law that came in a year or so ago. We have to check that tenants have a right to rent in this country so we need to see a passport, or driving licence. You know, something with a photo.'

Blake looked at Fenton and smiled. 'You take copies of these documents?'

The manager rolled her eyes: 'Obviously. Didn't I say that? We scan them in and upload them on to our computer. Give me a minute and I'll get them up.' She plodded over to her desk, sat down and tapped furiously at her keyboard.

Fenton stepped closer to Blake and whispered: 'How do you know about this stuff?'

'I need to know about it. I'm a landlord.'

'I take it you were right about the loft?'

'Of course I was right.'

Blake turned to Ricky and patted him on the shoulder. 'Thanks for your help, but we're done. Janice is sorting us out.' The young lettings agent bowed his head and walked slowly into the back office.

Both men walked over to the manager's desk and stood behind her. 'I'll be with you in a second, gents,' she said. She opened a folder tagged 'scans' and the screen loaded with files. 'These are listed as property addresses, rather than names, because I'm terrible with names.'

Fenton's heart raced as he bent forward to get a better view. The manager opened a file near the top of the screen. 'Bingo,' she said.

Fenton and Blake found themselves looking at a copy of a standard British passport opened at the photo page.

'That's right, I remember now,' the manager said. 'Peter Friel, that's his name. He was a real sweetie.'

Fenton and Blake weren't listening. They were fully focused on the photo. The image was grainy and few years old, but they were looking at a face they'd both seen before.

66

Am I mad or bad? Some would say both. Others would argue that if I'm mad I can't be bad because I'm not in my right mind. If I don't know the difference between right and wrong, I can't be held responsible for my actions. Bullshit.

I am not mad. I am not bad. I am dangerous.

I've been playing a dangerous game. It's been interesting, but it's getting to that time when I have to complete my mission.

The time is near for me to do what I did all those years ago. I need to shed my skin again and slide into the undergrowth.

The problem is, so far, nothing has matched the joy of my first kill. The lovely Lauren still dominates my thoughts. I've tried so hard to recreate that feeling. Maybe it's like first-love syndrome. I wouldn't know.

I don't like having to accept that I can't do something. If I need to kill Lauren Bishop again, then I'll find some way to do it. My brain is already working on it. I feel something stirring, deep inside.

67

Discovering the identity of a serial killer is no mean feat. Blake wasn't expecting a financial reward, to be hailed a hero, or even a pat on the back, but a thank you would have been nice.

Instead, he found himself sitting in the same police interview room where he'd been questioned twice about Lauren's murder, under the watchful gaze of a red-haired female police constable.

He'd spent the past two hours with Detective Sergeant Daly, detailing the events leading up to the moment he and Fenton found the photograph of Ray Partington. Throughout the interview, the detective ignored Blake's questions about the press officer, then left without comment.

Blake understood that the police wouldn't be overjoyed that he'd beaten them at their own game. In the end, all that mattered was that Partington had been exposed, flushed out like a spider forced from the darkness of its den.

The door opened and Fenton walked in carrying a coffee in a plastic cup. He was followed by a grey-haired woman wearing a uniform similar to the constable's except for the crown and commander badges on the epaulettes.

Fenton gave Blake a nod and handed him the coffee. 'Thought you might need a drink,' he said.

Blake took the coffee and placed it on the table. He said nothing. He was pissed off and he wanted them to know it. The older officer sat down opposite Blake. She wore a rigid expression, her nose wrinkled as if she had a bad smell under it.

'This is Assistant Commissioner Hall,' Fenton said. 'She's in command of the investigation.'

Blake didn't look impressed. That's because he wasn't. 'I've been wondering when someone was going to thank me. Now I know why it's taken so long. You've been waiting for an officer of suitable superiority to become available. How nice.'

Fenton opened his mouth to speak again, but Hall twitched her thin lips and raised a hand to silence him. 'I assure you, Mr Blake, that I'm grateful that you have discovered the identity of the killer. However, I'm afraid to say that knowledge came to us a bit late. Partington must have known you were getting close. He's vanished. Gone to ground. So you see why we've been too busy to congratulate you on your amateur detective work.'

Blake glanced up at Fenton. 'He's done a runner?'

The detective nodded. 'He's been off work sick for a couple of days. An armed-response unit was sent to his flat in Shoreditch to bring him in, but there was no sign of him.

The place was spotless. Sparsely furnished. You wouldn't think anyone's been living there. The neighbours say Partington didn't interact much, but those he did speak to say he told them he was a police officer. A detective.'

Blake picked up his coffee and sipped. It was weak and tepid. He pulled a disgusted face and took another sip. 'What happens now?' he asked. 'Yeah, he's bolted, but he can't hide for ever. We know who he is. What he looks like.'

'We're doing everything we can,' Hall said. 'In the next hour or so the newspapers and television stations will have a photograph of him. The whole country will know his face. We've also put airports, ferry terminals and the Channel Tunnel on alert. Of course, if you'd come to us sooner we'd have him behind bars now.'

Blake suppressed an urge to hurl his half-full cup of coffee at the wall. Not because of what Hall had said, but because she had a point. Instead, he directed his anger at Fenton.

'What have you been doing while I was being interrogated as if I'm some sort of suspect?'

Fenton didn't react. He simply stared at Blake as if he were an errant child throwing a tantrum.

'Like you, DCI Fenton has been questioned thoroughly,' Hall said. 'Your statements have been compared and they appear to match. He has a lot more to lose than you. Clearly, you broke the law entering Ince's home, but you're unlikely to be charged. DI Fenton's role in your unofficial investigation will certainly lead to serious disciplinary proceedings. He's still advising me at the moment but, once we have Partington, he'll have to face up to what he's done.'

Blake didn't like her use of the phrase '*unlikely* to be charged'. But he knew it was probably not a good idea to argue the point.

He downed the rest of his coffee and tried to refocus his thoughts on the hunt for Partington. 'Are you telling me that you're pinning everything on Partington's photograph and a public appeal? That's all you've got?' Fenton looked across at Hall. She gave him a go-ahead nod.

'There is something else we're working on,' he said. 'A few hours ago Partington posted online again. Another fake Twitter account.'

Blake tensed in his seat: 'He's killed again?'

'No. This is different from the others.' Fenton hesitated as he considered the best way to break the news. 'It's about Lauren.'

Blake stood up, felt his head spin and sat down again. 'Can I see it?'

Fenton turned and took a sheet of paper off the uniform. He glanced at it then placed it on the table. Partington had uploaded the headshot of Lauren the police had issued to the press at the start of the investigation. Blake looked down at the wide smile and blue eyes, and his throat tightened.

The tweet read: *Time to bring her back to life. Time to kill again #IKiller.*

Blake looked up at Fenton and frowned. 'What the hell is this?'

'We don't know yet. We're trying to work it out. We've got psychologists analysing his background. Hopefully they'll come up with something. It seems he spent most of his childhood in care. His real dad, Peter Friel, was stabbed to death by his mother.'

'My heart bleeds for him.'

Fenton shrugged and carried on: 'It seems he tried to join the Met four years ago, but failed the psychological evaluation.'

'Why doesn't that surprise me?' Blake screwed up the printout of the tweet and hurled it at the wall. 'Is there any chance your experts can come up with a likely target?'

Fenton hesitated for a moment and swapped glances with Hall. The assistant commissioner pursed her lips. 'We were hoping that's where you might be able to help, Mr Blake,' she said. 'DI Fenton thinks you have a special talent for getting inside Partington's mind. He's persuaded me to allow you to have access to all our reports.'

Blake wanted to take what he'd just heard as a compliment, but wasn't sure that's how it was meant. 'Are you suggesting I think like a psychopath?'

'DCI Fenton believes you can. It's not something to be ashamed of. I wish more of my detectives possessed that ability. After all, you did work out how Partington framed Ince.'

Blake turned to Fenton and gave him a long, hard stare. 'Thanks a lot,' he said.

68

Leah Bishop stood beside her sister's grave, bowed her head and wondered why she'd even bothered to make the journey. Lauren wasn't there. Wherever she was, she wasn't in the wooden box buried in front of the white marble headstone. That contained only decaying flesh and bone.

She had wanted to speak to Lauren, to tell her she was sorry for not being the sister she should have been. They'd been close as little girls, but adolescence brought on a hormone-fuelled sibling rivalry.

Leah turned away from the memory and headed back towards the car park. A thick blanket of cloud draped over the city, the air still and moist. Rain was on the way, but around the cemetery Leah could still see several people watering pots of flowers they'd placed around their loved ones' graves.

Approaching the entrance to the car park, she noticed a man standing in the middle of a row of gravestones about one hundred yards to her left. He wasn't tending a grave, or reading a headstone. He was looking directly at her. She stopped and returned his gaze. He was tall, with fair hair cropped close to his scalp and, despite the greyness of the day, his eyes were hidden behind a pair of wraparound sunglasses.

Leah was the first to crack. She turned away and continued walking to her car. More than anything, the man's stillness had disturbed her. It was only when she reached her car and slid behind the steering wheel that she realised she'd been holding her breath. She emptied her lungs with a loud sigh and looked through the passenger window. The man was still there. Still motionless. His hands tucked into the pockets of his black overcoat.

She started the engine and drove off. The traffic was slow-moving, but she was glad to be on her way. Driving north along the perimeter of the green expanse of Wanstead Flats, she found herself thinking about Blake, something she'd been doing more and more recently. He was good-looking in a rough-around-the-edges kind of way. They had chemistry. That was undeniable. But chemistry isn't everything. Lauren had seen the good in him. She'd wanted to save him. When it had become clear he didn't want to save himself she gave up.

Leah made a mental note that she needed to meet Blake and Fenton soon, to bring a formal end to their arrangement. They'd done what she'd asked them to do. Unmasked the killer. Now it was up to the police to hunt Ray Partington down.

The further west Leah drove, the more congested the

traffic became. As she reached the outskirts of Stratford, the clouds opened and dumped their rain. Big, fat raindrops pummelled the windscreen. Leah switched on the wipers, but for a split second she was driving blind. The downpour slowed the traffic to a crawl. An image of Partington's face slid into her mind and she shivered. It was hard to believe that the man who'd treated her so sensitively at the press conference had killed Lauren and the others.

Murderous hands had helped her to her feet. She'd been comforted by a deceiving smile. A wave of repulsion swept through her, and tears of anger coursed down her cheeks.

69

Running in the rain isn't a problem, as long as you run fast enough to generate the energy needed to keep warm. Slow down, or stop, when you're soaked and you're in trouble, as evaporating water droplets steal the heat from your skin.

The downpour had lasted no more than a few minutes, but its ferocity left Blake drenched to the bone. He slowed down as he approached Grove Road, and crossed into the western section of Victoria Park. The route around the park's perimeter was usually a big draw for runners, but that afternoon Blake had it to himself. Everybody else had been warned off by the dark clouds shrouding the east of the city.

It wasn't that he needed to run. He needed to think. He'd spent the morning reading the stuff Partington had posted after killing Vale, and his mind was churning with questions.

Delving into Partington's darkness scared him. It made him wonder if he had the capacity for evil himself. Does evil fill the void in the absence of good? Blake shivered. He picked up his pace as he approached the north end of the boating lake. He was never going back to that place, he told himself. He was never going to leave a void again.

Once he'd left the park, it took him ten minutes to run home. He spent another ten minutes in the shower, standing motionless as the hot water stung his skin. He dressed quickly, grabbed a bottle of beer from the fridge and sat down with his laptop at the kitchen table. Blake opened the file Fenton had sent him and started to read. Somewhere, there had to be a clue to Partington's next move.

After a few minutes, he stood up and walked to his bedroom, slid the wardrobe door open and pulled out a cardboard box. It was full of reporter-style notebooks. Most of them had been used and were full of notes he'd made while researching assignments. He took one from the middle of the pile and flicked through it. The scrawl was a mixture of longhand and shorthand. Nobody else had ever been able to make sense of his notes. The memory made him smile.

He rifled through the pile until he found a blank one, grabbed a ballpoint pen from the bottom of the box and returned to his laptop. A copy of Partington's last message was still on the screen. Blake flipped the notebook open. We were so close and he sensed we were coming, Blake thought. He read the message again, this time aloud . . . *bring her back and kill her again.* Plain crazy. But not to Partington.

A knock at the door disrupted his train of thought. He considered ignoring it in the hope that whoever it was would go away, but the caller knocked again, louder and more urgently. On his way to the door he checked his watch. It was early evening. He wasn't expecting anyone and didn't like surprise visits. The thought crossed his mind that a visit from Leah wouldn't be an unpleasant surprise, but when he opened the door Fenton stepped in without waiting for an invitation. 'We've got a problem,' he said.

Blake led him into the kitchen without asking what the problem was. He opened the fridge, took out a beer and offered it to his visitor. Fenton shook his head and waved a hand impatiently. 'Didn't you hear what I said?'

Blake put the bottle back and closed the fridge. 'I heard you. I'm waiting for you to tell me what's up.'

'Someone's sent me an email.'

'Wow. You're so popular. I'm jealous.'

Fenton scowled. 'It was from a generic address and said "Cubitt Town. The Dutton Hotel. Room 107. I, Killer".'

'And you believe it? You don't think it's some idiot winding you up?'

'I don't know what to believe.'

Blake sat at the kitchen table, nodding for Fenton to join him, but the detective stayed pacing around the room. Blake switched his laptop off and closed it.

'Why would Partington hide in a hotel on the Isle of Dogs? Every police officer in the city, no the country is looking for him. The Dutton Hotel is less than ten miles from his flat.'

Fenton shrugged. 'It's close to City Airport. There are daily flights to the continent.'

'So, let's check it out. What's the big problem?'

Fenton stopped pacing and sat down opposite Blake. 'The problem is I should call this in and let the Yard take care of it.'

'Well. Do it then.'

'That's the problem.'

'What problem?'

'I don't want to call it in. I want to check it out myself. If Partington is there I want him. I want him badly. My career's shot anyway. I'm not coming back from this. I might as well go out in a blaze of glory.'

Blake grinned. Fenton had fire in his belly after all. 'Have you got your car?'

Fenton nodded.

'And what about your daughter?'

'Sleeping over at a neighbour's, but the uniforms know and they're guarding the house.'

'What are we waiting for then?'

Darkness fell fast. Each autumn day shorter than the last. Blake's Mile End Road flat was only five miles from the hotel, but the traffic was bumper to bumper. He looked out of the passenger window and watched the haphazard streets of east London slide slowly by.

Fenton took his left hand off the steering wheel and switched on the radio. The lead item on BBC Radio 4's eight o'clock news was an update on the I, Killer murder hunt. It ended with Assistant Commissioner Patricia Hall insisting that Partington's capture 'was only a matter of time'. The second item was a story about Syrian refugees drowning off the coast of Turkey. Fenton turned the radio off.

'Did you read the reports?' he asked.

Blake nodded. 'The man's messed up. He's not going to stop killing until he's behind bars, and even then he'll be a danger to other prisoners unless he's in solitary confinement.'

'That passport he used to rent the flat next to Ince's was his father's,' Fenton said. 'He added his photo and doctored the birth date. By all accounts he was a nightmare child, but eventually managed to fool one foster couple. They adopted him. He took their name, changed his ways, they financed him through university to do, guess what? A computer science degree.'

Blake thought about what Fenton had said. It had suited Partington to hide his evil, bury it deep for all those years, letting it multiply like a virus. He thinks he can do it again, but he's not in control any more.

The traffic congestion eased as they turned left on to Commercial Road and Fenton accelerated. Blake stared at the headlights cutting through the darkness. They turned sharply on to Marsh Wall. They were ten minutes away from the hotel. Blake couldn't stop thinking about Partington playing the perfect son. 'What about the adoptive parents? Do they know what he's done?'

Fenton flashed Blake a sideways look. 'Would you believe Geoffrey and Jean Partington died in a fire at their home? The apple of their eye dropped out of university after a year and was back at home looking for a job. He was out the night the house burnt down. No definite cause was ever established. Police put it down to an electrical fault. They had no natural children. He inherited a pile of money.'

'Lucky boy.'

The Dutton Hotel was an ultra-modern, five-storey glass and steel building in Cubitt Town, an area of the Isle of Dogs named after a former mayor of London. Fenton pulled into the hotel car park and found a space close to the main entrance. The two men approached the revolving glass door in silence, Fenton leading the way as agreed. He was a senior police officer, and he looked like a senior police officer. He waved his warrant card at a smartly dressed young woman behind reception.

'Detective Chief Inspector Fenton, I need to speak to your manager, please.'

The woman's smile faltered a touch. 'Can I ask what this is about, sir?'

Fenton stiffened his jaw and gave her a stern look. 'I'm investigating a serious crime and need your manager here right now.'

The receptionist dashed into the glass-walled office behind the counter and picked up a telephone. Blake, standing a couple of steps back like a well-trained subordinate, was impressed with Fenton's performance. It was a big improvement on his effort at the lettings agency. The guy was a fast learner.

A couple of minutes later a short, slim man in his forties

strode across the lobby and introduced himself as Joseph Cook, the night manager.

Fenton got straight down to business and explained that he needed access to room 107. After tapping away at the keyboard of her computer, the receptionist confirmed that a Ray Bishop had booked into the room two days ago. She'd been on duty and remembered him as tall, with cropped blond hair.

Blake caught Fenton's eye. 'Lauren's surname. He can't resist playing games.'

The night manager took the lift with them to the second floor and led them to the room at the far end of the corridor. Blake stepped up to the door and raised his fist. Before he could knock, Fenton pulled him aside.

'This isn't a great idea,' he said, lowering his voice to a whisper so the night manager couldn't hear. 'Partington's killed four people. Neither of us is armed. This isn't the most sensible way of doing this.'

'I don't do sensible,' Blake said, stepping back to the door and rapping hard with his knuckles three times. 'Anyway, I'm pretty sure there's nobody in.' He waited a few seconds and knocked again. The room was silent.

Blake stretched a hand out to the night manager, who passed him the master keycard. He opened the door and stepped into the room. Fenton followed, signalling to the night manager to stay put.

It was a standard, mid-range hotel bedroom. A double bed, a television, a table, two chairs and a bathroom. There was no sign of Ray Friel, or Ray Partington, or Ray Bishop. Fenton walked over to the window, which had a good view of the office block across the road. It was late, but all the floors were still lit, and he could see several people working at their desks.

The room was clean. The only sign that it had been occupied was the unmade bed. Blake poked his head into the bathroom and beckoned Fenton over. A half-empty bottle of what looked like hair dye lay on its side in the sink and the floor tiles were littered with strands of dark hair.

When they emerged into the corridor, the night manager was standing with his hands behind his back, a nervous look on his face.

'It's empty,' Blake told him. 'I don't think your guest will be coming back.'

'But Mr Bishop hasn't checked out yet. He hasn't paid his bill.'

Blake shrugged and walked back into the room. Fenton followed and stared out of the window. 'Do you think it's definitely Partington?' he asked.

Blake sat on the end of the bed. 'It's possible he sent you the email. It can't be a coincidence that the man who booked in used the surname of Partington's first victim.' Fenton turned back to face Blake. 'What's he up to? He should be keeping his head down.'

Blake thought for a moment. He tried to put himself in Partington's shoes and work out what he'd have to gain, other than the satisfaction of pulling their strings. The answer he came up with sent his pulse rate into orbit.

'He wants to distract us. To know where we are. To make sure we're not somewhere else.'

The colour drained from Fenton's face. 'What are you getting at?'

Blake stood up. He knew he was right about this. 'He's going to kill again. Tonight.'

Fenton took his mobile out of his jacket pocket, all fingers and thumbs as he frantically punched in his daughter's number. It went to voicemail. 'Hi, Tess, it's Dad. It's late so I guess you're in bed asleep. If not and you get this, ring me back, please.'

'It's not your daughter,' Blake said. He could see in Fenton's eyes that he wanted to believe him.

'How can you be so sure?'

'Because I know who it is. The last I, Killer message. He wants to resurrect Lauren, bring her back to life and kill her again. He can't do that, but what's the next best thing. He's going to kill Leah.'

Fenton nodded slowly as Blake's words sunk in. His response was to lift his mobile and dial his neighbour's number. The call went to voicemail again. 'Hello, Tina, it's Dan,' he said. 'When you get this message please double-check that the officers who were on duty outside my flat have shifted to your place. If not call me back straightaway.'

Blake had been waiting patiently. He understood Fenton's concern for his child, but his patience was running out. 'We need to move,' he said, sprinting into the corridor. He barged by the bemused night manager and headed for the lift, Fenton close behind him.

The lift door was already open. Blake stepped in and pressed the ground floor button. Fenton slid in as the door closed. 'Millennium Drive is only a half a mile from here. I'll call Leah to warn her once we're in the car.'

'I'm not coming,' Fenton said.

Blake thought he must have misheard. 'You what?'

'I'm not going with you.'

'What are you talking about?'

'I'm driving home. I need to know Tess is safe.'

'I told you. It's Leah. He wants to recreate Lauren's murder. He used their surname to book the room.'

The lift stopped and the door opened. Both men stared at each other.

'I'm sorry, but I can't risk it. Partington got to Tess once before, remember?'

Blake tore his mobile out of his pocket, glanced at the screen, then back at Fenton. 'Do what you have to do, but call the police first.' He ran out of the lift and across the lobby, his mobile clamped against his ear.

70

Blake ran across the car park, slowing at the exit to study a map of the area on his mobile. He tried phoning Leah, but the call went to voicemail. He turned left and ran at a steady pace along Stewart Street, the cold night air stinging his lungs.

In his prime, Blake would have made it to Leah's flat in under two minutes. He'd be lucky if he made it in three. After a few hundred yards, he cut right then turned left again into Manchester Road. The pavement was wider, the street busier and better lit. According to the map, it was a straight run from here to Leah's street.

He checked his phone's screen again. It showed he had a quarter of a mile to go. He was already sweating heavily, his shirt sticking to his back, the palms of his hands damp. It wasn't all the result of physical exertion.

Up ahead, a couple holding hands stopped as they spotted him running towards them, and crossed hurriedly to the other side of the road, throwing nervous glances at him as he passed.

Blake clung to the forlorn hope that he might be wrong. That he'd misread the clues. But there was a twisted logic to Partington's fantasies. Despite the fact that his legs were screaming stop, he lengthened his stride. I can't let this happen, he told himself. Not again. He lifted his right arm and wiped the sweat from his eyes with the sleeve of his jacket. Up ahead, under an orange street light, a road sign marked the entrance to Millennium Drive. He slowed a little and tried to calm his breathing. He needed to save some strength.

At the sign, he turned left, and then left again. Leah's flat was in the first low-level block on the right. He crossed the road and approached the entrance. Still catching his breath, he found Leah's name on the intercom panel and pressed the button. There was no response. He pressed it again, holding it down for several seconds. Still no response.

He turned to the door, jammed his palms against it and pushed. It gave way a little before springing back into place. The bolts and hinges had been weakened by years of constant use. Blake had the strength to force it. He knew it would almost certainly set off an alarm and decided that would be a good thing. He took two steps back and shoulder charged the door. It gave way with an ear-splitting crack, the wood around the lock splintering into jagged shards.

Blake's momentum carried him through. He ran to the staircase and bounded up the stairs, the electronic howl of a security alarm ringing in his ears. When he reached Leah's flat, he found the door fractionally ajar. That was the moment all hope left him. Someone had picked the lock and deliberately not closed the door behind them because they wanted to keep their approach silent.

Blake had no need, or time, for stealth. He gripped the door, flung it aside and charged in. He turned into the living room and stopped dead. He was too late.

71

On her knees in the centre of the room, Leah's hands were bound behind her back, a thick strip of grey duct tape sealed her mouth. Her head slightly bowed, her eyes were fixed on the floor. Behind her stood Ray Partington. His long dark hair had been cut close to his scalp and dyed blond. His right hand was tucked into the pocket of his black coat. His left hand hung at his side, the serrated blade of a black-handled hunting knife glinted against his thigh. Partington smiled. 'I wondered what the commotion was,' he said.

His words caused Leah to raise her head. Her eyes widened at the sight of Blake standing in the doorway. He took a step forward. Partington raised the knife and placed the blade flat on Leah's head.

'At last,' he said. 'We've been waiting for you. The guest of honour. I don't like being kept waiting and it's not a good idea to get me angry. I'm not a particularly nice person, even when I'm in a good mood.'

He took his right hand out of his pocket, grabbed a

handful of Leah's hair and yanked her head back, exposing the soft flesh of her throat. She cried out, but the duct tape muffled the sound. Blake moved forward, but stopped when Partington slipped the knife beneath Leah's chin.

Blake's heart thumped against his ribs. He doubted he could reach Partington in time to stop him slitting her throat. The burglar alarm stopped. Blake prayed that one of Leah's neighbours would have called the police. Partington laughed softly, as if he could read Blake's thoughts and found them ridiculous. 'Don't pin your hopes on the police coming to the rescue. You know what this city's like. As long as people feel safe behind their own locked doors they'd rather keep their heads down and not get involved.'

He's probably right, Blake thought, but he trusted Fenton. 'The police will be here soon,' he said. 'I called them a few minutes ago.'

Partington laughed again. 'Nice try, but you're a terrible liar. Lauren is going to die. I've never killed in front of an audience before. This will be an interesting experience.'

'That isn't Lauren Bishop. You know that.'

Partington stiffened. He yanked hard on Leah's hair and pushed the blade against her skin. A single drop of bright red blood slid down her neck. 'I know a lot of things. I know that I'm going to enjoy killing her, but she's only the side-show here.'

Unable to make sense of what he was hearing, Blake glanced at Leah. Her eyes were shut tight, her nostrils flared as they sucked in air. He took two steps back. He wanted to give Partington space and time. Space to breathe and time to think. 'Believe me, Ray, I'm trying to help you. You deserve the truth.'

'I am the truth. You tried to deny me, but the truth can't be denied.' Partington smiled at the confusion on Blake's face. 'I thought you were supposed to be smart, but you haven't worked it out yet, have you?'

Keeping the knife against Leah's throat, he released his grip on her hair and used his free hand to pull a folded piece of paper from his jacket pocket. He flicked it in Blake's direction and it fluttered to the floor between them. Blake stepped closer, bent down and picked it up. It was an old, stained newspaper cutting. Under the headline 'Wife stabbed husband while he slept' was the reporter's name: Adam Blake. Partington took hold of Leah's hair again. 'Read it,' he said. 'Let's see if it jogs your memory.' Blake skimmed the text. The defendant was Rachel Friel, of Lewisham, south London. The victim Peter Friel. 'That was years ago. It must have been one of the first court cases I covered.'

Partington pulled the knife away from Leah's throat, wiped the blade on his thigh and placed it back under her chin. 'You do remember it then. Read me what it says, in paragraph eight, about my mother.'

Blake took a few seconds to find the right place and quickly read the paragraph to himself first.

Leah yelped under the tape as Partington jerked her head back. 'I asked you to read it out loud.'

'All right, don't hurt her,' Blake pleaded. 'I've found it. It says that the accused, aged thirty-five, has no children.'

'That's exactly what it says. Can you explain to me how, if that was the case, I am standing here?'

Details of the court hearing were coming back to Blake. It'd been his first murder trial and he'd been disappointed when it had been adjourned for psychiatric reports.

'I think there's a simple explanation for this,' Blake said. 'I take it you were put into care when your mother was arrested?' Partington didn't answer. 'Well, once a child is in care nothing can be printed that might identify him or her.'

Partington lifted his left foot and jammed it into Leah's back sending her crashing face down on to the floor. 'That's your justification for denying my existence?'

Blake held his hands up and took a step back. 'Okay, keep calm,' he said. 'Are you really telling me you're doing this because your name was left out of a newspaper report all those years ago?'

Partington's eyes narrowed. 'That cutting was in a box of my mother's belongings they gave to me when she died. She hanged herself. Killed herself because of that article. Because of what you wrote.'

Blake shook his head: 'You don't know that, Ray. I'm sorry that happened to you, but unless your mother left a suicide note there is no way of knowing why she did it.'

Partington pointed at the newspaper cutting. 'You don't get it, do you? That's her suicide note. You wrote her suicide note. When she read that, when it dawned on her that I no longer existed in her life, she knew she had nothing to live for. She put that cutting in the box with her stuff because she knew it would be sent to me. She wanted me to know so I could put things right. I kept it with me. I waited patiently, year after year. I knew the time would come and when it did I was ready. Your return from Iraq made the news big time, didn't it? That's when I recognised the name. That's when I knew my time had come.'

Blake's head was spinning, but things were falling into place. The coverage of his ordeal had been Partington's trigger. 'That's why you chose Lauren. That's why you started beheading your victims. But Lauren had left me by then. Why not come straight for me? Why did the others need to die?'

Partington sneered: 'I killed them because I wanted to. I am a killer. I exist. I, Killer. They were enjoyable diversions on the way to you. A demonstration of what I'm capable of. You've seen the hysteria on the internet, the newspapers. My followers adore me. No one can deny my existence now, can they?'

Blake desperately tried to recall every detail of the reports on Partington's childhood, searching for a weakness he could exploit. 'You've got me now,' he said. 'You don't need to harm Leah. You can let her go.'

'I can, but I won't. It's touching that you care so much, but that only makes me more determined to let you watch me deprive her of her existence, like you deprived me of mine. Like you deprived me of my mother.'

72

Time was running out. Blake edged closer, trying to put himself into a position where he had a chance of throwing himself between Partington and Leah. 'I'm asking you to think carefully for a moment, Ray. If this is some kind of sick revenge on the world then you're setting yourself up to be disappointed, let down again. Like all the times you were let down before. When you were a child. Little Ray Friel.'

Partington's head snapped back as if he'd been slapped in the face. Eager to press his advantage, Blake chose his words carefully, firing them like bullets.

'You know what I think? I think you've only got yourself to blame for the bad things that happened to you and your family. Your mother killed your father then herself. That's no one else's fault. Certainly not mine. From what I've heard, Ray Friel was a sick little bastard and Ray Partington is an even bigger, sicker bastard.'

Partington said nothing. He lifted the knife and stared at his reflection in the blade. His eyes darkened. Blake braced himself, aware that his chances were low. A knifeman as skilled and as fast as Partington could shred you in a heart-beat.

The shrill wail of a siren filled the silence, the sound close. 'They're coming,' Blake said, trying to convince himself as much as anyone else. 'The police know all about you. All about Ray Friel. What you are. Every pathetic detail.'

Partington sneered at him. 'Have you seen how many people have searched for and viewed my messages? What have you achieved? Who worships you?'

Blake said nothing, but edged closer. Partington mistook his silence for submission. He dug his right hand into his jacket pocket and pulled out a smartphone. 'Video time,' he said, lifting the mobile to get Leah in shot.

Blake took his chance and dived across the gap, driving his head into Partington's stomach. Both men crashed to the floor, the knife slipping from Partington's fingers. Blake grabbed it and staggered to his feet. Partington slowly hauled himself up, a pained smile on his face. Blake lifted the knife and pressed the point of the blade to Partington's neck.

'Go on, do it,' he said. 'You know you want to. You'll enjoy it. Trust me.'

73

B lake tightened his grip on the hilt of the knife. The weapon felt heavier than he expected. He pulled the tip of the blade away from Partington's throat, then jabbed it back. Partington smiled.

'You want to do it,' he said. 'What's stopping you? I'll give you permission, if that'll help. Go on. Do it.'

Is it evil to destroy evil, Blake wondered? Wouldn't I be doing the world a favour? Partington's smile widened. He seemed to have an uncanny knowledge of what was going through Blake's mind.

'What are you waiting for? You can say it was self-defence. It was me or you. You've got plenty of time to get your story straight. You'd better get on with it though, because she's choking pretty badly.'

Blake looked down and saw that he was right. Leah's eyes were bloodshot and bulging, and she was sucking so hard on the tape he could see the outline of her mouth. He quickly dropped to her side and used his free hand to rip the tape from her mouth. She coughed violently, gasped for air and retched.

Blake gave her a concerned glance, taking his eyes off Partington for no more than a fraction of a second. A fraction of a second was long enough. Partington's right foot connected with his left temple, sending him to the floor in a blur of semi-consciousness. When his vision cleared, he was lying face down. A couple of feet away, Partington stood behind a kneeling Leah, holding the knife against her throat.

'Glad to see you're back with us,' he said. 'I wouldn't want you to miss the show. My followers are impatient. I can't keep them waiting.'

Blake lifted his chin and started to push himself up. 'Stay down,' Partington snarled. 'You had your chance and you blew it.'

Blake slumped forward into a prone position. He could see Leah's lips were swollen and bloody, but at least she was breathing freely. He stared at the blade held across her neck, and thought about launching himself across the room. Pushing himself up on to his hands and knees, he tensed his body.

'Back on your belly, there's a good boy' Partington sneered. 'If you don't do as you're told there will be consequences.' Blake dropped to the floor, shaking his head in frustration and using the movement to disguise the fact that he'd managed to slide a few extra inches closer.

He wanted to keep Partington off balance. Keep him talking about the one thing that made him uncomfortable. 'So, your mother was sent to prison, Ray? I think I was working on another newspaper by the time her trial resumed.

I guess she was sent down for a long time. That alone is enough to make someone suicidal.'

Partington slid the knife gently back and forth across Leah's neck and Blake thought he'd overstepped the mark. 'The trial never restarted,' Partington said. 'There was no need. They locked her up on remand while they compiled psychiatric reports. They were never completed. It's amazing what you can do with a bedsheet and exposed plumbing when you're desperate. The funny thing is she would probably have been sent to a nice comfortable psychiatric unit anyway. But it was your story that did for her. She couldn't bear that I'd never be in her life again.'

'I'm sorry you see it that way,' Blake said. 'But killing us is not going to change what happened. You know there's no way out of here, so why take another life?'

Partington shook his head slowly. His left hand gripped the knife under Leah's chin, his right hand rested on her right shoulder.

'You still don't get it. Why take another life? Why not? You're not as stupid as you look, Blake, but you're not as smart as you think you are. I knew you would work out who would be next. I knew you'd come running. I knew. You don't think either of you are walking away from this, do you? Twice as gory, double the glory. Social media is going to explode.'

Leah's lips were still oozing blood, but it was her eyes that caught Blake's attention. Keeping her head as still as possible, she repeatedly rolled her pupils to peer down at the knife.

Blake raised himself up on to his knees. Partington glared at him. 'Back on your belly, or I'll bleed her out.'

'You're going to do it anyway,' Blake said. He stood up quickly and lunged across the room. Partington stumbled and Leah took her chance. She pulled her head back, dropped her chin and sunk her teeth deep into the mound of flesh at the base of his thumb.

Partington cried out, Blake saw the knife fall and turned his lunge into a full-blooded dive. His head hit Partington's shoulder and the two men crashed to the floor. Blake used his momentum to roll on top of Partington and pin him down. A knee smashed into his groin. Blake's stomach heaved. He was concentrating on not vomiting when Partington grabbed his shoulders and smashed his forehead into his nose.

The bone cracked and Blake tasted blood. He lay limp and helpless as Partington rolled him on to his back, and pressed a forearm across his windpipe. Blake coughed violently, choking as the blood from his broken nose filled his throat. He felt the pressure on his neck increase and looked up into Partington's eyes. They held no mercy.

His lungs burned from lack of oxygen and his eyes bulged in their sockets. Partington lifted his torso ready to bear down harder and finish Blake off, but instead he froze, the look of triumph on his face replaced by astonishment. He twisted to one side, slumped on to his back, and emitted a low guttural groan.

Blake gasped for air and pushed himself up on to his

elbows. Blood poured from a wound in Partington's side, between his hip and his ribcage. Beside him, knelt Leah, the bloodied knife in her hand. Blake turned on to his front and crawled towards her. She wept silent tears as he prised the knife from her fingers, gripped it in his right hand and flopped on to his back.

74

A paramedic wrapped a blanket around Leah's shoulders and led her away. Two others worked on getting oxygen into Partington's system and stemming the flow of blood from the knife wound. Nearby, stood two Metropolitan Police firearms officers, their semi-automatic pistols drawn and pointed at Partington's head.

Overkill, thought Blake. He's not going anywhere. The paramedic who'd taken Leah to the ambulance came back in and turned her attention to Blake. The damage to his nose looked spectacular, but it was a simple break. She ran her gloved fingers gently over his swollen throat, feeling for internal injuries. 'Can you speak?' she asked.

Blake considered the question for a moment. 'I think so,' he whispered. 'But it hurts like hell.'

The paramedic gave him a sympathetic smile. 'I'm not surprised. Lie still and we'll get you to hospital as quickly as we can.' Blake nodded at the two men working on Partington. 'Is he going to live?' he rasped.

The paramedic shrugged. 'Probably.'

Blake closed his eyes. 'Pity,' he said.

75

The trees, stripped of their leaves, stood black against the cloudless morning sky. Despite the early hour, the park bustled with families making the most of the weekend. Blake had been pleased to get a phone call from Leah suggesting that they meet. He was less happy with her suggested meeting place. The spot where her sister had died.

Two weeks had passed since Partington's arrest. It had been a hectic time. Blake found himself at the centre of a media circus eager to entertain the public with every detail of the drama. Blake's part in the killer's capture had been given prominence in most of the newspapers, despite his refusal to be interviewed.

He reached a line of skeletal oaks running north to south and walked between two gnarled trunks. In the distance, he could see the triangular patch of undergrowth near the park's Gore Gate, which had hidden Lauren Bishop's body. Taking a deep breath of cold air, he headed towards it

He'd seen Leah only once, a few days after the arrest, when he'd visited her in hospital. She'd not been seriously injured, physically, but the trauma had left her too frail and too frightened to return home. Blake recalled her lying pale and motionless in bed, unable to speak, or even look him in the eye. He'd sat beside her in silence until she fell asleep.

He reached the meeting place and looked at his watch. They'd agreed on 9 a.m. and it was five minutes past. He heard footsteps approaching the gate and looked up. His heart lifted when he saw Leah carrying a large bunch of flowers. She still looked a little frail, but her eyes were bright and her step brisk. He fought back a strong urge to go to her and stood his ground. When she reached him, she rose on to her toes and kissed him softly on the cheek. 'Thank you for coming,' she said. 'How's the nose? It looks painful.'

'It's not as bad as it looks. They tell me once the bruises go it'll be as good as new. Maybe even better.'

Leah smiled and it made Blake feel good. 'What about you?' he said. 'You certainly look better than when I last saw you.'

Leah furrowed her brow in mock confusion. 'Right. I think that's a compliment.' She looked at the flowers she was holding and a shadow fell across her face. 'Give me a minute,' she said.

Blake watched as she walked on and slipped into a gap in the undergrowth. A few minutes later she emerged, no longer carrying the flowers. She strode back to where Blake was waiting, her eyes wet but defiant. 'We did it,' she said. 'We got the bastard.'

Blake nodded. 'Let's hope he never gets out. He's confessed

to the lot. Proud of his work by all accounts. But he's slippery. He's got a good lawyer and they're talking about pleading insanity. He still gets locked up, but in a hospital rather than a prison.'

Leah shrugged. 'Well, if Partington is diagnosed as insane then maybe a hospital is the best place for him.'

'Partington, or Friel, whatever his name is, isn't insane. He knew exactly what he was doing.'

Leah closed her eyes and shook her head. 'The hardest thing is getting my mind straight. Trying to make sense of everything that's happened. I can't understand how someone like Partington can exist. How such a sick mind is formed.'

Blake reached out and took hold of her hands. Her fingers were soft and slender. 'He's not sick. He's evil. He was born evil. He'll die evil. There are plenty of people like him in this world. Too many people.'

Leah moved closer. 'Then it's lucky there are people like you in the world as well,' she said.

Blake let go of her hands. 'Have you been in touch with Fenton?' he asked.

'He came to see me in hospital and we've spoken a few times since. The police are pretty unhappy at all the credit you've been getting in the press. That's probably why they're taking it out on Dan. He's fighting it, but it looks like he'll be kicked out of the force. They say he broke the rules, so he's got to pay.'

Blake said nothing. The silence stretched. Leah was the first to speak. 'He told me what happened. He did the right thing. He had to put his daughter first. Surely you understand that?'

Blake kept her waiting, before nodding slowly. 'I get it,' he said. 'He had to put his child before anything else.'

'That's right. He had no choice. He's a good man. A decent man.'

'And I'm not?'

'I didn't say that.'

Blake took a deep breath to steady himself. He'd had enough of avoiding the issue. 'What are we going to do about us?' he said.

'I don't know. I need time to think. That's why I'm going to Italy for a few weeks. To sort things out. Flying out tomorrow.'

Blake resisted the temptation to ask if she was going alone. 'Why leave now? That won't solve anything. Surely, it's better to stay in London so we can talk this through. We've agonised over this for too long. I was damaged. Things are different now. I'm different now.'

Leah didn't reply. She stepped closer, kissed him softly on the lips, and walked away. Blake wanted to call out to her, ask her not to go. Instead he watched her until she disappeared through the gate. When she'd gone he headed back to the line of leafless trees.

76

Things aren't so bad here in prison. Naturally, I don't have the use of a laptop, but the wing is awash with smuggled mobile phones. I've been using mine for research, educating myself about the defence of insanity. I'm wondering if a hospital for the criminally insane might be a better option than your run-of-the-mill jail.

You might think that I'm looking for a way to avoid responsibility for what I've done. That isn't the case. The fact is, when you sit in a cell most of the day you get a lot of time to think, and when I set my mind to thinking, I can cover a lot of ground.

The long and short of it is, I'm reconsidering my approach to life. I'm prepared to accept the possibility that I might be afflicted with a personality disorder that could respond to treatment. I'm willing to try, at least. That's one thing the staff here like about me. I'm a trier. I'm trying to be a model prisoner, and they appreciate it. It's good to have a couple of wardens onside when you're inside.

One of my many powers is the ability to get people to

believe. You see, it's easy to think that if you believe some-thing then it must be true. The real truth is, that's rarely the case.

If I can convince the right people that I'm desperate for psychiatric help, that I want to change my ways, how can they refuse me? That would be inhumane. It wasn't my fault. Honest. My brain made me do it.

The police, with the help of the press, are still gloating about my capture. It's been going on for weeks. They've put me away. Stopped the notorious I, Killer in his tracks. If only they knew the truth. I may be locked up, but these bars cannot constrain an intellect as powerful as mine. The idea is laughable.

You see, my internet posts are still clocking up record viewing figures. With that kind of acclaim comes responsi-bility. I owe it to my public to keep doing what I do best. I can't let them down. My followers are loyal and I appreciate that. But among them are a few special individuals who want to do more than look. They have embraced the darkness and are eager to learn from the master.

Those determined to put a negative spin on this develop-ment would probably describe it as the birth of a cult. I like to think of them as my acolytes. They are lying low of course. They would be foolish not to. But they know, and I know, they will be my willing instruments. When the time is right I will make my selection and they will carry on my work.

Acknowledgements

I am truly grateful to everyone who has helped *Now You See* find its way to publication.

Many thanks to my amazing agent Madeleine Milburn, who saw potential in the raw manuscript, and all the members of her talented team, including the dynamic Hayley Steed.

Also, to Kate Stephenson, my editor, for her intelligent notes and insight, the 'part human/part firework' Ella Gordon, and everyone else at Wildfire, including the designers, marketing and sales.

I can't do this without thanking my late parents, who encouraged and nurtured my love of reading and writing.

Throughout the roller-coaster process of writing this crime novel, I feel so lucky to have had the complete backing of my wonderful family, my wife Valerie, and grown-up children Becky, John and Sarah.

Lastly, I want to give special thanks to my wife for her incredible support as an invaluable, dedicated and honest reader. I couldn't have done it without you.